www.eibonvalepress.co.uk
2007

A Thread of Truth

Nina Allan

'A Thread of Truth'
Nina Allan

Published in 2006 by Eibonvale Press
www.eibonvalepress.co.uk

Cover art and interior/exterior design by David Rix
www.eibonvale.co.uk

Printed by Lightning Source
www.lightningsource.com

Bird Songs at Eventide previously appeared in Interzone issue 199, TTA Press 2005

Terminus previously appeared in 'Strange Tales' from Tartarus, Tartarus Press 2003

ISBN
978-0-9555268-0-0

In memory of my grandmother, Hilda Lily Horlock,
who told extraordinary stories and
encouraged me to tell my own.

Acknowledgements

I would like to thank Naomi Drake, Helen Carpenter, Karen Denning, Leila Grayling and Will Travis for the unwitting inspiration they provided, Dev Agarwal for his staunch comradeship and willingness to indulge my taste in bad horror movies, Debbie Bennett, Trevor Denyer, Rosalie Parker and Andy Cox for their belief in my work at crucial stages in its development and David Rix for making this collection possible. My heartfelt gratitude to you all.

Contents

Amethyst

In the High Street they were selling sardines. When you see them *en masse* like that, laid out head to tail on one of the marble slabs in Leslie Grainger's window, you can almost convince yourself they were never alive at all. They look like designer jewellery or some expensive work of art. One Christmas one of Angela's aunts gave her a box of chocolate sardines. The box was made of cardboard but painted to look like tin. The chocolates inside were wrapped in foil and they were delicious in the way that novelty chocolate always seems to be, much more so than the ordinary bars. I ate three before the box was taken away from us. I was never able to find chocolates like that again even in Switzerland. I suppose it's a strange thing to want to find anyway, chocolates that are shaped like fish.

Angela sometimes used to buy things because she felt sorry for them. She invested rubbish with a life of its own. She once bought three plastic horses from Garston's Antiques in the run-down arcade off the promenade just because she was afraid of what might happen to them if she didn't. The horses looked bloated as if they had been inflated with a bicycle pump and had coloured nylon manes and tails. Someone had twisted the tails into dreadlocks. She paid £5 for the three.

"There's nothing wrong with them really," she said. "They'll look better once I get them clean." A week later I saw the horses standing on the bookshelf in Angela's bedroom. Their bodies were brightly coloured like small balloons. I noticed that Angela had managed to disentangle their tails. I sensed it must have taken her hours.

Garston's wasn't a proper antique shop. Mostly it sold junk, the kind of discarded bric-a-brac that wouldn't have looked out of place at a jumble sale. People seem to like shops like that because they never know what they might find. Angela's mother helped out in Garston's for a while at one point because she was friends with the owner. I used to wonder if that was where Angela got it from, her passion for superfluous things, or whether it was just a coincidence. Some of these things happen by chance and some are pre-programmed, at least that's what the scientists say. It's difficult to tell which is which. I might have learned more about that if I'd gone on with biology instead of switching to statistics but perhaps that was programmed too.

The name of our town came up in a television music quiz once. *Moon Landing on Silas Street* was in the Top Ten singles charts for six weeks the summer it came out, which was unusual because Amethyst were really a folk group who happened to use electric guitars. People knew the song was about our town because Lorna Samways had said so in an interview and after all she had been born there. It made the town famous for a while at least in a small way. I don't know who remembers it now.

> *Midnight at noon and the silent bells*
> *St Andrew on the run to the sea*
> *Life's on fire and there's no way home*
> *Moon landing*
> *Moon landing down on Silas Street*

St Andrews was the church at the top of the town and Silas Street ran from just opposite the churchyard down to the Nubia Pavilion on the seafront. The Nubia had been boarded up since before I could remember. Every other year squatters or teenaged boys broke into it and had to be turned out by policemen sent in specially from Deene. Our town didn't have its own police station. The Nubia Pavilion was a sort of poor man's imitation of the Royal Pavilion at Brighton. People in town were always trying to get the money together to have it reopened but it never came to anything. There were all kinds of stories about it. Some people said it was haunted but that's the kind of thing that gets said about anywhere that's inaccessible and dark. Nobody said anything much about Silas Street until the song came out. It was just a road that led downhill from the church at the top of the town to the sea at the bottom.

"What d'you think it means?" Angela said. "You can't have a moon landing anywhere else but on the moon."

The magazine had a full-page colour photograph of Lorna Samways. Angela was trying to unpick the staples that held the magazine together so she could take out the photo without tearing it.

"Pop songs are just like that," I said. "Most of the words don't make sense."

"Maybe she meant that Silas Street is like the moon somehow, empty and alien. Or perhaps it seemed that way, just for a second."

Lorna Samways had a plump moon face and a dimple in one cheek but she was beautiful when she sang. I went online recently and looked up some of the press that came out at the time. One reviewer compared her to the young Janis Joplin.

"She probably didn't write it herself," I said. "They probably paid someone to do it."

"Yes she did, she's a writer as well as a singer. Lorna Samways writes all her own songs."

I used to paint birds. I began by just drawing them, by copying pictures from books, and then one day I went to one of the shops in the Salt Street arcade and bought a large bound sketchbook full of heavy smooth paper called vellum. I painted in watercolour; there was a box of colours in the living room sideboard that had been there for so long it was impossible to say where it might originally have come from. I liked the way the watercolour paint seemed to blend with the paper but in spite of that it was the birds that interested me most. I've heard it said that painting isn't about what is painted but about the paint itself, the quality of line and brushstroke, the effects of colour and light. All I wanted to do was to make a record of the birds I saw. That I painted them was simply a matter of chance.

Angela would sometimes lie on the floor of my bedroom, turning the pages of the sketchbook as if it were a photo album.

"You could go abroad and paint more birds," she said once. "Foreign ones. Like the artists who went on that ship with Captain Cook."

I laughed but what she said shook me because it was that kind of life exactly that I sometimes imagined for myself. In the end I was able to paint well enough to consider showing the work to other people but by then I had given up the idea because I knew there was no money in it. On the other hand I could make sense of numbers almost without having to think. It seemed the best chance I had of getting away.

The thing that seems strange to me now is that I don't remember whether Angela's obsession with aliens began with Amethyst or whether it was something that had always been there. All I know is that soon after Lorna Samways appeared on a local news programme being asked questions about Silas Street Angela insisted we go and have a proper look at it.

"There would have to be a reason," she said. "She wouldn't have picked it for nothing."

"She picked it because it sounds good," said Angela's father. "It's the two s's. That's alliteration." Angela's father was a taxi driver but he had trained as a teacher. He spoke with a northern accent. When I once asked Angela where her father had been born she told me she didn't know. At the time I thought that was odd.

"Why don't you know?" I said. "Aren't you interested?"

"I've never thought about it," said Angela. "It's the way my dad speaks, that's all."

The first time I met Angela's father I couldn't help staring at him because I was sure he reminded me of someone. There was nothing special about him - he was a small wiry man with mousy thinning hair and pockmarked skin - and yet I was almost certain I had seen his likeness somewhere, in a film maybe or a television advertisement. He wore square framed steel rimmed glasses and had strange, almost colourless eyes. His eyes always made me nervous.

Every time he looked at me I wanted to look away.

The idea of us going to have a proper look at Silas Street was ridiculous of course, like going to have a proper look at your own living room. At the same time I could see what she meant. It's easy to stop noticing the things you see every day; you might think you know what they look like but really you don't. The fact that someone had chosen to put Silas Street into a song had made it special somehow and not just for Angela. Some people in the town hated *Moon Landing* on principle because of all the extra tourists but others said that Amethyst had made the town immortal. They mentioned Penny Lane and Bourbon Street and Scarborough Fair. It struck me then that these places would be as familiar and ordinary to the people that lived near them as Silas Street was to us.

At the top end, near St Andrews Church, Silas Street was broad and well kept with neat grey kerbstones. Beside the churchyard was a small uneven area of stubbly grass that was sometimes called Silas Green and sometimes Church Green. There were bushes around the green and several trees, beech trees I think they were, but all of these were lopsided and a bit stunted because of the hard salt winds that came up every day off the sea. A narrow cobbled path ran down between the green and the churchyard. In the black and white photographs of the town that were made into postcards and sold in the kiosks along the promenade you could see that at one time Silas Street had been cobbled from top to bottom. When the cobbles were replaced by tarmac I don't know.

A short way downhill from the church the road became narrower with houses to either side. On the left ran a terrace of about ten small cottages, their front doors opening straight onto the street. To the right was a row of slightly larger houses. Several of them had been turned into shops. One of them was a small chemist's that also sold photography supplies. The other two were antique shops full of china and glass and small, easily portable items of furniture. The things they sold were of a better quality than the junk in the Salt Street arcade. I suppose people came to know that, by word of mouth as much as anything else. I suppose that's how small shops survive.

Angela would sometimes stand in front of one or other of the Silas Street antique shops with her nose pressed against the window gazing in at some old teapot covered in roses or a silver cigarette case engraved in curly letters with the name Maria. She thought things like that were beautiful and would have bought them if she'd had the money. I stood beside her and looked but I couldn't really see the fascination. I could never get away from the fact that the things had belonged to people who were old or dead.

Below the antique shops was a narrow passage called Whitsun Lane that came off Silas Street at a right angle and connected it with Johns Road, where the doctor's surgery was and the old town hall. Whitsun Lane was really too narrow for cars and bollards had been set in concrete at either end to stop them even trying it. Downhill from Whitsun Lane Silas Street became shabbier and almost run-down. There was a fish and chip shop called the Jolly Roger that sold excellent food but whose red and white paintwork was peeling and tired. One of the small panes of glass in the door to the Jolly Roger had been broken for as long as I could remember. There was a square of mouldy hardboard in its place. Behind the Jolly Roger was a yard where they kept the dustbins. The yard always smelt of mildew and overcooked fat. At the bottom end of Silas Street, where it came out onto Westwind Road by the Nubia Pavilion, there were a couple of larger houses that had been made into flats. These houses were white and well-kept, with hanging flower baskets and large plastic wheelie bins instead of dustbins, but between them and the Jolly Roger Silas Street was a jumble of tatty three-storey Victorian terraces and garages built out of breeze blocks. One of the houses had a sign outside that said Margaret's B & B but the downstairs windows had been boarded up and the gate was padlocked shut. Behind the garages was a dirty alleyway where boys sometimes kicked a football or threw stones at empty beer bottles they hauled out of the dustbins.

"It's a very old road," said Angela. "You can see that."

"Those garages aren't old," I said. "They're just ugly."

"But the ground under them is old. I mean whatever was

here before them. There was something here. I expect it was all pulled down."

She scuffed the sole of her shoe on the concrete at the side of the alley and I saw then that she was right. Parts of the tarmac had broken away and under it was the remains of some other kind of walkway made of red bricks laid side by side in a herringbone pattern. I had been behind the garages before but this was something I had never noticed. It disturbed me rather, although I couldn't have said why. It was the same feeling I had when I looked at the things in the antique shops, the sense that I was looking at something dead. I went past St Andrews four or five times a week and often walked through the graveyard as a shortcut to Angela's house on Kennmore Terrace but I never thought twice about that. Cemeteries and gravestones are at least open about what they are; you could almost say they're an advertisement for death. These other things – the old teapots and the herringbone brick – were different, the kind of things that might surprise you in the dark.

Lorna Samways's song wasn't really about aliens, at least not that I could see. A lot of the words weren't in proper sentences and it was hard to work out what they meant. If it was about anything at all it was probably about breaking up with a boyfriend. That's what most pop songs are about but when I said that to Angela she said that wasn't the point.

"Anyway, it's not a pop song," she said. "It's a folk song. Folk songs are based on ancient myths and legends."

"There's not going to be an ancient myth or legend about aliens, though, is there?"

"Aliens have been here for centuries. Some people think humans evolved from aliens and not from apes at all."

"Something could definitely evolve from the stuff in some of those dustbins," I said. I wanted to make a joke of it but she wouldn't laugh. By that time Amethyst had brought out their first album, Holy Grail. Angela knew it by heart. She told me she wanted to write songs of her own but didn't have a notebook to put them in. I went with her to look for notebooks in the Salt Street arcade but she refused to buy any of them.

"I'll know it when I see it," she said.

Angela's mother hated the magazines that Angela brought home, about sightings of UFOs and the threat of alien invasion.

"It's enough to give anyone nightmares," she said. She gathered the magazines from where Angela and I had been reading them, spread over the rush matting of the floor in the breakfast room, and made Angela take them upstairs. Each time she picked one of them up she held it by the corner as if it were soiled. When she moved her hands her rings caught the sunlight and made rainbows on the walls. One of the rings had a large pink stone in it that Angela said was amethyst. I thought it was too pale to be amethyst, that it was probably just rose quartz, but I didn't say anything to Angela. I noticed that Angela's mother bit her nails.

Angela bought the alien magazines at the newsagents next to Grainger's the fishmongers. I was amazed that such magazines existed and that Angela had known where to find them.

"You don't really believe in these things?" I said. I half read, half flicked through an article about a woman in Cromer on the North Norfolk coast who claimed to have definitive proof that the manager of one of the local guesthouses had been replaced by an alien invader.

"He sounds just the same but there's a smell about him," she said. "A smell you can't quite put your finger on, like mushrooms or eggshells. Everyone's noticed but nobody dares to say." There was a grainy black and white photograph of the hotel manager coming out of a supermarket. He was balding and running to fat.

"Not all of it," said Angela. "But there's a lot of things that can't be explained."

"That doesn't mean aliens are the answer."

"No," she said. "But they might be."

When Angela insisted we go to Silas Street after dark her

mother wasn't keen on the idea but her father seemed resigned to it.

"There's nothing to be afraid of," he said. "I can easily make a detour and bring them home." Angela's father sometimes bought in help if he was especially busy but he did most of the pick-ups himself. When he was at home in the house he wore old cord trousers and baggy t-shirts but when he was driving he often wore a shirt and sometimes a tie. Occasionally I wondered why he had given up teaching to become a taxi driver but I didn't ask Angela about it and the truth never occurred to me. There are some things you don't think about unless they happen to you.

It was cold. I had my hands pulled up inside my sleeves. We came to the top of Kennmore Terrace and then took the short cut through the graveyard. The moon was full and St Andrews appeared to glow. I remember thinking how irrelevant that was. Things always seem different at night.

"It's beautiful," said Angela. "Isn't it?"

"I suppose," I said. "I'm freezing."

We turned into Silas Street and began to walk down the hill. The air was sharp in my lungs, heavy with ice crystals. I thought that was strange. It was rare to see ice in the town. The salt on the wind normally kept water from freezing.

There was nobody about. From further down the hill I could hear the sound of cars on Westwind Road, a chorus of wolf whistles from the youths who gathered under the streetlights outside the Nubia Pavilion. But up by St Andrews Silas Street was silent and still. Lights had come on in some of the cottages. From behind one set of curtains came the flickering bluish glow of a colour TV.

"What are we looking for exactly?" I said.

"We're not looking for anything," said Angela. "We just want to find out how it feels." I laughed a little, hoping she would laugh back but she had already turned away from me and was looking through the window of one of the antique shops. The shop was called Chalmers. There was a display of antique linen in the window:

embroidered pillowcases and handkerchiefs, a nightdress edged with broderie anglaise.

"My mother had some just like that," said Angela. At first I thought she was talking about the lace nightgown and I hated the thought of that, of wearing something that had belonged to someone dead. But then I saw she didn't mean the nightdress at all. She was looking at something else, at a bone china coffee cup that had been placed among the linen like a prop in a period film. The cup was tall and narrow with birds of paradise on it and a narrow band of gold below the rim. The saucer had a gold rim too but otherwise it was white. I noticed a darker wavery line across it, running at an angle to the base. It looked as if the saucer had been cracked and then later repaired.

"Does she like to collect old china?" I said. "Some people do."

"I don't really know," said Angela. "They're all smashed anyway now. It happened in the kitchen. She threw them against the wall." She laid her hand next to the glass, blocking out her view of the porcelain cup. Her hand looked tiny, bluish-white and star shaped like something that had been washed up on the beach. When she took it away it left its outline in mist and a dark clear patch at the centre like a hole.

"All mothers are mad," she said then. "Don't you think so?"

I shook inside my skin, a liquid faltering lurch that had nothing to do with the cold, but when I turned to look at Angela her eyes had a faraway look as if she were half in a dream. She might have meant nothing by it after all.

"Can we go back now?" I said.

"No," she said, then smiled. "We have to go all the way down."

The Jolly Roger was closed. In summer it was open every night but during the off season they seemed to shut up shop whenever they felt like it. The dingy concrete yard smelled just the same.

"There's nobody here," Angela said. I asked her what she had expected but paid no attention to the answer. I was afraid she had found out the truth about my mother.

By the time my mother actually died I was long gone. Somewhere in the decade before she forgot my name. Angela went down the hill ahead of me. Her red wool coat was the colour of tinned tomato soup under the streetlamps. She had owned the coat for as long as I could remember and it was too small for her. I followed her down the street and saw her disappear into the narrow passageway that cut through to the access road behind the garages. I smelt the peculiar, somehow chemical smell of damp breeze blocks. When I came through into the alley Angela was not there but several of the garages were open and I supposed she had gone inside. Most of the garages were of the usual kind with up-and-over doors but two of them were the older type, built of brick rather than breeze blocks and with double doors that opened sideways like the doors to a room. One of these garages was closed up and secured with a padlock but the other was easy to get into because one of its doors was hanging off the hinges. From where I was standing I could see dark squarish shapes that looked like piles of boxes and the silvery corrugated curve of a bicycle wheel. I could also hear sounds, a sort of scuffling-scraping that I presumed must be Angela.

There were security lights on everywhere but I still felt nervous. I wondered what might happen if anyone came. It seemed suddenly very quiet. I could no longer hear the boys outside the Nubia Pavilion nor the hum of passing cars on Westwind Road. I trod on a crisp packet and made it crackle. It was yellow and blue, the colours of salt and vinegar. I wanted to call Angela's name but I knew my voice would come out sounding too loud.

I wondered why Angela's mother had smashed her coffee cups. I tried to imagine it, the fine bone china shattering against the wall, and found it was something I couldn't quite believe in. Angela's mother wore long floating dresses made of Indian cotton. She always sounded slightly breathless, especially when she answered the phone. I imagined loud noises would startle her. I breathed on the back of my hand and felt the skin there go warm and then damp. I could have worn gloves but I had never liked the feel of them. They made me feel helpless somehow, as if I'd lost the use of my hands.

In the end I had to go into the garage because Angela didn't come out. I'm not sure how long I waited but it seemed a long time. The garage smelled strongly of creosote and was full of the things people usually store in garages: folding garden furniture, tea chests full of newspaper, rusty pitchforks and broken spades. There was a moped underneath a tarpaulin. I didn't see Angela, at least not at first. For a moment I felt convinced that she was gone.

I sensed movement behind me and turned. There was no time to be afraid. Someone was standing by the boxes. The light from outside shone on the red coat and the fine, slightly wavy hair but even so it took me a couple of seconds to realise that it was Angela. Perhaps that was because she didn't seem to know me either. She was so still she didn't seem real. I didn't dare touch her. I thought she might shatter like glass.

I said her name and started towards her but she didn't move. I blew air into her face. It obscured her features for a second and then disappeared. Suddenly she moaned. Her voice was the voice of a child.

"I know it's still in here," she said. "It won't let me get away."

I felt freezing all over. I stepped away from her and put my hands on the moped. I felt icy water spreading across my palm.

"That's rubbish," I said. "There's nothing here apart from all this junk."

I turned again to face her but then I realised there was something after all, something that scuttled away from me out of the light. Hard air punched into my lungs. I tried to look away but then I saw that the thing was only a cat. It was a largish animal, a scrawny-looking long-limbed tabby. Its eyes were furious and golden. When it saw me staring it arched and hissed. I managed a laugh. The animal darted away.

"That's all you saw," I said. "It was just a cat." I went to her then and took her arm. Almost to my surprise she was breathing and warm.

"Let's go," I said. "You're cold."

She put both arms around me and held on. It was something she had never done before. She gripped me tightly, much more tightly than I would ever have believed possible. All I could think was that if we had been in the sea we would both have drowned.

"I didn't know what it would be like," she said. "I didn't know I'd be so afraid."

I moved her backwards towards the door. She still held me tightly but I thought she was beginning to relax. When I got her outside she looked up at the moon, shading her eyes as if against sunlight. She suddenly let me go and I almost fell down.

"My God, you must be freezing," she said. Her voice sounded normal again and it was only then that I realised I didn't have a coat on. I tugged the sleeves of my sweatshirt down over my hands and tried to remember what had happened to it. It was possible I had come out without it but I couldn't have said for sure. I blew air through pursed lips and watched my breath escape into the dark. We started walking away. On Westwind Road there was a group of boys sitting in a row on the steps of the Nubia Pavilion. All of them were smoking roll-ups but none of them said a word. Each time a car went past their faces turned to gold in the headlights.

When we got to the top of Walton Road, which was the back way to Kennmore Terrace, Angela ground to a halt.

"Can I stay round at your house tonight?" she said. She glanced at me and then looked away. The suddenness of the question caught me off guard.

"It's best if you don't," I said. "My mother hasn't been very well." I tried to smile at her and we began going up Walton Road together. When we came to her house she made as if to go up the path but then unlatched the side gate instead.

"I'll go in the back way," she said. "I've forgotten my key."

The next day she was off school. Her mother rang in and said she had a cold and none of that surprised me. She was off a lot though after that and that surprised everyone. She began to get behind in some of the lessons and I suppose in the end one of the teachers must have kept her back after class and asked her about it. That sort of thing was unusual then. Not the thing itself, I mean, but the teacher noticing. People didn't talk about it then. These days they give teachers checklists of things to look for: altered behaviour, alleged sickness, a drop in grades. Angela displayed all of these but even so it was a long time before anyone said anything. Angela changed towards me too and I was angry. I thought she was spending her time with other friends.

Angela's father moved out of Kennmore Terrace for a while but it was Angela who was sent away for good. I didn't know about that until it had already happened because by then there was hardly a day when she wasn't off school. I saw her mother once, coming out of Miriam Sanderson's office carrying a pile of textbooks and a stack of the coloured folders we used in our English lessons. Her head was lowered over the books and a strand of her wavy hair hung into her eyes. The hair was a pale blonde colour, much lighter than Angela's. I don't know whether she saw me. I turned away before she could catch my eye.

About a fortnight afterwards I got a postcard from Angela. It came in an envelope, an ordinary white business envelope with a Deene postmark. It had been franked though, not stamped, as if someone had posted it for her. The postcard was of Lorna Samways, dressed in a t-shirt and jeans with her guitar resting in her lap. The guitar was black all over, a wired-up acoustic flatback with twelve steel strings. It was one of her trademarks. I remembered the postcard well. Angela had sent off a coupon from one of her music magazines and they had sent her a pack of twelve. The back of the postcard was covered in Angela's perfectly aligned tiny writing. The writing was so neat and even it could almost have been taken for print. She wrote to me about things and people I had never heard of. I supposed it must be the news from her new school.

There was no return address. There was a logo on the envelope, a sycamore leaf and a single word, 'Raymont.' The logo was printed in red. It was impossible to tell if Raymont was the place the postcard had come from or just an advert for something but I wrote a letter anyway and addressed it to Angela at 'Raymont, Deene.' I chose a card with seagulls on it. It was just the birds and the sky in the photograph, no land or water or people of any kind. I wasn't sure what to put in the letter so I told Angela I'd decided to drop my Art 'A' level and take up Computer Science instead. I told nobody I had sent it and I never received a reply. I presumed the logo had been an advert after all.

I saw a TV interview with Lorna Samways a couple of years ago. She still had her old black guitar. The interviewer asked her how the band got its name and was it true that she had violet-coloured eyes. Lorna Samways laughed. She sounded carefree and natural, the laughter of someone young.

"People always ask me that," she said. "But my eyes are really dark blue. We called the band Amethyst after my birthstone. My birthday's in February. I'm a Pisces."

She said that amethyst was a protection against drunkenness and went on to tell a story about how the Greek goddess Diana transformed a girl called Amethyst into a pillar of rose quartz to save her from being eaten by tigers. For some reason Bacchus had poured wine over the quartz and turned it purple. Lorna Samways had written a song about Bacchus and Amethyst. She called it Cup of Roses and was going to sing it live in the studio but I didn't watch the programme through to the end.

When the interviewer started asking her what it had been like having a single in the Top Ten when she was only nineteen years old Lorna Samways laughed again.

"I never thought about it like that," she said. "I just

wanted to write the song. What happened afterwards was just lucky because it meant I could write more songs without having to worry about where the money was coming from. The important thing has always been the songs."

I wondered if the interviewer would ask her about the town she had grown up in but he didn't. He probably had never heard of Silas Street except in her lyrics. I turned off the television and logged onto the Internet. There were hundreds of links for 'Amethyst,' both the semi-precious stone and the band. I read that as well as being a charm against drunkenness amethyst could also temper evil spirits, help to overcome addiction and stabilise mental illness. It was the touchstone for sincerity, a protection against poisons and thieves.

My coat wasn't at home. I hoped that maybe I had left it at school but I hadn't. I had another coat I could wear, a belted woollen houndstooth that had belonged to my mother. I hated it because it looked so old-fashioned and because it had once been hers. I wanted my parka but it was gone. There was no way I could ask for another.

When I went back to the garage on Silas Street a month later I told myself I had gone to look for my coat. That sounded unconvincing even to me. I don't know why I went there other than that I missed Angela. It was late November. The cold snap had suddenly ended and the weather had turned windy and wet. I had no umbrella. The woollen houndstooth coat felt damp against the backs of my knees.

There were puddles in the alleyway behind the garages. Oil floated in some of them, making rainbows beneath the lights. I could hear water dripping from somewhere even though the rain had stopped. The wooden door was still hanging off its hinges but I saw at once that the boxes and tea chests had mostly gone. I realised that if my parka had been in the garage there was no hope of finding it now.

The moped was still there and so was the bike. The remaining boxes and tea chests had been pushed to the back. The floor was a dirty grey, the concrete spotted with oil. There was no sign of the cat nor anywhere for it to hide.

It was cold in the garage, colder than it had been outside. I supposed that was just the damp. I folded both arms across my chest and held onto my sides. There was a deep crack in the concrete, running the length of the garage and between my feet. I shivered. I knew it hadn't been there when I first came in. As I watched a large black beetle emerged from between two tea chests and started across the floor. When it reached the crack it seemed to hesitate for a second and then fall right into it. I leaned forward to look closer but there was not enough light to see.

At that moment the light cut out completely and I became aware that I was not alone. I should have been afraid but I felt relieved.

He came forward and let in the light. Its yellowness spun off his glasses and dazzled my eyes. Once again I had the feeling I recognised him from somewhere, that maybe I had seen him in a film.

"Jane," he said. "I was watching you come down the road."

I knew that Angela's father's name was Ian but I had never called him by it. He was speaking softly, almost whispering, as if he were afraid of being overheard. He took a step forward.

"It wasn't like you think," he said. "It wasn't like everyone said." He started to come closer. He had one hand outstretched towards me. I don't know if that was meant to calm me or restrain me but in any case I never found out.

"No," I said. "You can't."

Perhaps he saw the fear in my eyes or perhaps he thought someone might come. He was still a few paces away from me but suddenly I could smell him, the bitter, chromatic odour of underarm sweat. He looked about to speak again but then didn't. He turned his back on me abruptly and went away.

The air in my lungs was icy. I had been afraid he might

step on the crack.

I moved my foot carefully sideways then looked down. There was a dirt-coloured stain on the concrete, a thready twisted line like a broken vein. There was no longer a crack in the floor. I supposed it had been a trick of the light.

When I went back outside I found it had started to rain.

The first thing I noticed was that they had opened up the Nubia Pavilion and turned it into a four star hotel. Its outer doors were open and I caught glimpses of an open plan reception area with large leather armchairs and a mosaic-pattern stone or marble floor. With the Salt Street arcade to one side and the shabby entrance to Silas Street on the other it looked ridiculously grandiose. It was hard to see how they could afford to keep it alive.

"It's really too big for the town," I said later. "It must be expensive to stay there, I can't imagine they get all that many guests."

"I love the floor in there," said Angela. "There's a notice that tells you about it. It's an exact copy of the Victorian original, which was based on a mosaic in a French chateau. They saved bits of the old floor and put them into some of the bathrooms. I go down there sometimes to have coffee. I like to sit and look at the sea."

She was thinner. The veins stood out on the backs of her hands. She had kept her hair long – it trailed slightly below her shoulders – but it had already begun turning grey. She was wearing glasses. When she came to the door I recognised her at once but the oval steel-rimmed glasses gave me a shock. After a second or so I realised it was her father she looked like. I knew then that it had never been Angela's father who looked like the film star but Angela herself. She looked just like Vinnie Stebson, who had played Morna Crewe in The Dollmaker. Morna Crewe had killed six people and the film had kept me awake for half the night.

"I only use them for reading," said Angela. She took off the glasses and tucked them into the pocket of her skirt. The skirt was a patchwork of colours, the kind of thing her mother used to wear. I wondered what had shown in my face.

The first of her postcards had reached me at college. I don't know who sent it on. After that there had been others although sometimes a year would go by with nothing and I would think that was the last of her. I wrote back to her, the bland and careful letters of someone who has made a friend later in life and isn't certain whether to relax their guard. In essence I told her nothing. The letters were just a way of holding on. I wondered how much of Angela there really was left or whether I was making her up as I went along.

Her postcards to me conveyed no news at all. The cards themselves were mostly photographs, pictures of places neither of us had ever been to or had ever talked about – Cleethorpes, Llandudno, Tralee. They were old – sepia tinted and yellowed around the edges – and I supposed she had picked them up in the Salt Street arcade. On the backs of the cards there were poems. For a long time I tried to find the source of these poems, in books of quotations and modern anthologies. It never crossed my mind she had written them herself.

"I work full-time at Chalmers now," she said. "You know, the antique shop just below St Andrew's."

"Are you the manager?" I said.

"I'm in there on my own. There's nothing to manage really. I just like old things."

She said this to me as if it were something I didn't already know, as if we had only just met. My heart ached in my chest and my saliva tasted sour as if I were ill.

Before driving up to Kennmore Terrace I had parked the car in one of the half-hour spaces across from the Nubia Pavilion. The wind coming off the sea smelt fresh and clean. At the bottom of Silas Street there was a new brick wall and then a side entrance to a fifty-space car park. 'Westwind Lodge Patrons Only,' said the notice. I had to think for a moment before realising that Westwind Lodge must be the new name of the Nubia Pavilion. The alleyway and the garages were gone.

The car park was all black tarmac and freshly painted

yellow lines. The surface was smooth and unmarked. I stood there for several minutes and looked at the cars. I imagined bulldozers and hammer drills tearing up the pale grey concrete and herringbone brickwork that had been there before and that should have comforted me but it didn't. While I was standing there a young man in linen trousers and a raw silk shirt came out of one of the new back entrances of the Nubia Pavilion and strode towards one of the cars. It was a beautiful car, a Jaguar convertible in a soft, almost luminous grey.

"Can I help you?" he said. "You look lost."

"No thank you," I said. "I'm waiting for someone, that's all."

He nodded and got into the car. I waited until he had driven away and then walked back down Silas Street and crossed the road to my own car. I thought about how easy it was to invent reasons for doing things, lies that sounded convincing and less troubling than the truth.

Angela's mother had died of an overdose and Angela inherited the house on Kennmore Terrace. There were a lot of things I recognised – the yellow upright piano, the oak veneer sideboard, the Habitat kitchen chairs – but there were other things too, things I supposed Angela must have brought home from Chalmers. There was one object in particular I couldn't stop staring at, a carved magazine rack in the shape of an angel blowing a trumpet. The house felt cluttered. I couldn't have stood to live in it myself.

There were pictures propped up on the mantelpiece, photographs from an exhibition of Twenties fashion and sepia tinted postcards like the ones she had sent to me. In amongst them was a photo of Angela and her father. It had been put in a frame, a gilt-edged cardboard surround. It was Christmas in the picture. There was a blurred foil tree in the background and Angela's father wore a party crown made of red tissue paper. He had his arm around her shoulders. In one corner of the frame someone with a silver pen had scrawled 'Aldershot' in untidy capitals.

Angela looked her age or somewhere near. Her father looked no older than when I had last seen him: scrawny and innocuous and pale. They were both wearing their glasses. If I hadn't known them I might have said they were brother and sister.

"I've tried writing songs about it," said Angela. "I've been trying to write it down for most of my life."

She had put down her teacup and was looking at me looking at the photograph and of course I thought she meant the thing that was supposed to have happened with her father. I felt myself blushing. I had no idea what I would say if she started to talk about that but it wasn't what she meant at all. What she took from the sideboard was a pile of notebooks. The covers were soft and pliable, made of some sort of coloured plastic. I recognised her writing, the anodyne too-perfect script that looked like a child's.

"I don't know how to write music," she said. "I can only put down one line."

I had never learned to read music. The notes she had spaced on the five ruled lines were just dots to me. I ignored them and read the words.

> *Stone heart*
> *What happens when*
> *A stone heart opens*
> *Stone hearts crush everything*
> *And don't know*
> *What they've done*

As well as the notebooks she had a recorder. I watched her fit it together, the three sections sliding into each other like bits of some antique machine. The wood was dark and polished like old furniture. The sound that came out of it was deeper than I had expected. It had a low brown softness that was like the wood. I don't know which song she played, whether it was the one about the stone heart called Cold Night or one of the others but she played for what seemed a long time. Near the end she made a noise on the recorder that was like a bird twittering. I don't know how she did that, whether it was something she had made up herself or whether somebody had taught her. I looked at her hands fluttering above the holes, the thin nervous fingers, and remembered her mother's breathless voice and bitten nails. I wanted to tell Angela she should get her songs typed up and sent to a publisher but I didn't. There seemed to be so little of her. The songs were really all that was left.

"What did you see?" I said instead.

"I don't know," she said. "It was cold that night, that's all."

She looked almost old. I wondered how I looked to her.

"You must come and visit," I said. "Soon."

She said nothing. She pushed back her hair and took off her glasses. It was only then that I noticed the ring she had on, the faceted stone in the gold setting that had belonged to her mother. I had once meant to tell Angela that the stone was rose quartz but I realised I had been wrong about that in any case. I'd remembered it being pink but when I looked at it now I saw it was the bottomless translucent purple of amethyst.

Ryman's

Suitcase

Derek Ryman had run away to the Congo because his wife had been having an affair. That was what I was told later, although Maxted maintained at the interview that Ryman's flight to Africa was more in the nature of a pre-planned sabbatical. When I asked Maxted how long he might be needing a locum, he told me he wasn't sure.

"I would guess at six months, " he said. "Although it might be as long as a year."

Ryman's suitcase, when it came, was stuck with a multitude of self-adhesive airline labels and addressed to Colin Maxted, care of the practice. Maxted delivered it into my keeping because I was using Ryman's room.

"There's not enough room in mine," he said. "I hope it won't be in your way."

Even though Maxted was the senior partner it was Ryman who had the largest room, a corner room on the ground floor with a shutter-lined, triple bay window. He had been in the practice the longest; he had occupied the room for twenty years. Once Maxted had gone I picked up the suitcase and put it away in the deep triangular cupboard beneath the stairs. I pushed it all the way to the back and then shut the door on it. It had not been particularly heavy. If I thought about it at all I presumed it contained things of his, clothing perhaps, that he didn't want to get rid of entirely but wouldn't be needing in Zaire. By then I didn't want to dwell too much on the subject of Derek Ryman. Less than one month earlier I had fallen in love with his wife.

My first emergency callout in Horsfall was to a children's birthday party on the new estate. The house was an end-of terrace: double-glazed PVC windows, red-shingled pantiled roof. The party was round the back. They had hired an outside caterer and a well-known local conjuror called Clive Latimer. A nine-year-old girl had fainted and wouldn't come round. She was lying unconscious beneath a large green-striped marquee.

"Her name's Abigail. Everybody calls her Billy." The woman who opened the door looked approximately forty years of age. Her long russet hair was liberally streaked with grey. She led me through an orderly cream-painted house and into the garden. I thought at first that she was the sick girl's mother; though I found out soon enough that wasn't the case. As we came out onto the lawn, people drew aside, staring at us. At one point the woman clutched my hand.

The child lay on her back in the grass. Sunlight passed through the marquee, casting long, irregular stripes across her face. I pushed past a collective of little girls in party frocks and a loitering, clownish figure dressed mostly in black. Some time later I realised he must have been the magician. I felt for the child's pulse and checked inside her mouth for any obstructions. Her temperature was normal. I couldn't find anything wrong.

"What happened?" I said, looking at the red-haired woman.

"She just fell over," said a clear, high voice at my elbow. "The magic just freaked her out." It was a plump-faced, sturdy child with savagely-cut brown hair. She wore square-framed purple spectacles and shiny red patent leather shoes. She put out a foot towards Billy; her mud-streaked sole brushed against the prone girl's dress.

"It's been very hot," said the woman with the greying red hair. "They've been running round all day long."

"Have they had enough to drink?" I asked her.

"I've put out bottled water by the gallon," she said. At that moment the child in the grass shook rapidly all over like a dreaming dog, then sat upright and opened her eyes.

"I want some more jelly," she said. Then she got to her feet.

"She's bonkers," said the glasses girl. "Billy's bonkers." She withdrew her foot.

I made Billy sit down again and then checked her over. Her breathing was steady. She looked at me with grey-brown eyes.

"Your daughter seems fine now," I said to the woman. "She must have got over-excited with all the games."

"Billy's not my daughter. My daughter's over there." The woman pointed to another girl standing some distance away. She had a gold foil crown on her head with a pennant that read 'nine today.' She was hand in hand with the magician.

"She's Billy Ryman," said the fat girl in glasses. "She's bonkers. That's why her mother ran away."

In the wake of that afternoon the villagers seemed to accept me and began calling me 'the new doctor.' Some of them maintained I had saved Billy Ryman's life. There would be people in my position who might well discourage such a rumour but I was not one of them. I had heard it was often difficult to integrate oneself into a small community such as Horsfall; I needed all the help I could get. I had been a junior houseman at St Thomas's but had decided to take the plunge into General Practise. I had taken a post at a surgery in Clapham but then had been made redundant due to cuts. The locum's job at Horsfall had come along at just the right time but I felt out of my depth away from London. I had never before experienced the peculiar and unavoidable intimacy of life in a village, and therefore felt strangely exposed. When you meet someone in a city they might disappear forever unless you arrange it otherwise; if you make a new friend in a village you are certain to see them again. I ran into the woman with the long red hair less than a week following the incident with Billy Ryman. She was standing on the pavement in the High Street just outside the chemist's. She touched me on the hand as I went by.

"I never really thanked you over Billy," she said. "I suppose it was just the shock."

"It doesn't matter," I said. "That's really quite alright." I felt awkward and even embarrassed. I could not remember a single incident in London where I had encountered one of my patients on the street. "How's Billy doing now?" I put both my hands in my pockets and glanced down at the ground.

"She seems fine." The woman ran a hand through her hair, exposing roots that were almost white. "She's living with us at the moment. At least until one of her parents decides to come back."

I offered to buy her a drink without really knowing why. It was as if I were thanking her for something rather than the other way around. I was surprised when she accepted, enough to almost regret what I had done. As I followed her inside the saloon bar of a pub called the Harlequins I wondered what we might find to talk about. Before I had time to get nervous she was telling me about Sonia Ryman.

"I think it's an absolute scandal," she said. "How a woman could leave her own child." She took a sip from her glass, which contained mineral water with a dash of vodka. "I can understand anyone wanting to get away from Derek, but there's no excuse for deserting Billy too."

I was unsure how I ought to reply. I was wary of taking sides in a matter on which I was all but ignorant. However I found myself intrigued.

"Where's Billy's mother now?" I said. "Is she maintaining any contact with her daughter?"

The woman shook her head, moving it emphatically from side to side. The grey hair rustled. For a second she laid her fingers on my arm.

"Not a word since the day she left. It's no wonder that Billy had that turn. I suppose I should get her to talk about it, but it's difficult to know what to say."

"Does anybody know where she went?"

"Not even Clive Latimer. At least he says not, and I for one believe him." She shook her head again, but with diminishing emotion. "Clive's a magician, you know. It was Clive that Sonya was seeing."

I stared at her, feeling foolish, not quite understanding

what she meant. Then I realised she was talking about the conjuror at the birthday party. I felt myself blushing. I had never met Derek Ryman but he was still in a way a colleague. I didn't like the thought of betraying his trust. I gulped down the last of my beer and rose to leave.

"Surgery starts at two," I said. "It's time I went." The woman gazed up at me, the red-brown hair falling back to reveal her neck. The skin of her throat had begun to sag slightly, suggesting scrawniness. I realised I didn't know her name.

It was about ten days after that when I found the photograph of Sonya Ryman. Maxted's consulting room had been recently refurbished in leather and steel; Ryman's still had an aura of the pre-war. It had been cleared for my use before I came, but in a room of that size and temperament it would have been all but impossible to remove his every trace. The things that remained I discovered with time: a stack of old calendars, each of them depicting scenes from the Scottish Highlands, a Rubik cube made of polished, painted wood, a black lacquer box that must have contained close to a thousand gold-wire paper clips. In the cupboard under the stairs I found a trepanning iron. I had seen such things before, of course, in the pages of medical textbooks, but never close at hand. The discovery shocked me; I wondered if Colin Maxted knew it was there.

I found the photograph of Sonya in the top drawer of Ryman's old desk. The desk was enormous, a roll-top model made of oak that had been obsolete for decades. The picture had been turned face downwards, but the curlicued silver frame was still very bright. For a long strange moment I believed I had seen her before. Then I realised that it was just that she looked like Billy. It was an old-fashioned face: no visible make up, a wide, pale forehead, straight dark hair tied severely back. There was an agelessness about her, something that gave me the impression she could have no life beyond the photograph. Almost without thinking I stood it upright on the desk. She looked back at me calmly, as if approving my decision. I had always imagined Ryman as old and the scraps of esoteric rubbish that had been left behind in his consulting room served only to confirm me in this impression. The woman who had become Billy's guardian had made no secret of the Rymans' unhappy marriage. Looking at Sonya's serene, almost stoical image I began to feel the first stirrings of what I then considered to be pity: a woman such as she, condemned to an obscure existence at the side of an ageing eccentric. I wondered what had drawn her to Ryman in the first place. I wondered what had made her run off and leave her daughter when she was supposed to have found happiness with Clive Latimer, the magician.

In London I had spent my leisure hours in cinemas and galleries, drinking with acquaintances, having occasional dinner with friends. Horsfall provided few of these diversions. Before my arrival in the village, its absence of metropolitan facilities had worried me greatly; in the event I was surprised at how little I missed. I quickly discovered a hitherto unknown enjoyment of long walks in the surrounding countryside. Colin Maxted became my hiking partner whenever he could get the time off.

"This is an unexpected pleasure," he said to me on one occasion, when we first made it to the summit of Hanna's Fell. "I know it's a cliché, but I always imagined a chap from London would be accustomed to more sedentary pastimes."

"So did I," I said. "But needs must when the devil drives." He laughed at that and I responded in kind. Hanna's Fell was the highest peak in the district and the view from the top was like nothing I'd ever seen. From where I stood I could just make out the houses and businesses of Horsfall, scattered like cardboard boxes at the foot of the green ravine. On the far horizon I could see the grey smudge that was the city of Winterton, a smeared and oily thumbprint against the blue. The climb had taken over three hours, and as we descended it began to grow dark. The change was so gradual that my eyes grew accustomed to the dusk without my even knowing it, but by the time we had negotiated the rockier parts of the climb I realised I could hardly see my feet upon the path.

"We should have brought a torch," I said to Maxted.

"There's really no need," he replied. "I've done this climb so often I could find my way blindfold." It was true that he seemed unconcerned. He carried on talking as if we were walking in bright daylight; I tried not to look about us, and kept as close to him as I could. The lower slopes of the Fell were densely wooded and in places the path disappeared almost entirely. Wood-rodents scuttled noisily in the leaf litter; the night-blackened trees seemed to whisper to one another as we passed. The dark threw twisted shadows and made things huge. I reasoned to myself that if we lost our way we would soon come upon habitation, but even faced with this logic I did not feel entirely calm. The woods seemed to stretch endlessly in all directions and it seemed to me that we might walk in them forever. I listened carefully to Maxted and tried to focus on what he was saying. Our boots thudded on the path like the footsteps of a cavalry. Whenever I answered one of Maxted's questions I spoke louder than usual, as if to prove to myself I was still there.

We came back into Horsfall suddenly. When Maxted suggested we should eat together in the Harlequins. I agreed at once. I felt that I needed a drink. It was only when I came to sit down that I realised I was also hungry and tired. For a while I left the talking mainly to Maxted. I was content just to sit in safety and light, lulled by the babble of voices at the bar. When the food came I began to feel more like myself again. The Harlequins served real ale, which had a loosening effect upon my tongue.

"Where were you before?" I said. "Or have you always lived at Horsfall?"

Maxted laughed. "This is the kind of place you run away from rather than stay in. I came here as a promotion. The only trouble now is how to leave."

"Ryman left," I ventured.

"He'll be back." Maxted leaned back in his seat and took

a swig of his beer. "He came here as a young lad, you know. He knows the fells and woods like the back of his hand." He sighed and stretched his legs. "It was Derek who got me started on the hills."

"Derek Ryman?" I said. "He must be quite fit for his age."

Maxted turned his face towards me as if in surprise. "Derek was only fifty," he said. "Only five years older than me." He wrinkled his brow. "What made you think he was old?"

"I don't know." I shrugged and then sipped at my beer. It struck me as odd that Maxted had spoken of Ryman in the past tense, as if he might not be returning after all. I had no idea why I had presumed that he was old. I wondered if it had been a convenience for me, if it made me feel less guilt with regard to Sonya. Suddenly I realised I was desperate to ask Maxted about Sonya, and yet I did not quite dare. I put down my glass and scraped my feet back and forth over the floor.

"How come Ryman wasn't head of the practice?" I said, before realising I had used the past tense as well.

"He would have been, but he was ill." Maxted closed his eyes and crossed his arms behind his head. "Or rather Sonya was ill. He took a lot of time off to look after her. That was just after Billy was born. Shortly before I came."

"So you took over his post?"

Maxted nodded. "It was five years before he came back full time."

Now that Sonya had finally been mentioned I felt ill at ease talking about her. I recalled her photograph, the fragile transparency of a woman who looked as if she had lived out her life before the war. I supposed she had suffered some kind of postpartum disorder. I could have asked Maxted to confirm this but I disliked the idea of gossiping about her. It would have felt like I was being disloyal. "Did you know he had a trepanning iron?" I said instead.

Once more, Maxted laughed. "Did you find that in one of his cupboards?" he said. "I can't say I'm all that surprised." He told me that Ryman had had a passion for medical ephemera and outmoded hospital equipment. "He used to go to auctions," he went on. "He would buy up all this stuff they had there – doctor's bags and apothecary chests, that sort of thing. Sometimes he'd get me to come into his room and look at them, then start enthusing at how beautiful they were. I don't imagine he ever actually used any of them, but then again you can never be sure." He paused. "There are still some doctors who will swear by trepanning. It's illegal of course, but then so are a lot of things." He went on to recount an anecdote of a contemporary of his at medical school who had been caught trying to germinate cannabis in the airing cupboard of the nurses' home. Soon after that the evening drew to a natural close. Outside the pub Maxted clapped me on the shoulder and passed some comment about good beer being a lot more beneficial than any mere hole in the head. It took me a moment to realise that he was referring to the trepanning iron. I tried to laugh without quite succeeding, covering up my failure with a cough. Maxted turned from me then and ambled off into the night. I watched him for a moment – his slightly hunched, aquiline shoulders, fingers knotted together behind his back – then made off in the direction of the cottage I was renting at the far end of Vaughan Street. The character of night in the village differed so greatly from the glimpse I had had of night in the hills that I hardly even noticed it was dark. I had heard that there were some villages in the district that still had no streetlights but Horsfall was not one of them and I was glad. A procession of orange lanterns led me almost all the way to my door.

The space inside the house seemed somehow darker than the narrow street outside. I turned the hall light on quickly and made my way straight upstairs. I flung open the door of my bedroom and switched a lamp on in there too. I undressed and then went back and forth several times across the landing to the bathroom, firstly to go to the toilet, then to clean my teeth and wash my hands. I found that I was making an unnatural amount of noise, as I had done on the darkening hillside earlier. I felt a curious sense of relief at being in bed.

I did not turn off the light at once. Instead I reached

beneath the bed for the concise edition of Weills Medical Encyclopaedia I habitually kept there and leafed through it to the entry on the trepan. It was a bulky volume; the weight of it constricted my chest. I read what I already knew: that the trepanning iron, or trepan, was a portable cylindrical saw that had been used to bore small holes in the human skull. There was a fine line diagram of the device, with arrows indicating the various moving parts. It looked exactly like the thing I had found under Ryman's stairs. The text maintained that the primary purpose of trepanning had been to relieve a build-up of pressure within the brain. Ancient tribes had once trepanned their enemies, and kept the resultant discs of bone as war trophies. In Central European occult medicine trepanning had been employed as an exorcism for demonic possession, although by the eighteenth century such arcane practices had all but died out. The physicians of the Enlightenment stopped blaming the Devil and concentrated instead upon solving the equations of blood pressure and biorhythms. The article contained part of a verbatim report by a Dr Thomas Henscher who had practised in Leipzig in the 1850s, claiming that the trepan had proved uniquely efficacious in providing a cure for chronic migraine headaches. 'I have seen grown men, strong as bulls, reduced to the status of whimpering children by this insidious *dolor*,' I read. 'All treatments have provided but temporary respite, with the notable exception of the trepan.' Henscher went on to describe a particular case in which he had bored three small holes into the skull of a man named Friedrichs, who had been subject to rages brought on by headaches of such violence and intensity that other physicians had given him up to brain cancer. 'Following my treatment he was a changed man,' wrote Henscher. 'Within three days of surgery Hans Otto Friedrichs had returned to his former profession of watchmaker, in which he enjoyed profitable success until his retirement some fifteen years later.' Henscher described the process of trepanning in some detail, thereby acquainting me with a salient fact that I had not known: namely that the patient was usually practised upon without the use of an anaesthetic. The final paragraphs of the entry were headed 'Modern Applications' and seemed to suggest that the trepanning iron had been a regular component of the doctor's armoury until after the First World War.

My wrists had begun to ache and I returned the book to the floor. Before turning out the light I gazed for a moment at the silver-framed photograph of Sonya Ryman which I had brought home from the practice and now stood on my bedside table beneath the lamp. I wanted to meet her eyes with an expression of intelligence and fortitude but in fact was aware of little save my own exhaustion. My eyelids slid closed and I had trouble in opening them again as I groped for the light switch. In the final split second of brightness I imagined that Sonya was really looking at me; the stoical serenity of her features now seemed helpless and somehow resigned.

There were six of us at dinner: an older man and his very young wife, who I understood to be involved in local politics, a couple from the estate who ran their own courier business, the red-headed woman, and me. The red-headed woman was called Yvonne Nancy, and she had delivered her invitation through the post. I didn't know how she had got hold of my address and I did not particularly want to be her partner at dinner. I went because I wanted to see Billy and there seemed no other way to bring such a meeting about. Yvonne opened the door to me before I had time to ring the bell.

"The girls are already in bed," she said. "Come in and I'll pour you a drink."

My heart sank. There was as yet no sign of the other guests and I wondered if that had been intentional. It had just gone seven-thirty and there was no sound from upstairs. I had little experience of children outside the surgery but all the same I found it difficult to imagine how Ms Nancy had conspired to keep two active healthy nine-year-olds so quiet. I perched myself on the edge of one of her beige velvet armchairs and sipped at the *fino* sherry she had put into my hand. I tried hard to listen to what she was saying but found I was becoming increasingly fixated on the silence in the house's upper floor. I pressed my fingers hard against the slender stem of my glass.

"....the village?" I heard her say.

"I'm sorry?" I replied. She was wearing a low-cut rust-coloured evening dress that was uncomfortably the colour of her hair.

"Do you think you'll stay on in the village, or are you aiming to go back to Town?"

"I suppose that depends on Dr Ryman. It's his job after all, not mine."

Before she could say more the doorbell rang and I was being introduced to the middle-aged man with the beautiful wife. Shortly afterwards the other couple arrived and we all sat down to eat. Yvonne Nancy proved to be an exceptional cook and for a while I forgot my original purpose in coming. The middle-aged councillor dominated the conversation expertly throughout the first two courses and I was pleased not to be under an undue strain. It was only as the dessert was brought in – a tarte tatin of sculptural beauty and a delicious piquancy of flavour – that attention reverted to me.

"What's your opinion, Doctor?" said the politician. "Is it nature or is it nurture, and do we have the right to even ask?"

I came back to myself with a rush, dimly aware that they had been discussing NHS funding and the financial morality of providing free treatment for deliberate self-harmers.

"The NHS should be free at the point of delivery, that's its founding principle," I said. "If you start to tamper with that, where might it end?" I used the maxim often in such debates, although in quieter moments I had sometimes begun to wonder if it was something I still believed.

"Forgive me, Doctor, but in this day and age we have no choice but to begin asking just where it ought to begin," said the politician. "Surely the founding principle of democracy is that there are no rights without responsibilities."

"I'd like to question that," said the self-made man. "Where is it written down?" He was a small man, with sparse, sandy hair and the beginnings of a paunch, but his unusual yellow-gold eyes glowed with a peculiar light.

"It's the whole person you've got to treat in any case," said his wife. "People have nothing to work for any more, that's the real problem. How do you suggest we pay for that?"

I looked from one of them to the other, uncertain of what to say. I had heard all the arguments so many times before that the discussion itself did not interest me.

"We must treat as we find," I said, wondering how best to extricate myself without causing offence. "There's really little more that we can do."

"Goodness gracious," said the politician's wife. "For God's sake, somebody, catch her." The woman had covered her mouth with her hands; her haul of expensive rings flashing coloured fire in the candlelight. I quailed under her gaze, uncertain as to what I had done. Then I realised she was not looking at me at all but at something behind me. I turned round rapidly, almost upsetting my chair. A child in a pink flannel nightshirt was standing at the top of the stairs. She was swaying back and forth like a sapling caught in the breeze. Her loose brown hair lay about her shoulders in a spidery tangled mass. It was Billy Ryman. I could see she was just about to fall.

I was across the room in what seemed less than a second. I mounted the first five steps of the staircase, my arms spread wide as if to prevent the girl from getting away. The child seemed unaware of me. Her eyes were open, but she stared blankly ahead of herself like a blind girl. I crept upwards slowly, the stairs creaking under my feet. The child's bare toes were curled around the lip of the stair-tread, as if she could somehow sense her plight and yet do nothing about it. I wanted to speak to her, to utter some soft words of protection or comfort, but was afraid to do so in case they shocked her awake. Once I was close enough I took a firm but gentle hold of her upper arms. She trembled slightly under my fingers and I was reminded of a dog I had helped to save once, injured at the side of the road. I propelled her gradually backwards, out of harm's way. Those in the room behind me released a collective sigh.

"Billy," I said quietly, crouching before her. "It's time for you to go back to bed." She looked down at me then, although I don't think she actually saw me. I put out a hand again and used it to stroke her hair. "Can you show me where your room is?" I said. The hair was sticky with sweat. I smoothed it across her temple and tucked it behind her ear. As I withdrew my fingers I felt something strange, something that ought not to have been there. Using my fingertips as antennae I traced a line backwards from her temple and round towards the midpoint of her skull. There were three slight depressions, the openings to three small holes. I felt a savage chill bloom in my chest, as if I had been forced to drink ice-water. Then Billy Ryman spoke to me, her high voice fragile but clear.

"Everyone's out in the woods," she said. "I mustn't be late, or they'll go."

"No Billy, it's time to go back to bed." Yvonne Nancy had crept up beside me without my knowing. I was so startled by her voice that I came close to toppling backwards down the stairs. Almost at the same moment a door on the upper landing opened to reveal Yvonne Nancy's daughter, the girl I had first seen in the garden wearing a crown.

"Billy's got out again," she said. "I can't make her come awake." In contrast to Billy, she looked bleary-eyed and tousled, her round cheeks ruddy from sleep.

"Billy's just coming, Amanda," said Yvonne Nancy. "I want the both of you straight back to bed." She herded the children through the open doorway and into the bedroom. When she came downstairs two minutes later the other guests were rising to go. There was a multiple exchange of forced goodbyes. I hovered on the periphery, uncertain of what to do. Eventually the front door closed and the two of us were left alone.

"Perhaps it would be good if you stayed," said Yvonne Nancy. "For Billy's sake, I mean." She laid her hand on my arm. She was wearing a loud, aldehyde-based perfume, overlaid with the scents of powder and base foundation. Her hair had more red in it than it had done when I first met her. "The room next to mine is the spare room. I can easily make up a bed."

"There's really no need to worry," I said. "Sleepwalking is actually quite common, especially at their age." I told her to call me if anything untoward happened then made my escape. There were lights in the windows of some of the buildings but there was no-one at all to be seen. I walked quickly away from the house. I went the long route home, by way of the new sports centre and the supermarket car park. I took no notice of the dark. I was thinking of Sonya Ryman.

The house was cold. I went upstairs and into the bedroom. The photo of Sonya stood in darkness, a dark upright oblong in the shadow of the unlit lamp. I touched the frame, but did not turn on the light. The metal was chilly with a hint of condensation. The luminous dial of the bedside clock told me it was long after midnight. I found that I had lost all sense of time. I went back downstairs and out into the night.

Vaughan Street stood utterly empty. I turned onto the High Street, suddenly convinced of the necessity that I ought not to be seen. Some of the shop fronts were covered by metal shutters. Others lit up their wares in blurred haloes of soft amber light. As I went past the chemist's a dark car swerved towards me from the entrance to Latten Street. For one brief moment I saw my reflection spreadeagled across its windscreen. Then it too was gone.

I let myself in at the side door and turned off the alarm. I stood in the passage and tried to listen, but the sound of my blood and my breathing cut me off from extraneous sound. I tiptoed through to the waiting room. Plastic seats lined the walls, a strap of moonlight revealing their emptiness. I tried the door of Maxted's room but it was locked. The door to my room, Ryman's room, stood slightly ajar. I could not remember if I had left it that way. I closed my fingers around the handle and slowly widened the angle of aperture. Everything seemed to be the way I had left it. There was nobody inside.

There were things in the understairs cupboard that needed

moving: a rolled wad of rubber sheeting, the yellow Dyson hoover, an overhead projector and its hood. I hauled them into the open and pushed them aside, then bent myself double into the narrow triangular space. Ryman's suitcase was still at the back. That surprised me a little. However illogical it might have seemed I had almost prepared myself to find it gone. I took hold of the handle and pulled it towards me then dragged it to the centre of the floor. It was a medium-sized suitcase of the older kind: solid-sided, with a small brass padlock and gold-coloured catch. I broke the padlock with a screwdriver. The safety catch itself had not been secured.

There was an almost audible exhalation of damp, stale air. The checked paper lining looked dingy and discoloured, like something that had been stored in an outbuilding or cellar. There were clothes in the case, women's clothes, folded together neatly in a pile. I lifted out a blouse in fine grey cotton, a narrow circle of lace set into the neck. It was an old-fashioned garment, and had begun to smell faintly of mould. Beneath the blouse was a white cotton petticoat hemmed with *broderie anglaise*. In places on the pale blue stitching there were faint reddish stains that could have been traces of blood.

Under the clothes was an unbound sheaf of paper. The handwriting was purposeful and elegant, but for some reason still difficult to read. From what I could make out it formed a series of nature-notes, detailing the breeding locations and habitats of an insect called the ichneumon fly. I knew little of natural history but I had heard of the ichneumon fly. It was a large solitary insect that laid its eggs in caterpillars. When the larvae hatched they became parasites, feeding off the body of a still-living host.

At the bottom of the suitcase I found a Swan Vestas matchbox that contained several hard white discs that felt like bone. There was also a pack of playing cards with a pattern of swirling stars on each reverse. The inside flap of the pack had been signed 'C. Latimer' but the signature was in pencil and was already more than half-way gone.

Bird Songs at Eventide

For when the dusk of dreams
Comes with the falling dew
Bird songs at eventide
Call me to you.

Royden Barrie

When she took over from Dennis Marchont there were six dragons out on the sward. The sward was five acres square, a scrubland of lichens and sarg hemmed in on all sides by stands of blood oak and phosphor-weed. It was Billings who had named it the sward, and even though Billings had died the name had stuck. From the air the land looked corrugated, like a wrinkled greenish piecrust, or a scab.

"Quilla and Percival have been out there most of the day," said Marchont. "Lydia's just arrived. It's all in the log." He put up his hood and pulled the zipper of his yellow bush-jacket all the way to the top so that only his eyes and cheeks could still be seen. "Can you sign me off straight away or should I wait?"

Dennis Marchont liked to abide by the rules, a trait that sometimes made him tiring to work with. Isabel found it interesting and strange that such scrupulous pedantry should sit so blamelessly alongside the species of bashful wonderment that made him unable to resist naming the dragons. His delight in the Fendrics was spontaneous and inexhaustible but his diligence sometimes amounted almost to prudery. She supposed that in many respects he was still a schoolmaster. She put down her rucksack and keyed her password into the microlap. She entered the date and time then told Marchont he could go. In the beginning they had shared the watches. Six months on that seemed extravagant and unnecessary. Schwarowski had all but lost interest in the bush. The sward was mostly quiet and the dragons seemed as morbidly unadventurous as zoo animals. He had shifted his attention to the crill lakes and the vast underground cave complexes that perforated the hills below North Fall. Isabel thought that if she had wanted to abandon the hide then Schwarowski would most likely have let her.

Percival and Quilla were always together. Dennis Marchont thought they were a pair. The smaller pink-winged dragon, Lydia, stood close beside them, tearing up roots with her overgrown carbon-coloured nails. On the other side of the sward three others were grazing on sarg, resting their forelegs against the trees like overgrown dogs. Two of them were occasional visitors, Fendric 7 and Fendric 20. She thought the third was the six-toed male that Marchont referred to as Gulliver but until she unpacked her glasses she couldn't be sure. In the open space just in front of the hide Percival spread his wings, testing the humid air as if for flight. His scales were a dull slate blue with a sprinkling of pinkish-white patches across the back. His wings, stretched tight, were translucent and membranous, as soft and pearly grey as the wings of bats. Despite all evidence to the contrary Dennis Marchont was still convinced that the dragons could fly. Most of their colleagues were sceptical. Schwarowski didn't care.

Isabel took off her jacket and dug down inside her rucksack for her thermos and field glasses. There were glasses in the hide but she preferred to bring her own. On top of the thermos was a grey fleece but she was unlikely to need it. The hide was constructed of pli-glass. Schwarowski said that pli-glass had a molecular hardness comparable with that of diamond, that the only thing capable of making a hole in it was a heat-gun. So far the bush had not presented them with anything large enough to test that theory but Isabel was in no doubt that it kept out the cold.

Her watch would last six hours. Towards the end of that time it would begin getting dark. The cabin was equipped with UV lights but in spite of the one-way pli-glass Isabel preferred not to switch them on. On the far side of the Sward the phosphor in the blood oaks began to glow. The light it gave off was greenish, sickly and impotent as marshfire. As the sky darkened Isabel watched the dragons. From time to time she made entires in the microlap, measuring the tea in her thermos against the time left until Evan Jalister returned to collect her in the buggy.

She had moments of terror before she woke, a recurring dream in which she was pursued by something febrile and monstrous that crackled as it moved. When she woke she was nowhere. She grappled for a sense of herself only to have it retreat into the darkness until it was gone altogether. She caught brief mind's eye glimpses of her Spitalfields apartment, the bungalow, the seafront at Swanage. She imagined those places clearly even though she knew that the people she had known there would mostly be dead. The medics in pre-flight counselling had warned her about the nightmares. Her personal physician had been a horse-faced woman with long heavy hair and large dark glasses called Lisa Bernhardt. She had told Isabel that the nightmares were part of the adjustment.

"All that will pass," she had said. Isabel had made notes and nodded. She supposed that Dr Bernhardt was probably dead now too. She must have been forty when Isabel had last seen her; the voyage to Menhir Magna took fifty-six years. She wondered how often Dr Bernhardt had thought about her clients, speeding towards Menhir Magna while she herself went towards death. She wondered if such thoughts had been comforting, whether they granted her some promise of escape.

They had packed very little because Stevie had insisted that would be best. He had taken the disc of photographs out of her hand.

"It's a new beginning, Izzie, like being born again," he had said. "There won't be any use for the past." That was before the flight, before he had seen Sophie Pellow. There were times now when Isabel longed so fiercely for a photograph that she wondered if longing alone might not be sufficient to restore one. It was the photograph of her sister that she wanted most, her sister Melanie with spokes of yellow straw caught in her hair. Melanie had been sixteen then; now she would be seventy-two.

Stevie was in the canteen. He had a tray with two bowls of kasha and was filling two beakers with tea. When he saw her coming her smiled.

"How's it all going?" he said. "How are the dragons?"

"Hector's disappeared," said Isabel. "Dennis thinks he's flown away." Stevie smiled again and put a hand on her shoulder. Isabel watched as he carried the tray to one of the side tables and sat down next to Sophie Pellow. She wondered if complete happiness made people somehow immune to the misery of others.

The dragons were changing colour. The green scales on Mozart and Gustav had started to turn yellow along the margins. Percival had amber patches amidst the blue. When he rubbed himself against one of the blood oaks gold specks came off on the bark and fell to the ground.

"It's probably seasonal," said Dennis Marchont, even though there had been no perceptible change in the weather. Menhir Magna was a huge planet, almost ten times the size of Earth. Away from the crill lakes the atmosphere was humid. In the depths of the bush the rain sometimes went on for days. The dragons rolled in the puddles, shaking themselves dry afterwards like greyhounds. Isabel used the grab-arm to collect some of the yellow scales and scoop them into a vac-jar. In closeup they were hexagonal like the floor tiles in the canteen lavatories. When she shook the vac-jar gently back and forth they made a ringing sound on the glass like gravel or coins. She wondered if the dragons were moulting. She had once been to Indonesia to write a paper on Komodo Dragons. The Komodo Dragons had been many times smaller than the Fendrics and yet sloughing their skins had made them sluggish and carmudgeonly as crocodiles. The behaviour of the Fendrics appeared unchanged.

Stevie had worked for Fitzwilliam Cartographers. He was helping to chart the surface of Menhir Magna. So far they had mapped the crill lakes and the rush plain and the tiny tract of bush that bordered the sward. She had heard that Schwarowski wanted them to leave off mapping the barrens and turn instead to the possibly fertile land beyond North Fall. In the weeks that followed their arrival Stevie had talked about his work a lot. Most likely he still did; it was just that he now talked to Sophie and not to her. She had lost all track of their progress. She kept to the hide, to the bush and the sward, restricting herself to watching the Fendric dragons. She saw Lydia arch her wings and dart forward, nipping the neck of her best friend Fendric 30. The gesture seemed affectionate although she hadn't learned enough to know for sure. Isabel recorded the incident in the log. She wondered what Earth had felt like to live on before Columbus had discovered America. The mapped world had been tiny, as the mapped lands around North Fall were tiny, at least within the context of Menhir Magna as a whole. She seemed to remember that women at the time of Columbus had largely been discouraged from studying science. She had decided to christen Fendric 30 Judith. Judith had beheaded a man and had several operas written about her. Strong women still frightened men. Isabel couldn't decide how she felt about that, whether she was glad of it or sad.

The bush was full of life besides the dragons. She had seen leaf-changers and oakvoles, and the giant blue centipedes that Jalister had nicknamed Boxworms. There were hamster-sized red-faced monkeys with long prehensile tails and naked toes. At first they had expected to find other things too: larger primates, maybe, or even men. Five years on that now seemed unlikely. She knew Schwarowski hoped they were alone. There were three thousand people living in the cabins and bunkers around North Fall; in five years' time they expected a thousand more. Things were complicated enough without natives coming out of the woodwork.

"Are they chitinous, do you think, or do they contain actual metal?" Schwarowski held the vac-jar to the light, watching the golden fragments flash and burn. The amber glow had not diminished. Isabel suspected it might even have grown.

"That's not my department," she said. "I'm being paid to find things, not to find out what they are." She liked Schwarowski because he was a brilliant man who had never become arrogant. Not knowing something didn't seem to unnerve him in the way it did others, younger pretenders like Henderson and Cathcart. She thought perhaps he had stopped being afraid of anything since the death of Hermione Lakeman. Hermione Lakeman had died of blanket fever. As far as Isabel knew Schwarowski had been alone ever since.

"You're a marine biologist anyway, not a dragonslayer," he said. "We could do with you up at the lakes."

"You've got Morton, and Lucy Vicinnicus."

"I know, but we still need you." He was still holding the vac-jar, passing it back and forth in front of his face. In the strange yellow glow from the scales his deep-set eyes looked green instead of blue. "You should consider it, anyway," he said. "There are plenty of other sods who can work with Den." He put the jar down on his desk and crossed to where Isabel was standing and reached for a file. As he did so his brown-stained fingers brushed her hair. His hands had been attacked by some sort of suction-weed they had fished out of the crill lakes. The skin damage appeared permanent but thus far at least it did not seem to be cancerous. Stevie's hands were the hands of a draughtsman. They were lean and soft like Sophie Pellow's, unblemished and silky-white like the hands of a child.

"It's too soon for me to think about that," said Isabel. "Dennis would hate it, anyway. You know what he can be like." People thought Dennis was boring because he talked about nothing but dragons. That was why Isabel liked him: she wanted nothing else, at least for now. She turned to go, leaving Schwarowski alone with the personnel files and the vac-jar full of dragon scales.

Stevie was out with Jalister. She hadn't seen him for days.

North Fall had lost more than a hundred of its settlers to blanket fever. They had vaccines now that alleviated the symptoms but whilst working in the bushlands few people went out of the hide. Isabel had been outside briefly, twice, when something had gone wrong with the grab-arm. On both of these occasions the dragons had stayed away. The dragons occasionally ate oakvoles and treemice, but mostly they stuck to greens. Sometimes they stood still in front of the hide, gazing at the one-way glass as if they guessed there might be somebody behind it. The microphones picked up their breathing and the muffled sounds of their feet among the leaves. Percival and Quilla had gone entirely amber. When the sunlight caught their backs their hides turned to gold. Isabel collected more of the scales into vac-jars. She stacked the jars in neat rows at the back of the hide. They glowed at her weakly, like headlamps gliding through fog.

As the night came on the sounds of the bush increased. The blood oaks rustled, the hamster-monkeys whistled, the ivy cracked open its flowers. From everywhere came the sweet, keening vibrato that Dennis Marchont had attributed to glassflies. From the tallest trees came a yammering cacophany that reminded her a little of birdsong. They had looked for birds on Menhir Magna but so far they had found none. Isabel turned up the microphones, letting the riotous sounds of the bush invade the hide. She thought of summer twilights in Swanage, the carriage light over the door, the air in the lane made vibrant with the sound of swifts. She had seen the martins, too, waiting in line on the rooftops and the telegraph poles. When she had asked what they were doing her father had told her it was the birds' way of saying goodbye.

"The summer's almost over. It's time for them to leave."

"How do they know where to go?" she had said. "How do they know it's time?"

"Nobody knows that, Isabel. Birds have always flown

south for the winter. They've been doing it for thousands of years. We don't know how they know. Perhaps something calls them. Perhaps they get a message from the sun."

He had told her the flying south was called migration. He had shown her pictures in a book, photographs of African wildebeest and Monarch butterflies, extinct American bison, snow-bellied Greylag geese.

"It must be a marvellous sight," he had said. "The birds against the sky as the sun goes down."

There was a record he used to play sometimes, an old CD on which a reedy tenor voice sang a ballad about birds singing in the evening and a girl who was far away. Her chest felt tight. She wondered if there might not be birds singing in the blood oaks after all, birds that were like the glassflies and could only be seen from one side.

Out on the sward the dragons had stopped grazing. Percival lifted his head and after a moment's stillness opened his wings. They snatched at the last of the light, shimmering a deep red-gold. Isabel disengaged the vacuum seal and stepped outside.

The algae beneath her feet were soft and leached of colour. Clouds of insects rose around her knees. The dragons stood with their wings out, seemingly in thrall to the twilight. Percival made a low grunting sound in his throat that made him sound like a wild boar. When Isabel touched him on the flank he lowered his head like a horse and nuzzled her arm.

His back and sides were golden. His flank felt warm and cold together like some precious metal alive with the heat of its wearer. She moved her hand back and forth across his scales.

The evening grew deep around her. She realised with a spasm of panic that she could no longer remember the words of the song about the birds. She allowed her attention to wander, hoping it would come back to her but all she could bring to mind was the title. The song had been called 'Bird Songs at Eventide.' She had never asked her father who had written it. It hadn't seemed very important, at least not then. As the stars began to come out the sounds in the trees began to die. Suddenly she was aware of a new sound, the whirr and grind of the buggy. She leaned her cheek against Percival's flank then left him and went back inside. She signed herself out of the log. By the time Dennis Marchont appeared she was ready to go.

"They're silicon-based," said Schwarowski. "The lab boys are really on fire." A jar of the scales was open on his desk. As Isabel watched he poked them with one of his pens and began to stir. They cascaded over one another like chips of yellow marble. The vac-jar glowed with a solid amber light. "Perpetual energy," said Schwarowski. He removed the pen from the jar and rapped it against the glass. "If we can learn how to tap it who knows where it might lead."

"Can you reconstitute the element?"

"Maybe in time. Until then we can harvest it at source." He glanced at her quickly as if to gauge her reaction. "Do you think the Fendric dragons could be farmed?"

"That's impossible to tell, since we know next to nothing about them," she said. "I thought you wanted me off the Fendrics, anyway. You said the project was a waste of time."

"That was before." He put the lid back on the jar and twisted it shut. "Do they present any risk?" Since Hermione Lakeman's death Schwarowski had not cut his hair. It grew coarse and grey like a wolf-pelt. There were no wolves on Magna. It was hard to remember exactly what they were like. As Schwarowski leaned towards her a strand of the hair fell forward across his face. He swiped at it with one hand as if he were swatting a fly. "I can let you have more people," he said. "Once Thorsen comes back from the caves." The patches on his hands seemed darker. In places they looked almost black.

"We can't put people in danger," she said. "We can't

afford to." She glanced down at his hands then looked away. Schwarowski folded his arms, almost knocking over the vac-jar. He was a big man, seemingly undiminished by hardship or age. Hermione Lakeman had been small in stature but in other ways she had been Schwarowski's equal. Isabel felt suddenly close to her, though she had known her only slightly when she was alive. She remembered the way Percival had brushed her hand with his mouth, the cold-warm feel of the luminous amber scales. He had seemed almost to recognise her. In any case he hadn't been afraid. "It takes a long time to domesticate a species," she said. "Sometimes it can take many years." They still didn't know how often the Fendrics bred. Since they had been on Magna they had seen no young dragons born. The smaller Fendrics all had pink wings like Lydia but there was no way of knowing their age.

"We should bring one in for dissection," said Schwarowski. "It would tell us how they react to being caught." He uncrossed his arms and once more picked up the jar. "You should come over one evening," he said. "We've got a lot to talk about."

Outside Schwarowski's office Isabel came face to face with Sophie Pellow. Her fine blonde hair had a greenish cast, like the light from the phosphor weed. She moved lightly, almost without a sound.

"We heard about the scales," she said. "That's really amazing." She was carrying a rack of floppies and used the word 'we' casually, carelessly, without emphasis. Sophie Pellow was a geographical statistician from Dublin. She spoke with an Irish accent that reminded Isabel of the red-headed actress she had seen once in an historical TV drama about the Troubles.

"It's all been Dennis, really," she said. "Lizards aren't strictly my field." She thought about the word Schwarowski had used: dragonslayer. There had been more than a dozen people using the hide at first and that was what everyone had called them although there had been no plans then to kill anything. The island people of Rinca did not kill Komodo Dragons because the animals were sacred.

The blanket fever victims had been incinerated quickly to prevent contagion and then scattered on the rush-plains beyond the camp. When Hermione Lakeman had died there had been a funeral of sorts but so far as Isabel could remember the word 'sacred' had not been used. It was hard to believe in anything so far from home. From the vantage point of North Fall the universe seemed larger than it had been before. During her time on Earth Isabel had never really thought about God; now Menhir Magna seemed too big to accommodate him.

"It might well be a breakthrough," said Sophie Pellow. "Stevie says it could change everything." She used his name as an everyday object, a bedsheet or a spoon, a shirt, a knife.

"There's a long way to go," said Isabel. "Anything could happen."

It was twelve hours until her next shift. In her room she downloaded the last of the five piano concertos by Beethoven and booted up her microlap. She wondered if she might be able to use the graphics function to reproduce the photograph of Melanie. She had never been particularly skilful at graphics but there was plenty of time now to learn. She had heard a rumour that Schwarowski had once gone in for oil painting. She wondered if it were true.

The nights had grown longer and colder. Lars Thorsen's party would soon be returning from the caves. When that happened Schwarowski wanted Thorsen to put up some kind of electronic barrier around the Sward.

"It shouldn't be too difficult," he had said to her. "Not when they can't fly out." Schwarwoski had taken to shaving more regularly and tying back his hair with a piece of frayed cord that looked like an old bootlace. Sometimes he played cards in the canteen with Henderson and Cathcart. The younger men made jokes about his hands.

There was no moon on Magna but the stars were spread

thickly across the sky like moth-holes in a horse blanket. Instead of the black tissue paper monsters Isabel dreamed mostly about her sister Melanie. In one dream Melanie ran across the road in front of a car. Each time the car reached her she was gone. Sometimes there were sheep in the dream. Melanie unlatched a gate and soft white bodies poured out onto the road.

"It's alright," said Melanie, when Isabel tried to stop her. "The sheep know their own way home."

When she woke in the night and drew back the pro-blinds the stars shone down with a hard silver light that was as bright as moonlight. During the warmest of the summer evenings she and Melanie had sometimes taken blankets from the airing cupboard and spread them on the lawn. They had lain on the blankets talking and looking up at the sky. Isabel knew the constellations by heart. Melanie liked giving the stars names of her own.

"I can see someone looking down," she said. "The Great Dog-Warden of Highersloth."

"He'd be dead by the time you saw him," said Isabel. "The light from that star takes a hundred years to get here. Or maybe it's a thousand. I can't remember for sure."

"Don't tell me that. I think it's sad," said Melanie. They heated up milk in the kitchen and drank it from the striped blue and white bowls that were normally used for their breakfast cereal. They pretended it was goat's milk, the same as in the *Heidi* films. Melanie always played the part of Heidi because she was the youngest. Isabel had to be Clara, the sad, serious German girl who had lost the use of her legs. At the end of the film Clara had suddenly stumbled to her feet as a column of goats streamed past her down the Alm. Somewhere in the distance someone had been ringing a bell.

When Stevie came back from the lakes he had grown a beard.

"I heard about the project," he said. "Well done." His voice sounded different as if he had changed it to go with the beard.

He spoke as if he had forgotten who she was.

"I didn't really do anything," she said. "Has everything been OK?"

"It's the best thing I ever did, coming out here." He looked over her shoulder along the corridor. When Isabel turned her head there was no-one there.

"We're seeing things for the first time," said Dennis Marchont. "Nobody's done that for centuries, not since Columbus or Vasco Da Gama. I find that makes up for a lot." He zipped up his swamp-boots but left his jacket hanging open. The sleeves of the jacket were stained green around the cuffs. Isabel supposed that Dennis had been going outside.

"Everyone's forgotten us," said Isabel. "We may as well not exist."

"As long as we write it all down we'll be OK." He touched the logbook briefly with his outstretched hand. The backs of his fingers were flecked with age-spots. She thought of Schwarowski's hands, the long ridged fingernails blackened as if by tar. Once Dennis had gone she opened the microlap to Dennis's last entry. He had been sketching diagrams showing the Fendrics' wings. 'Juvenile,' he had written, and then 'mature.' On the previous page there was a list of calculations and a table detailing recent changes in weather conditions. At the foot of the page there was a graphic showing a crowd of stick figures and a flock of what looked to be birds. The stick-figures all had crowns. Beneath the drawing Dennis had written 'seasonal exodus,' underlining it twice in red. When she looked at the drawing again she saw that the things in the sky were not in fact birds but dragons. The stick-men raised their arms to them as if in welcome. Isabel wondered who they were meant to be.

The dark now came almost at once, like a cloud passing over the sun. When she took off her swamp-boots the algae beneath her feet felt damp as grass. As the stars began to come out the dragons unfolded their wings. It was Percival who took off first; leaf-litter swirled in his wake as he left the ground. Quilla stared up at him, then gathered herself and flew. The rest rose in a body and suddenly the air was dense with them. Their wings glowed strident as bronze in the light from the stars. They wheeled in convoy like a flight of Monarch butterflies above the Atlantic. They cleared the copse of blood oak and then they were gone. Smaller things flitted amongst the leaves, a stiff tangled jumble of wings. The constellations were nameless. The shadows between the trees made enormous pockmarked faces against the sky.

The doorstep grew cold in the dusk and the moon was full. The damp air made the old woman's bones ache but still she stood in the twilight and gazed at the stars. Her hair lay smooth and white against her cheek. Behind her in the trees the night-birds had begun to sing.

"Can you think where they might have gone?" said Schwarowski.

"It's a big planet," said Isabel. "They could be anywhere."

Queen South

The town where I grew up was called Middlehampton. It was a middle-sized town with a middle-sized population, hemmed in on all four sides by middle-sized roads. At the top of the town was a t–junction and a bus depot. The roads that formed the arms of the 't' were Queens Road North and Queens Road South. That was how they were designated on the map anyway, and on the signposts on the bus depot wall. Most people who actually lived in the town called them Queen North and Queen South, summoning images of something spacious and skyscraper-lined, like avenues in some American city. I've sometimes wondered since if it is minor deceptions like this that make middle-sized provincial backwaters bearable to live in. For a while I liked this idea but later on I discarded it as irrelevant. People rename things all the time, especially as children. It is simply a way they have, a way of laying claim to their world.

It was five years ago last week that I last saw her. She was standing at the far end of Queen South between the bus depot and the piece of waste ground with the burnt-out car on it. She had her red rucksack hanging from one shoulder and she was waiting for the coach to London. I could have called out to her but I didn't. Instead I hid in the wide covered entrance to the boarded-up shop that had once been Baxter's DIY and waited there until the bus came. She scraped the toe of one trainer against the kerb as if trying to erase the grass stains. When the coach drew up she got onto it without looking back. It was only then that I began to wonder if she knew that I had been there all along.

They caught up with her before she got to the airport and that was the end of that. Term began at my new school in Ealing. The leaves had started falling from the trees. I had returned to Middlehampton to do my teaching practice because it made good financial sense to live with my parents. I didn't go back there afterwards though, not even in the holidays, not even when it caused a row. I made sure I always had an excuse ready: vacations with Lisa, a study trip, even an illness. One winter I had pneumonia. I was taken into hospital for a fortnight because Lisa was booked to speak at a conference in Stuttgart and couldn't look after me. The nurses served turkey soup and tried to make jokes with me about Christmas crackers. At night I stared at the ceiling and listened to the sound of the rain. Each time a vehicle went past a bar of light pushed its way through the curtains and slid slowly down the opposite wall. I thought about how different the beams of car headlamps always appeared in wet weather: more ominous somehow, more golden. I thought about the excess water running down the sides of the road. Queen North sloped downhill into Queen South and when the rain was heavy the gutters filled up with water like mountain streams. Litter span on the rapids, the wrecked and breakable bones of miniature ships. I remember her stooping to pick up the rubbish, smoothing the soaking cellophane between her hands. There was a crackling sound, as if she were unwrapping a parcel.

"It's beautiful," she said. I saw red and yellow stripes, diagonal, like the colours in a candy cane. Her fingers looked white and cold. She folded the small scrap of paper and put it in her pocket. One of the nurses said I had been delirious but I remembered nothing. I asked her not to mention it to my wife. When Lisa came back from Germany she told me she was pregnant. Seven months later we had a baby girl and called her Rosalind. It was July. I went down to the post office to buy fifty first class stamps. There was a traffic jam on the High Street and I thought about the way buses used to sit back on their brakes when they came out of the depot on Queens Road South. In July the hot air at the top of town always used to smell of diesel. She wrote her name on the side of a bus once, licking the end of her finger and dabbing at the yellowish dust. Beneath the dust the bus-metal was bright green. The tip of her finger went black. She looked at it as if it was something unknown to her then wiped it clean again against her jeans. She noticed colour everywhere the way she noticed paper. She was determined to go to Japan.

"The Japanese build things with paper," she told me.

"Like they build things with ceramic or stone." She showed me pictures in an exhibition catalogue where everything was made from paper: miniature temples and newspaper dragons, tiny octagonal boxes with varnished lids. The names of the artists looked cumbersome and impossible to read yet she pronounced each with confidence like the names of the other people who lived in her street. At other times she said little. She touched things instead, running her fingers over broken down fence-posts and old masonry. It was as if all things were extraordinary to her, as if she saw them for the very first time. When she first saw me naked I could sense her looking at me with surprise as if I were some new beast. When she undid my shirt-cuffs she pressed the buttons hard between finger and thumb, testing their reality. They left impressions of themselves against her skin.

If she had been in one of my classes it would never have happened. Some people have revolution folded into their substance like a layer of red tissue paper but I have never been one of them. It was the summer I qualified but I didn't yet have a car. When I wanted to spend time with Lisa I had to go to London on the bus. I first saw the blonde girl from the window of one of the bright green coaches as it turned in at the depot from Queen South. It was July and term had just finished. She was wearing scuffed red trainers over bare ankles and held a large plastic bag in one hand. The plastic was so white it made her knuckles look dirty. She gazed up at the bus, not at the people on it but just at the bus. I wondered why I had never seen her at the school.

When I came out of the depot she was still there. She had put the bag down on the ground and was scanning the pavement in front of her as if she had dropped something.

"Have you lost your ticket?" I said, aware of the crumpled scrap that was still in my hand.

"No," she replied. "I was just looking at the ground."

Mica sparkled in the granite. I saw striations of pink and grey. A tendril of lichen hauled itself upwards through the green-edged hairline crack between two stones.

"Oh," I said. I sidled past her, almost treading on the carrier bag. It was only when I got to the bottom of the road that I realised I was still thinking about her. The next time I saw her was in the newsagents on Gull Street. Her footprints were outlined in dust on the square black tiles. She was looking at the greetings cards and gift wrap and counting coins from a torn leather purse. Her hair straggled downwards, obscuring her hands. It was wispy and slightly dirty, the colour of a tarnished penny piece.

"Must be a birthday coming up," I said.

"No. I just like the paper."

We left the shop together and I tried to ignore the fact I had forgotten what I went there to buy. It was hot on the street outside and the pavements shone.

"It's the mica that makes them do that," I said. "It's like walking on quartz." I kept my eyes on the ground, knowing I would never have said anything like that to Lisa. Lisa knew all about mica in granite; there would be no need to comment on it at all. The blonde girl didn't speak but I could sense her still there beside me. I turned round in the end, hoping she would say something. I caught her using the roll of gift wrap to look at the sky.

The following week I went to London to visit Lisa.

"Things should be easier in September," she said. "Once you get an actual job." She was wearing the watch I had given her for her birthday. It had a thin silver bracelet strap and she had told me that it kept perfect time. I had no reason to doubt it. She never came out with anything unless it was true. When I asked her to marry me she said nothing at first. Instead she had just nodded, as if my question were not a surprise.

"I love you Tim," she had said then. "I think it's a good idea."

I made love to her there on the bed, and admitted to myself that I had been afraid of losing her even though we had been together for more than three years.

"What are you thinking?" I asked her afterwards. Her black hair had already fallen back into place.

"I was wondering if I looked different," she said. "Now that I'm engaged." She laughed. "Let's get up," she said. "I want to speak to Dad."

She was on the phone to him for almost an hour. I lay back on the bed, flicking through *Architectural Digest* and thinking yet again how alike they were, Lisa and Malcolm Bell. Not just in the shiny black hair they had but also in the linear lucidity of their thought patterns. Lisa's father had won international acclaim for his work on the Brunswick Rotunda. The drawings Lisa had submitted for the Annersley Award had been shortlisted for the student prize. I had not really tried to understand the drawings even though I loved the things that Lisa made them with: the set of chrome compasses, the propelling pencils, the multi-joint anglepoise lamp in stainless steel. There were similar drawings in *Architectural Digest* but I didn't look at them. I stared instead at photographs of buildings constructed of aluminium and glass. The caption on one of them marked it out as the Newman Library in Oxford. The architect was David Reed. The building looked a bit like a beehive and was governed by solar power.

"Who are you?" she said. "What do you do?" She had asked for mineral water. It came in a frosted glass bottle with an oval patterned label on the side. I stared at her fingers as they worked at the label, trying to lift it free. I told her I was going to be a teacher but when she asked me what I liked to read I found it hard at first to know what to say. It was the kind of question I would usually have answered without thinking, but I wanted to give an honest reply.

"I've done a lot of work on Shakespeare," I said in the end. "But I like books that are set in the future instead of the past."

"With rockets in them, you mean, and alien worlds?"

"Yes." I looked down into my pint, a foam-flecked amber disc that snatched at the sun. Her face was reflected in it next to my own but it was difficult to gauge the way she felt.

"I've read books like that." She spoke slowly, as if thinking aloud. "I can't remember the authors' names. The one I liked most was about a girl who went to prison for leaving home. She wanted to learn to fly spaceships but it was forbidden for women to do it. The story was set on Earth but I didn't understand that until the end."

When I looked across at her I saw she had managed to free the label from the side of the bottle. It was intact except for a small ragged hole close to the centre. She held the label up to the sky, squinting at the sun through the hole as she had done earlier through the sheet of gift wrap. "I could try and make a spaceship out of paper," she said. "It would be interesting to see how it came out."

"Why do you like paper so much?" I asked.

"You wouldn't have your books and spaceships if there weren't any paper," she said. "Paper's a bit like bread: the most important thing under the sun." She smoothed the label against the table and then slipped it into her purse. "Most people treat it like rubbish, but I think it's a beautiful thing." She slid her finger into the neck of the bottle and spun it in a circle around my hand. "I want to go to Japan," she said. "They make the finest paper in the world."

"We'll have time to go travelling later," said Lisa. "We'll be able to do it in style." I watched the back of her head as she looked at herself in the mirror. Her hair spread out like an ink stain as she drew the hairbrush downwards and then away. "Anyway," she said. "You wouldn't want to give up on teaching. You know you've always wanted to teach."

I went up to Ealing for the interview but there wasn't time to go and see Lisa. It was a new school and a good one; they offered me the job there and then. On the journey back I read Lewis Spader's

Mammoth and wondered what the blonde girl might think about it, the idea of a planet turning to ice. With less than ten miles to go I put the book away in my briefcase and took out a notepad instead. 'Frozen,' I wrote. 'A metaphor for indecision.' Then I jotted down a list of words that had some association with frost. I ended with three colours: 'aqua,' 'opalescent,' and 'blue.'

She was standing at the kerb. I saw her as soon as the coach turned off Queen South and swung into the depot. I caught my breath. I think I imagined she had come to meet me, but then I saw she was only watching the buses. There was a rucksack on the ground between her feet. I crossed the tarmac, walking towards her because there was nowhere else to go. She didn't seem surprised to see me and I ended up wondering if she had somehow been waiting for me after all. I looked down at her rucksack, a faded cherry red. The drawstring trailed in the dust; its whitened ends had started to fray.

"I've got something to show you," she said. I saw her glance with surprise at my briefcase and that made me want to throw it away. She bent down and undid the rucksack. I expected her to take out a book but she took out a rocket instead. It was like a child's drawing of a rocket: slim and silvery with three triangular fins and a tapering nose. The surface was covered in foil, not in a single sheet but in snippets and shreds tessellated together to form a whole. I recognised the multicoloured wrapping of a make of Belgian chocolate, the coarse pressed silver of milk tops, the red and gold zigzag of a Mars Bar's capital 'M.' Partly submerged under the foil was the blue label from the bottle of mineral water she had drunk on the afternoon I had met her in the newsagents on Gull Street.

"Is it heavy?" I asked. She put the model into my hands and as she did so her fingers brushed mine. Her skin was warm with a texture that was matte and somehow grainy. I imagined it tasting of salt as if she had been swimming in the sea. The rocket seemed to weigh nothing. It rested on my outstretched palms, its nosecone pointing straight at the sky.

"It's made out of paper not card," she said. "You have to

let each layer dry before adding another or else the whole thing would collapse. It's the only way of getting it so light."

There was a red transparent circle around the nosecone, a section of a polythene bag. I held it level with my eyes and looked through it into her face. She appeared ruby-coloured and slightly distorted, like somebody in a cathedral seen through stained glass.

There had been no rain for almost a month and the meadows that bordered the town were yellow and dry. I couldn't get inside her at first. She had her arms folded across her chest as if she wanted to push me away. I felt myself failing. Then she took hold of my hand.

"It'll be alright in a minute," she said. "I'm not afraid." She put my hand between her legs, linking our fingers and penetrating herself in a manner so urgent I wondered if it might have caused her pain. She shook all over, inhaling through her teeth as if breathing were hard. Then she opened to me, suddenly and completely, as if something had given way at the seams. I wondered if it was blood I could feel but it turned out not to be. Afterwards we walked back into town along Queen South. Suddenly it began to rain. The raindrops felt heavy like mercury. Her hair clung in sodden fronds to her breasts and back. A pungent animal smell seeped out of it like the smell of dogs cavorting in a river. The impacted ground at the roadside hissed as the water soaked in. The gutters filled up instantly. My eye was caught by something spinning on the current, something that looked glittery and bright. When I bent to pick it up I saw it was just a sweet wrapper. It was coloured yellow and red with thin bands of gold. I was about to throw it back in the gutter but she took it from out of my hand.

"It's beautiful," she said, smoothing it out.

"I could teach in Japan," I said suddenly. "I could teach English and perhaps I could write on the paper." Her hands streamed with rain. I put her fingers in my mouth and sucked them dry. I could feel her knucklebones against my teeth and I almost wanted to chew on them, as if they were something foreign and delicious to eat.

It was Edward Blanchard who told me she'd killed her sister, the same Edward Blanchard who had taught me elementary maths. He was at the graduation party and when I saw him I mentioned her name. I had never said her name out loud before. I wanted to find out how it felt.

"It was one of those ridiculous accidents," he said. "They'd had a fight over something stupid and Adeline died. But Nicky Taylor was always a strange girl. There was an inquest and she missed all her exams. I can't think how you know her anyway. I thought that she'd left school for good." I told him I'd chatted to her once at the bus stop on Queens Road South. I left the party shortly after. The sky was so clear it seemed to go on forever. The stars hovered somewhere high above me, suspended on invisible strings. I went home the long way, taking streets I hadn't been on in years. I walked as quickly as I could, a little afraid. By my watch it was almost eleven. I didn't want to meet her in the dark.

"We were right outside the depot," she said. "It was raining. She slipped and then fell in the road." Adeline was hit by a bus and bled to death on Queen South. Nicky might have answered my questions but I didn't ask any. There was nothing else I wanted to know. Lisa's wedding dress was blue, the breathless mythical hue of an August sky. When I first saw her at the altar my breath stopped in my throat and I felt cold. Her black hair was sprinkled with white; I thought someone had been throwing confetti in advance of the vows. Then I saw it was just flowers in her hair, not paper. The flowers were tiny and lovely, like distant stars. I was reminded almost violently of a book I had owned once, *The Child and the Spaceman,* in which the spaceman asked the moon to be his bride. Later on I disentangled some of the flowers from Lisa's hair. They smelled strongly of her perfume and it was difficult to tell if they'd once had a scent of their own.

By the time I came out of the post office the traffic jam had cleared but the air was still muddy with fumes. A red double decker swung past me, groaning as if from the heat. Pasted along its side was an advertisement for Mars ice cream. I turned my head away, not wanting to breathe in the smell of diesel. There was rubbish in the gutter and on the road. I saw shreds of old newspaper, some orange peel, a burst supermarket bag. The newspaper flapped in the wake of the bus and I caught sight of a photograph, a picture of a girl in a loose summer dress. The caption above her said 'Missing' in heavy black type. For some reason I thought immediately of Rosalind even though the girl in the photograph was twenty years old at least and maybe more. She had been torn partway across the face and I wondered if she was still missing or had since been found. I bent down and picked up the paper. I felt the decaying newsprint come off on my hands.

When I got home I went into the spare room and hid the torn sheet of newspaper amongst the back issues of *Architectural Digest* that Lisa kept there. Later that evening after I had come back from the hospital I took it out and looked at it again. The girl had wispy fair hair and a smile that looked fragile, as if it had lasted for just one moment and then disappeared. 'Adeline,' I wrote in the margin. 'Wants to be a space captain, but can't.' It didn't seem to matter that someone else had had the same idea before me. I had read somewhere that it wasn't the story that mattered but the art in the tale. I had also read that there was no such thing as an original plot-line, not since human beings had stopped living in caves.

It rained hard that night. I lay on my back with my eyes open and tried to come up with fifty words that had to do with water. I fell asleep before I got to thirty. The last word I thought of was 'drought.'

The Vicar with
Seven Rigs

"I just want a fuck, that's all," said Justina. "I don't want any messing around."

"We could go over there then. We could do it right under that tree."

"No," she said. "You've got to take all your clothes off. I want to have a look at what you've got."

I knew what she was like, I'd known her for more than four years, but I couldn't help staring at her. It wasn't just because of the things she said, it was the way she was. Anyway, most people you passed in the street tended to stare at Justina because she was beautiful. Then there were the clothes she was wearing, the thin red spaghetti-strap t-shirt and the real blue denim jeans. The jeans had darker blue stitching and were tight across her behind. I don't know if it was being beautiful that made her behave like that or if she would have done it anyway because of her father. I used to wonder what it would be like to be her, to just open your mouth and come out with whatever you thought.

When I looked at Derek Peters I saw he was looking at me. Our eyes met briefly and then he looked away. I thought he was blushing but he might have just caught the sun. It was such a hot day that day. I kept looking at Justina's skin, watching for sunburn. I told myself I was looking out for her but really it was just an excuse to carry on staring at her, to see how her arms and shoulders were turning brown.

It was the first time I had met Derek Peters. He was a friend of Schaef Barrett's and that was really all I knew. Apart from saying hello he hadn't spoken a word and I didn't know if he was shocked by Justina or whether he already knew what to expect. Schaef Barrett I had met before but only because of Justina. He was tall with gangling limbs and never slow. Whenever he moved his head his long hair fell into his eyes. On that day he was wearing knee-length Wisdom shorts and a pair of Benedict trainers that looked brand new.

"Let's get inside then," he said. "I know somewhere we can go." He glanced across at Derek Peters but Derek Peters avoided his eyes. Derek Peters had white-blond hair that was silky-looking and shorn down into a crew cut. There were freckles in a fan across his nose and more of them in a band at the back of his neck.

"I'm not walking back to yours," said Justina. "Not in these shoes." She was wearing the red patent leather heels we had found in the seconds bin at Sally Swanage's. The shoes had been cheap because one of them was missing its buckle. The buckle on the other one was in the shape of a star and covered in fake diamonds. The heels were three inches high. The path between the Fences was dusty and Justina's red stilettos were covered in a brownish scum.

"You don't have to walk back to my place. I'm talking about somewhere near."

"It had better not be a henhouse."

"Who said anything about a henhouse? We can get in the back of the Vicar with Seven Rigs."

"I'm not breaking into the Rigs," said Derek Peters. "It's not worth the risk." His voice was mud-coloured and deeper than I had expected. The blond hair and the freckles had made him appear to be younger than he was.

"We don't have to break in," said Schaef Barrett. "There's a window that's always open. No-one will suspect a thing"

"Would you have broken in though, if we'd have had to?" said Justina. "How much do you reckon I'm worth?"

She was like it because of the weather. Under a hot sky everything wants to lay itself open to the sun like a mud butterfly or a gecko. People don't like to take their clothes off in winter but as it was Justina reminded me of one of the half-wild yellow dogs you sometimes see down by the level crossing: there was a matted look about her and every step she took seemed to give off heat. From the way she was talking it seemed like it would be the first time she had done it with Schaef Barrett. She talked to me about boys often, but I wasn't completely sure how far she would go.

"You're worth everything, Jus," said Schaef Barrett. "I'd have broken in for you like *that*, and if you wanted me to I still would." He made a gesture with one hand as if he were throwing something away and then looked straight at Justina, his dark hair falling forward across his face. He had blocked the rest of it out somehow. It was as if Derek Peters and I had ceased to exist. Justina spread her hands on her hips and put her head on one side. I thought she was about to laugh but in the end no laugh came out.

"OK," she said. "Let's do it." She set off again along the Fences, trying to avoid the potholes with her shoes. Schaef Barrett had to put on a spurt to catch up with her. I wondered if he would take her arm but when it came to it he didn't. They walked side by side in silence, neither of them saying a word. I walked beside Derek Peters. His open-toed sandals made a soft shuffling sound on the dusty path. I thought about what Schaef Barrett had said about Justina being worth everything. I repeated the words to myself inside my head and it seemed to me they had a rusty smell about them, and a harsh indelible colour that looked like blood.

I had heard of the Rigs. I had never been there of course but I knew enough to know that no-one ever called it the Vicar. As far as I knew it was west of Rydon but Schaef Barrett said that the Fences made a short cut around the back.

"It'll all be OK," he said. "It should be a laugh." Then he looked at Derek Peters and nodded his head. Derek Peters avoided his eyes and stared at the ground.

A lot of people avoided the Fences because they were a grey area. I had always felt at home there despite this. I had lived in Thakeham Village all my life. In winter the Fences was a damp narrow alleyway floating with rubbish and bounded by high brick walls. On that afternoon in August it was a wide dusty path hemmed in by rusty barbed wire. On the other side of the wire you could see people's gardens, their yellowing pockmarked lawns and moth-eaten sheds. Every now and then there was a breach in the wire and a way through to what was most likely Moreton or Red Lion Street. I realised by the way Justina kept looking over her shoulder that she was nervous of being there but I knew she would never admit to being scared.

When I was a lot younger I used to take my child's plastic spade down on the Fences and dig there for buried treasure. Usually I found nothing except pieces of broken crockery and a few earthworms but one day I found a whole glass jar. The jar was tall and green and had six sides. If you turned it into the light it glowed bright blue. I kept it in the back of my wardrobe but one day when I went to find it the jar was gone. After that I stopped digging for things. I never saw the green jar again.

On the face of it the Rigs was just a two star hotel, the sort of place that had fly screens across the windows and sold alcohol at the bar. At some time or other I had heard that the people who ran the Rigs made money on the side by taking in illegals but I had no idea if this was really true. Had I been on my own with Justina I would probably have asked her about it but with Schaef Barrett there I thought it was unwise. I could imagine the look on her face and the way she might laugh at my ignorance. In any case she might know less than me. I thought Schaef Barrett would most likely have heard something but I didn't know him well enough to ask. If it was true about the illegals the landlord could be prosecuted twice, for trafficking and for blasphemy. It struck me then that some people would set aside anything for the sake of money. It was the first time I could remember having had such a thought and I hardly understood what it meant. Schaef Barrett and Justina had drawn some way ahead of me and Derek Peters and from time to time their fingers touched as if by accident. They were talking to one another by then but I couldn't hear what they were saying. Justina spoke in a soft low voice I had never heard her using before. Her voice was usually topaz yellow, hard and clear and bright just like a jewel.

The further we went the larger the houses became. I had never been that far along the Fences; there had never seemed any need. Although the houses were larger they did not look very well kept. The gardens were sectioned off with panel fencing. Some of them had been concreted over. There were piles of plastic bin bags by the back doors. The rest of the gardens were overgrown, a wasteland of grasses and weeds. The backs of the buildings were zigzagged with washing lines and fire escapes. There appeared to be no-one around. In spite of the sunshine and the greenery the hot air smelled of onions and frying food.

"Fuck knows where we're going," said Derek Peters. "Do you want me to take you back?"

His voice and the coarse words startled me and I looked straight up into his face.

"What do you mean?" I said. "We can't just leave Justina behind."

"We wouldn't be leaving her," he said. "She would be leaving us." We carried on walking. Our sandals left tracks in the dust as if it were sand. We passed a few more of the large red houses and then there was a break in the wire. Schaef Barrett came to a standstill and put a hand on Justina's arm.

"This is where we turn off," he said. "Be careful you don't tear your clothes." He ducked down, folding himself almost in half, and then he stood up again behind the wire. I had a strange feeling seeing him there. It was as if there could be no return. Justina took a step forward and then looked back at me. I pulled ahead of Derek Peters and went to her side. One of the fence posts was down. The wire had been pulled upwards and away from it, forming a kind of rough arch.

"If I cut myself on that I'll kill you," said Justina. It was hard to tell who she was speaking to, Schaef Barrett or me.

"You're not going to cut yourself," said Schaef Barrett. "Get down on your hands and knees." His voice sounded different, thinner somehow, as if he were speaking from behind a pane of glass. I saw that the hem of his shorts was filthy, caked in some thick black dirt, although the ground around the break appeared to be dry. Justina crouched down on all fours and crawled under the wire. When she stood up again she gave a small laugh and brushed her hands briskly downwards against her jeans. I watched for mud stains to appear but the pale blue denim stayed clean. She raised a hand to her hair and stroked it although it still seemed immaculately smooth. Derek Peters went next and then I followed. As I got to my feet he held out his hand to me. The smooth skin was dry and warm. I looked back the way we had come and saw the ground sloping away. There was a twenty-foot drop to the path.

On the other side of the wire there was a road. The tarmac was grey and broken with weeds pushing up through the cracks. To the left of us a pit had been dug. There were oil drums in the pit, and around its edge were heaps of orange sand. On the far side of the workings stood a tractor without any tyres. Hogweed and red campion grew out from under it, slowly working their way into the cab. Further along the road stood a group of large detached houses. The sun beat down on them, draining them of colour. I rocked my foot back and forth on a pebble then used the edge of my sandal to knock it away.

"The middle place is the Rigs," said Schaef Barrett. "It's as ugly as fucking Satan."

He looked at Justina, his murky eyes half open behind his hair. She started to laugh and then put her hand over her mouth. He took hold of her shoulder and shook it slightly. Then both of them ran off along the road. Derek Peters and I looked at one another in silence. Then he shrugged.

"I suppose we'd better go if we're going," he said. He started down the road and I followed. I examined the back of his neck, the bar of reddish freckles, the silvery line of down where his hair had been shaved close to the skin. I felt less embarrassed to look at him than I had done. Although I still hardly knew him I sensed a growth of fellow feeling between us, the comradeship that had come from being abandoned by our friends.

One of the buildings beside the Rigs had been shut up; the narrow ground floor windows were boarded closed. Those on the three floors above had all been whitewashed. They stared down like blinded eyes. The sight of them made me uneasy for some reason, as if the house had something to hide. The Rigs itself had a despondent, almost derelict air. To one side of the house lay strips of bare earth that I realised might once have been flowerbeds. The paintwork was colourless and cracked. The window closest to the road was half way open. Mottled grubby curtains hung limply down. For a moment it seemed to me that I heard laughter from the window or voices, but when I tried to listen more closely I heard nothing at all. I stepped up to the house and laid my palm against the wall. The brick was hot to the touch as if something had been set on fire inside it. A gritty reddish dust came off on my hand.

"Do you think that's where they've gone?" I said, looking at the open window. Derek Peters nodded and then shook his head.

"Come here and I'll give you a leg up," he said. "When you're inside you can help pull me in too."

He made a cradle for my foot with both his hands. I clutched at the windowsill and then felt myself lifted up. I slid my stomach across the window frame and almost before I knew it I was in the room. I half fell, half rolled onto the floor. When I stood up and looked out I saw Derek Peters waiting. The front of his cotton shirt was covered in dust. I leaned out of the window and grabbed hold of his outstretched hands. For a moment I felt the full weight of him as his sandals scrabbled for purchase against the wall. A second later he managed to get his knee across the windowsill and was able to let go of my hands. Both of us were breathing heavily. The effort of getting in had made me stop thinking about what we were doing there in the first place.

"Do you think we should try to find them?" I said.

"I don't think they'd thank us if we did," said Derek Peters, and laughed. "Let's have a look around."

The room we were in was barren and square. Apart from a blue formica table and a stack of old newspapers in one corner it was completely empty. For some reason the door had been taken off its hinges and stood at an angle balanced against the wall. Through the doorframe I could see chequered vinyl flooring and the bottom of a flight of stairs. Somewhere on the floor above somebody was playing the cello. I glanced at Derek Peters; he had his head turned in the direction of the music and seemed to be listening. I wondered if he recognised the tune.

The staircase had no carpet. On every other step someone had put down folded newspapers and I supposed it was an attempt to damp down the noise. To either side of the stairs were doorways boarded over with nailed-down planks. The hallway itself ran on a little way past the further door but after that it came to a dead end. There appeared to be no way out except up the stairs.

"Where did they go?" I said. "They can't have got very far." I tried listening for noises, for talking or muffled laughter but all I could hear was the cello. Minerva Kraicek played cello in the school orchestra but I had never heard it sound like this. Every now and then two notes would be struck together and my heart would leap up in my chest. The noise the cello made was somehow desperate, stuck somewhere between a growl and a cry.

"What is that?" I said.

Derek Peters didn't answer and I wondered if I had spoken aloud at all. I opened my mouth and breathed out through my teeth, wanting to convince myself I could still be heard. Derek Peters stepped past me and laid both hands on one of the boarded doors. He smoothed his palms back and forth across the boards, probing the nail-holes with his fingertips like a blind man.

"This has been done recently," he said. "There are splinters at the edges of these holes."

I couldn't see why that mattered or why it might interest him but I came and stood beside him and felt the wood. It was warm to the touch even though it was cooler in the dusty hallway than it had been outside. I looked at the shape of my hand next to Derek Peters's hand. My own was so familiar to me it seemed squarish and stubby-fingered; his – larger, paler – appeared graceful by comparison. The fingernails looked delicate and almost transparent. Quite suddenly I found myself wanting to touch the back of his hand, to cover it with my own. He had gripped my hands tightly when he pulled himself in through the window but that had been different.

"Do you think it's a radio," I said. "Or is somebody actually playing?"

"It's someone playing," he said at once. "You can hear them moving their feet."

I looked at the ceiling above us. It was a grubby off-white and there were cobwebs matted thickly in all the corners. The thought of feet moving on the floor above unnerved me but I couldn't hear anything apart from the music.

"There's nothing to worry about. This is a hotel. It isn't somebody's house."

I supposed he might be right and that we probably wouldn't be noticed. Strangers were what hotels were all about. Derek Peters had spoken without looking at me. He had his ear to one of the boarded-up doors.

"Can you hear anything?" I said.

"I don't think so," he said. "Let's go."

I thought he meant that we should leave again by the open window but he stepped away from the door and went up the stairs. I found myself following. It seemed less daunting somehow to be with him than staying by myself in the empty hall. I took the steps two at a time, trying to keep my feet on the folded newspapers. Even so our footsteps sounded loud on the hollow unpainted wood. The music up above us suddenly stopped. I noticed a sort of half-landing and an open cupboard stacked with tartan blankets and thin-looking pale blue sheets. Then we reached the top of the stairs. The bare landing gave onto a long hallway with a window at either end and a green lino floor. There were doors to either side of the corridor, some of them closed tightly, a few of them standing ajar. There was nobody in sight and as we stood there looking about us the cello music started up again. I realised then that it had not been coming from this floor at all but from one of the floors above.

"It's massive," I said. "And this is all just one floor." I counted ten doorways. From the outside the Rigs had seemed much smaller. I had heard of buildings like that but had never been inside one. It would be a good place to hide illegals. For what seemed the

first time in many minutes I thought about Justina. I tired to get a
sense of where she was but felt nothing. I supposed she and Schaef
must have gone into one of the rooms but it was impossible to tell
which one. I thought of Schaef with his half-open greedy eyes and
his new Benedict trainers. I wondered what it was Justina saw in
him, what it was that made him different from all the rest.

It was easy to look into the rooms that were open and all
of them looked mostly the same. Each had a bed with a hump of
pillows at one end and a bedspread in dingy maroon candlewick.
Each had a scrappy green rug on the floor, a rickety desk and a chair
beside the bed. One of the rooms had a tarnished silver coffee service
on a tray just inside the door. Another had a picture on the wall, a girl
in a blue dress bowling a metal hoop along a road. None of them
showed any sign of being occupied. I supposed there were other
rooms, grander rooms perhaps, at the front of the hotel. Derek Peters
bent down to look at the coffee set. His back made a long curve
against the dirty white of the wall and I could see the nodules of his
spine through the thin khaki cloth of his shirt. His transparent
fingernails rattled gently against the silver. Quite suddenly I came to
realise why I had been brought here. My mouth filled up with saliva.
I sat myself down on the bed.

"I'd better shut the door," said Derek Peters. Once he had
it closed I saw there was a tiny metal bolt on the reverse. He slid it
into place, locking us in. When he turned and came towards me the
freckles on his nose and the upper part of his cheeks stood out redly,
like burn marks; his lips and the rest of his face looked very pale.

"It's alright," I said. "I want to." I wanted to ask if he'd
done it before but I thought that might make me look stupid and so
didn't dare. He started to unbuckle his sandals. Crossed bars of
white divided his feet into diamonds. His toes, always uncovered,
were a mud-coloured dust-streaked brown.

He knelt above me on the red candlewick. I felt him
lifting aside my skirt then pulling down my pants. I lay with my head
turned to one side on the covered pillow and let him do it. I expected

it to hurt more but all I felt was a sort of insistent pushing and then a sense of something giving way. I brought my hand around and touched the place where we were joined; I felt the solid, rhythmic movement of what was inside me, the lips of me rucked up to either side. On the pillow beside my face I could see one of his hands. The pale skin was stretched tight across the back of it, the narrow bones stood splayed like the legs of a spider. Then his breath hitched in his chest and he went very still. We still had most of our clothes on. I could see the circles of sweat stains under his arms. I felt him slide out of me and lift himself away.

"That was no good," he said. "No good for you."

"It didn't hurt," I said. "It was alright." I moved my hands slowly along the bedspread, pulling my skirt back down to hide my knees. Then I did what I had wanted to do earlier and covered the back of his hand with the palm of my own. I could feel the bones inside it and the tiny golden hairs that grew out of his skin. I noticed that the cello was still playing somewhere. The sound came down through the ceiling in a series of soft low groans, pricking at the nape of my neck. I had heard enough of it; I wished that it would stop. I sat up and pulled on my underthings. Seeing them made me blush. Justina wore panties made of a soft shiny fabric that stretched to an exact tight fit. My own underwear was of the usual sort: baggy cotton knickers with a drawstring waist. It crossed my mind that Derek Peters might tell Schaef Barrett about them just to set him laughing but I got rid of the thought. It didn't seem the sort of thing he was likely to do.

I sat beside him on the bed. Afternoon sun the colour of marigolds came in through the window and glinted off the silver coffee pot.

"We ought to be getting back," I said. "It's getting late."

"I don't think it's that late," he said. He rubbed his freckled nose with the back of his hand. "It's not like this out the front." I looked at him, not understanding. I thought that he was talking about his nose.

"The Rigs, I mean," he said. "It's different when you see it from the front."

"Have you been there?" I said. "It's the other side of Rydon." I said this as if it settled everything, as if I was accusing him of being a liar. If he lived in Thakeham Village he would have no business to be in Rydon. Not unless he had been to the hospital there. I glanced at his fragile hands.

"I've been with my dad," he said. "He delivers food." He looked at the ground as he said it as if he were somehow ashamed.

"What's it like then?" I said quickly. I felt bad that I'd made him say more than he'd wanted to. I hoped that he'd still tell me about the Rigs.

"There's a massive front door with metal bars across it. You have to ring a bell before they let you inside."

"Is it true then, about the illegals?"

"Who knows." He shrugged his shoulders. The tip of his nose was sunburned. In a day or two it would probably start to peel.

"Why is it called the Rigs?" I said. "What does it mean?"

"A rig was an old sort of sailing ship, with masts and crows' nests and that. Otherwise it's slang for an HGV. You know, a goods lorry, a haulage outfit. With seven rigs you'd be rich, I suppose, like all of them." He rubbed his nose again. "It's also a word for prick. The vicar with seven pricks. You wouldn't be surprised though, the way some of them carry on."

I laughed. An hour before I would have found it difficult to say anything but after what had just happened I found I could laugh. I felt I had earned the right to find it funny. I lay back on the bed again and ran my hands downwards over the bedspread. The fabric was ridged, a pattern of wine-coloured waves. I had been to the beach only once when the school had taken us to Dover Castle. Some of the boys had taken their shoes off and gone wild on the shore but the girls had not been allowed to go anywhere near the sea. The tide had been out and there had been ghost-waves all over the sand. I had never tasted wine at all.

"Is Schaef really in love with Justina?" I said suddenly.

"A lot more than she is with him," he sighed. "He talks about her all the time."

"She is beautiful though."

"Yes she is."

"Is that why Schaef likes her?"

"He's in love with her image I think. She's like a sort of icon to him, something that can keep him going, through the longest night, through anything. He'll still have that even when he can't see her any more. He'll have that forever, even when he's forgotten the things she said."

"You make her sound unreal."

"Well she's not real is she? For her it's all just a game." He sounded almost angry. His voice had a rough edge to it and the trace of an accent I didn't recognise.

"You're not from here," I said. He snatched his hand away and turned on me. I could see how skinny he was really, under his shirt. I wondered what he would look like with it off.

"We're not illegals. My dad's got a contract."

"I just wondered where you were from." It was the second time he had mentioned his father and I found I could imagine him easily, a thin-ribbed, worried-looking man in FresCo overalls and a crew cut the same as his son's. I was less certain about his mother. I suddenly began to wonder is she was dead.

"I was born in Nottingham," he said. "So was my dad."

"Does Schaef know?" I regretted the question at once but Derek Peters only laughed.

"Schaef wants to become something. I think he's envious. He thinks coming from the North gives you an edge."

"What do you mean he wants to become something?" I thought of Schaef Barrett's long hair and expensive fashions and the way he had of wanting to be in front. He liked to lead people even if he didn't have much love for them. I supposed it was at least possible that someone as young as Schaef might consider the Church. The black long-line jacket, the high-necked vermilion shirt – they were clothes that would suit him, even if he had to lose his hair.

"I don't think he knows what he really wants. He just wants to get out of here." He leaned forward where he was sitting, his arms folded across his knees. "He's not as immature as he seems."

He ran his fingers through his close-cropped hair and I found myself wanting to touch him again, to reach up and take hold of his hand.

"Do you know who Justina's dad is?" I said instead.

"How else could she get away with wearing those clothes."

He bent down to me and kissed me on the forehead and then on the mouth. I tasted salt on him, the salt of the sweat from his pores.

"You realise what we've done," he said. "If you tell anyone what's happened you'll put us at risk."

There was no-one in the hallway. As we went back down the stairs to the lower floor I noticed how dim the light had grown. I thought at first it was because night had come early but when we got back to the bare little room with the old newspapers and the blue formica table it was to discover that the window we had come through had been boarded shut. I drew in my breath; chalky motes of dust seemed to fill up my lungs. When I looked at Derek his face was in semi-darkness. It was hard to tell if he was frightened. I wished he would speak my name.

He turned away from the window without pulling at the boards. The doors to either side of the staircase were still blocked off. A thought came suddenly to my mind, flooding it like an inrush of tepid water: the rooms on the first floor could never be used because nobody could get to them. There was no way out from the ground floor and so no access up to the next. The open window had been the only way in; it was strange I hadn't seen this before. In a way the room we had been in didn't exist. The heat on the ground floor was stifling. I wondered what had been imprisoned behind the two doors.

I thought once again of Justina. I thought about her red high-heeled shoes.

Derek Peters came to stand beside me. I felt his fingers briefly brush my hand.

"We'll have to go back upstairs," he said. "All those rooms up there that no-one can get to. There has to be another way out."

We went past the first floor landing and carried on up to the second. At some point I realised the cello music had stopped and been replaced by the sound of an orchestra playing something tuneless and loud. It was obviously coming from a radio and I wondered if it had been a radio all along after all. The second floor hallway was very different from where we had been. A soft red carpet covered the floor. The walls were a clean bright white, rising to a high white ceiling. In the angle between the ceiling and the wall there was a moulded plaster frieze of gilded flowers. There were fewer doors, five or six at the most, each of them numbered in brass. At the far end of the hallway was a pair of heavy fire doors and then there was another flight of stairs. There were brass stair rods against the red carpet and a polished wooden banister.

"We can't go down there," I said. "There are people down there. We'll be seen." I couldn't hear voices exactly but I could sense that there were others very close. Derek put his hand on my arm. I think he meant to reassure me but I could feel the tension in him, feel his quick pulse beating right down to his fingertips.

"We have to go down," he said. "It's the only way we can go."

I passed a hand across my skirt and blouse to smooth them. Derek waited, not looking at me. I saw him blink, watched the rise and fall of his curled, reddish lashes. We had no plan but I realised it might be better that way. Plans could very easily go wrong.

"We'll say we were looking for friends," Derek said. "We'll say we came in by mistake." It was as if he had read my thoughts somehow but that didn't frighten me. The thing that frightened me was that he seemed more nervous than I was.

"Let's go quickly," I said. "It's best if we act like we're meant to be here."

I went first. The banister was smooth and cool and round under my hand. I could hear Derek close behind but I didn't look back. There was a first floor landing but the flush white door was barred. On the ground floor below I could see a square tiled vestibule. Leading out from this was another door. There was a pane of reinforced glass that overlooked the hallway beyond. When I looked through the glass I saw we would be alright.

The room on the other side of the door was obviously the main reception area and it was crowded with people. There were enough of them for us to lose ourselves, so many of them that we would be invisible in their midst. Derek was right behind me. His breath felt hot and fast on the back of my neck.

"Let's go," he whispered. Both of us leaned on the door.

The reception hall of the Rigs was large and dark, panelled in a blackish wood and lit with chandeliers. The carpet was blue and yellow, a design of crescents and stars. There were polished brasses on the walls and a stand of thornless roses in a huge Chinese urn but the thing that took your attention was the picture. It hung on a chain behind the massive marble-topped reception desk, a gigantic full-length portrait painted in oils. The Vicar was tall. The size of the portrait made him seem unnaturally tall, the high-topped boots he wore made him even taller. The vermilion shirt was buttoned to his throat, the narrow white band of silk clearly visible at the collar. He had his arms folded across his chest; the gold cross and chain gleamed dully on his black lapel. He wore the wide-brimmed Homburg that marked him out as Bishop Advocate. He stared out of the picture with narrow leaf-green eyes, cat's eyes, a stubbly regrowth of hair on his close-shaved temples. Behind him were the ships. They were not the rigged galleons that Derek had talked about but streamlined white cargo liners with ion drive and towering red mess-funnels. The ships had been painted in less detail than the figure in the foreground but you could see them and count them quite easily, seven in all.

"What do you think's going on," said Derek. His body was pressed close against mine, his words were hot and breathy in my ear. I forced my attention away form the picture and realised we were in the midst of it all, a heaving throng of people all straining to see. What they were looking at was in the far corner between a hatstand and a potted Yucca palm. My view of it was blocked by the woman in front of me, a large grandmotherly figure in a nylon floral tent-dress, but when she moved to the left slightly I saw it was Justina and Schaef. Justina was crying. The strap on one of her red shoes had snapped at the ankle and the single diamond buckle appeared to be gone. As Derek came alongside me in the crowd he caught sight of Schaef Barrett and gasped. At the same moment Schaef raised his head and saw Derek. He stared at him for perhaps ten seconds and then looked quickly away. His face was set and pale. He drew his fingers slowly downward through his hair.

I felt for Derek's hand and we worked our way along the margin of the crowd. I remembered what Derek had said about the metal bars across the front of the Rigs, about how you had to ring a bell before they would let you in. But when we got to the entrance it was a set of revolving doors in chrome and glass. We slid ourselves sideways into one of the wedge-shaped bays and pushed until we came to the pavement outside.

It was a dusty city street. The air was densely humid, reeking of diesel. A line of vehicles waited at the traffic lights: an open topped LandRanger, a red Lambretta with a dented sidecar, a lorry with Tesco in letters two feet high. On the corner by the Visilink kiosk a youth in a black sleeveless t-shirt was lighting a cigarette for a girl. They leaned in close together as if they were about to kiss, the girl's fair hair hanging down to shield her face. She had a round pink handbag that was covered in coloured sequins. The youth's t-shirt had a stencil of a guitar on the front. White letters spelled the single word 'Play.'

I looked up at the building behind me. It was shabby and grey and called The Ship Hotel. A scrap of cardboard had been sellotaped to one of the ground floor windows. They were advertising for kitchen staff. I stared at the notice, at the blobby blue ink, at the florid wide confident hand.

I looked at Derek Peters and he looked back at me. There was dust on his feet and on his sandals, a brown-red powdery scum between his toes. He gazed up at the sky as if checking it was still above him then glanced at the handwritten notice and shook his head.

"We can't go back in there, Nonie," he said. "I think we'd be better off trying somewhere else."

Heroes

The sound of the blaring horn had made him cry. Wail, his mother had said. That was the first time and he had been five. He had always been a sensitive child.

The sky had still been black when they saw him off. Wal Carter drove out of the depot at seven o'clock; the load was due in London by nine. For Finlay Carter the word London had a terrible ring to it. Two equally ominous syllables, heavy and blackened as death knells. He had never been to the city but for years he went there often in his dreams. The people that he saw in the doorways always ignored him. The streets were lit with a murky orange light. He told no-one about the dreams, not even his mother. When the spring came the nightmares grew less frequent. When they waved goodbye to his father the sky was bright.

His mother's name was Romany but most people called her Ro. When his father was on the earlies she took Finlay out to the ring road most days of the week. He grew used to the sound of the traffic and learned to point to his father high up in the cab. It seemed strange to him that once he had been afraid. The walks out to the ring road went on until Finlay was almost thirteen. After that his mother still got up early but instead of going outside she sat alone at the kitchen table in the dark. Finlay went up by himself sometimes although he never discussed this with Ro. There was one time in early April when he saw her, standing by herself at the edge of the road. The HGVs thundered past, casting an orange glow across her face. When Wal Carter's Leyland came down the outside lane she didn't wave but stood quite still, staring after it as if its existence amazed her. The lorry lumbered past sounding its horn. His mother's face had grown more distinct by then, the beginnings of morning sunlight streaking her hair. She looked after the lorry, keeping her eyes on its lights until they were lost. After that she turned and went down the hill. Finlay stayed where he was, behind the row of sheds on the Bounds Hill allotments. He didn't come into the open until she was gone.

Threep and Somerville Gazette Thursday 5th March 2006
Locals Fight Rearguard Action in Allotment Feud

Residents of Raisin Terrace, Threep and members of the Bounds Hill Allotments Trust disrupted a council meeting in Sheffield yesterday as an act of protest in the continuing row surrounding the proposed compulsory purchase of Raisin Terrace itself together with the entire site of the Bounds Hill allotments.

"The cottages in Raisin Terrace are in excellent condition," said Mrs Eliza Burton who together with her husband Tom has lived on Raisin Terrace for 25 years. "Many of them have been recently refurbished. This is not the slums clearance of the 1960s. It is an affront to democracy that ordinary people may be forced to give up their homes." She went on to say that the proposed rehousing of Raisin Terrace residents in executive townhouses on the Nannerfield estate was yet another incidence of the high-handed arrogance of the current city council. Others among the protesters were quick to agree with her.

"You can't tell people where they should want to live," stated cutlery salesman Horace Wilbur, himself a resident of Raisin Terrace as well as a long-time member of the BHAT. "I thought this sort of thing went out with Joseph Stalin and Chairman Mao. Perhaps I was wrong about that."

When questioned about the proposals Councillor Peter Godwin remained circumspect. "No final decision has been taken vis a vis Raisin Terrace and it goes without saying that the opinions of local people shall remain central to the decision-making process. It is not the physical condition of Raisin Terrace that is at issue here but the requirements of the village as a whole. Nobody disputes the need for a new incinerator and refuse site and there are few who would argue that the position of Raisin Terrace, cut off as it is from the main hub of the village and with its environment already severely prejudiced by the existence of the A399, makes it an ideal location for such an enterprise. The positioning of the site elsewhere in Threep would present obstacles of an even greater dimension and there is little question that the Bounds Hill allotments are an anomaly."

"Anomaly," said Marten. "Irregular or abnormal. Something that doesn't fit."

Finlay hadn't asked if Marten was the man's first name or his surname and when he had spelled it out he hadn't said. "Everyone gets it wrong. They always put an 'i' instead of an 'e.'" Marten wrote his name in black biro in the margin of the newspaper he had been reading. Finlay thought the 'e' made it look foreign. It gave the name something extra. Something anomalous.

There were often articles in the local paper saying that the Bounds Hill allotments were about to be concreted over and Raisin Terrace demolished and turned into an incinerator site but so far it hadn't happened. There were people who said it was only a matter of time. Raisin Terrace was the last road in Threep. Behind Raisin

Terrace there were long back gardens where some people still raised rabbits but most preferred to grow nasturtiums and wallflowers. Behind the gardens were the allotments. Beyond the allotments was the A399. The territory between the two was uncertain, a scanty random scattering of stones.

"It's like a No-Man's-Land," said Marten. "A battle line between people and machines. It's difficult to know who's winning. If you close your eyes you can almost hear the guns."

Marten lived at 14 Raisin Terrace and he kept racing pigeons. He spoke slowly and seemed to pay each word individual attention. It was almost as if he tasted words as a chef might taste a sauce or perhaps a wine.

"The traffic, you mean?" said Finlay.

"The traffic, and something behind it. Something that never stops, even at night."

"What do you mean?" said Finlay.

"It's the Universe unfolding," said Marten. "I can hear it turning over in its sleep."

From the cracked concrete path that ran down the centre of the allotments you could see the flyover and the hard shoulder and the traffic streaming down the A399. Finlay tried to imagine what the allotments must look like from the air: a tiny green thumbprint in the middle of a sea of striated grey. He wondered what Marten had meant about the Universe and its sleep patterns. The books he liked best were novels set in foreign countries such as Alex Garland's *The Beach* or Joseph Conrad's *Heart of Darkness*. The writers of these books seemed to be suggesting that people could lose their sanity by getting too close to nature. Finlay wondered how these same authors might feel about the A399 ring road. There had been a pile up once out on the ring road, with twenty-five vehicles destroyed and six people killed. Finlay had been ten at the time. Two boys that lived in his road, Darren Baker and Carl Sillitoe, had dashed by the Carters' windows on the way to the scene. The curtains had been drawn but Finlay had recognised them by the soft shadows their hair made and the excited sound of their voices, unusually high. Soon after he heard the sound of police sirens and ambulances. Ro Carter had made Finlay stay indoors.

Not all of the allotments were in use. Those that had been abandoned, those closest to the ring road, sprouted thickets of bramble and hogweed eight feet high. Wooden sheds still loomed on some of them, overrun with spiders and feral cats. In summer the grass hummed steadily with the sound of insects. There was a smell of sage and cow parsley and hot asphalt. On the ring road there were motorhomes and caravans and estate cars pulling sailing yachts as well as the usual traffic of HGVs. Mostly they headed west towards the Peak District or the Welsh Marches. The rhythm of thousands of wheels was like a stampede.

On the disused allotments Marten collected poppy seeds and groundsel and the seedheads of wild oats and plantain and the tall yellow grasses that grew up by the fence posts and the sheds. He had several bags or pouches made of a rough brown tweed. He put each different type of seed in a separate bag.

"You can buy a special seed mix now," he said. "They have sacks of it in the pet superstore over in Somerville. I depend on it in winter but there's nothing quite as good as picking seed fresh."

Finlay supposed that all seed, even the bought kind that came in sacks from the pet superstore in Somerville, must have originally been picked fresh but he didn't say anything to Marten. It occurred to him that a lot of things that grew on the Bounds Hill allotments might be contaminated by the cars on the ring road, by a fine black invisible dust that drifted down. When you put your face against the stands of willowherb and campion they smelled tart and green like the rocket salad his mother made sometimes or like the punnets of cress and chives she grew on the windowsill in the kitchen. But it was hard to tell if things were really clean. Nuclear fallout was colourless and odourless. So was carbon monoxide or bottled helium. Clive Bailey the science teacher had brought a cylinder of helium to school once to use in an experiment. When he went out of the room to fetch a tape measure Carl Sillitoe had dashed to the front of the class and sucked a mouthful of the gas direct from the cylinder, putting his mouth around the small brass tap. When Clive Bailey came back and asked him what he was doing Sillitoe had laughed. The laughter, high and pure as a girl's, had acquired a quality that was liquid and flawless and somehow ghoulish.

"I could have danced all night," he sang, fingers curled upward and palms outstretched. He looked like some ageing starlet. The class exploded. Finlay had found the whole thing simultaneously hilarious and terrifying. The helium was invisible yet for a space of whole minutes it had changed Sillitoe into something else entirely.

Threep had a Sheffield postcode but the ring road cut it off from the city. Wal Carter had been keen to buy a house there because it was convenient for the depot. He had let Ro choose it, a large red end of terrace on Barraclough Road. Barraclough Road lay at the centre of the village, as far as you could get from the motorway flyover and the ring road. The year after he set up his own haulage franchise he had brought home a brochure describing the new-build executive homes on the Nannerfield estate. Ro waited until he left on an overnight and then put them straight in the bin. Later the next day Finlay had emptied the kitchen waste into the large cast iron dustbin in the back yard. As he did so he glanced down at the brochures. The floor plans showed the size of each room and the number and position of electrical sockets. There were photographs of the kitchens and numbers you could call for financial advice. The paper was glossy and smooth. All the rooms in the show house were painted white. He dropped the brochures into the belly of the dustbin. They fell in a body, heavily, pages closed.

When he went back into the kitchen his mother was there.

"We could go and have a chat with your teachers," Ro said. "If that was something you wanted to do."

She was tall and somehow stately, magnificent like her name. Finlay knew what her name meant and had known for years: Romany: gipsy or wanderer, outcast or foreign spy. His mother's parents lived in a village called Fulton, close to Guildford in Surrey. Fulton was a village with a recreation ground and an antiques market, not a smattering of mismatched houses like Threep. Hugh and Shirley Woolerton had never been inside the house on Barraclough Road. Romany went south to visit them two or three times a year. When Finlay was younger she had taken him too but now she left him behind with his father. Once when he had been in Fulton his grandmother had taken him for an afternoon of pitch-and-putt at a miniature golf course nearby. His grandfather had walked him to one of the shops in the village and let him pick out a penknife. The shop had been dark with small windows and curved oak beams. The penknife had two blades and a corkscrew and a carving of a steam train on the side. Finlay wondered which of his mother's parents had chosen her name.

Ro stood at the kitchen table twisting her rings. There were three of them: the gold wedding band and ruby engagement ring wedged together on the fourth finger and an iridescent opal on the third. Wal Carter had given her the opal as an anniversary present four years ago. Prior to that she had worn a different ring on the same finger, a chunk of polished amber in a silver surround. She had had the amber ring for as long as Finlay could remember but since she had put on the opal he hadn't seen it again.

Her hair was thick and dark brown, the colour of horses. So far it seemed unmarked by grey. Finlay couldn't imagine that she coloured it. It wasn't something Ro would ever do.

"I don't have to decide yet, " he said. "There's still plenty of time." He thought about the end of summer, of hitching a ride on a lorry and heading south. The first time he had been in a lorry he had been six. His father had belted him in and driven him in a wide circle around the depot and then around the car park of the service station.

"I don't want you doing that," Ro had said to him. "It's dangerous." His father had undone the seatbelt and handed him down, swinging him from his hands like a marmoset.

"She met him in Buxton," Finlay said to Marten. "It was

a Saturday in August. She was in the car with her parents, a cream Ford Granada. She got out to ask for directions. He had just come out of a café at the side of the road." He didn't know why he was telling Marten except that Marten seemed the kind to appreciate stories. When you were talking he looked straight at you as if what you were saying really mattered, as if there were nothing more important in his world.

"What was she doing in Buxton?" said Marten. "I thought your mother came from the south?" He said 'the South' as if he meant somewhere exotic, South Africa or the South China Sea instead of just Surrey. As always he spoke slowly, rolling the words he had chosen across his tongue.

"They were on the first day of their holiday. They were driving to the Lakes, to Scarfell Pike."

He himself had heard the story from Ro.

"I ran right into him," she had said. "It was like running into a wall." Each time she told the story the details were slightly different. But it always ended with Wal Carter sprinting across the road in front of a car.

"It was a blue car, I remember that. I didn't ever know the make."

Wal Carter had ignored the car, had probably not even seen it. Instead he had tapped on the right hand rear window of the Woolerton's Ford Granada and waited while Ro wound it down. He had asked her for her number and her address.

"His clothes smelled of creosote or tarmac. I can never smell those smells without thinking of him."

"Lorry drivers have a macho image, I suppose, like highwaymen or pirates," said Marten. "The old-fashioned word is brigand. A new-fangled knight on a new-fangled metal steed."

"I think she just liked him, that's all," said Finlay. "She liked the way he looked and the way he smelled."

Most people thought Wal Carter's Christian name was Walter but in fact it was Walesa, after Lech Walesa the hero of the Gdansk shipyards. He had had it altered by deed poll at the height of the Polish unrest. Finlay often had the urge to ask his father what his name had been before that and also what had happened in Poland to make him change it but it seemed too personal somehow, almost rude. He supposed he could ask Marten about the Iron Curtain. He had no doubt that Marten would know a lot about such things but he felt wary of saying anything. It would have felt like going behind his father's back.

"She wants me to decide on my 'A' Levels," he said instead.

"She's an exceptional woman," said Marten. "She walks like an Inca queen."

Finlay hid his face in the grass. It tasted bitter and rank as if one of the feral cats had scalded it with urine. He felt that the man had no right to the things he said. When he turned over again a small white cloud was hovering high in the sky.

"Have you always raced birds?" he said at last. He wanted to ask Marten what his job had been before his retirement but putting it so directly didn't seem right.

"My sense of time is skewed," said Marten. "But I've been raising and racing pigeons for fifteen years." He was doing what he called ringing a bird, putting a metal band onto its leg. The band had a number stamped into it, the number 1503. He held the bird in the crook of his arm. It extended its legs towards him, yellow toes scrabbling. Marten pinched its toes together and slipped on the ring. The pigeon was gunmetal grey with gold-rimmed eyes.

"1503," said Marten. "Ginette Neveu." He recorded the name and number in a slim black hardbacked book. "Do you know who Ginette Neveu was?" Finlay said that he didn't and shook his head. Marten told him that she had been a world famous violinist who had died in a plane crash.

"Don't you think it might be unlucky," said Finlay. "Giving her that sort of name?" He put out a finger and touched the pigeon's head. The feathers there were closely packed and soft like eider down. Marten's pigeons were not like the scruffy and sometimes misshapen street pigeons that gathered in the shopping precincts and under the park benches in Sheffield. They were lean and sleek, their necks longer and their beaks more yellow. They came to Marten's hand like children or dogs.

"The air is a theatre of war," said Marten. "Anyone who ventures there is brave." He opened his hands and the bird flapped free. He ran a finger down its back, making it tremble and preen. "The girl lived by who she was. Nothing is worth more than that."

"How old was she when she died?"

"Thirty," said Marten. "She was a musical prodigy."

Finlay wondered if Marten also had been something of the kind but the concept was hard to sustain. Marten's hands were spade-shaped and boxlike, the thick fingers stubby and short. They were almost a workman's hands yet the idea of Marten undertaking any kind of manual labour was incongruous, even absurd.

"Can I come out and watch," he said. "The next time she's in a race?" He had no idea what happened on the day of a pigeon race but suddenly he was eager to know. He imagined birds careering down the sky like horses galloping the length of a field. It seemed unlikely that birds could be trained to do such a thing but he supposed they would have to be. He wondered how he could find out. He didn't want to look foolish in front of Marten.

"That one won't race for a while, she's still too young."

Finlay blushed.

"Hero's the one I fly now," he said. "People get her name wrong too."

Finlay said nothing. He thought it was wisest to wait. After a moment's silence Marten told Finlay that Hero was a character in an Ancient Greek legend. He pronounced the name with a short, lifted 'e,' like the 'e' in 'help' or in 'Helen,' and a slightly longer deeply rolled 'r.' "She was a woman," he said. "She had a lover called Leander,"

"Was she a goddess?"

"No, a mortal woman, a priestess. She had moderate psychic powers and was what they called a sensitive. She was handmaiden to the oracle at the temple of Aphrodite in Sestos.

Leander was a nobleman who came to Sestos with his friends to celebrate a religious festival. He fell in love with Hero as soon as he saw her."

An image came suddenly to Finlay of his father outside a café. The café was called Michelle's. The name was painted in swirling cream letters across a green awning. His father stood in the doorway looking out across the road. His long hair was tied back with a bootlace and his stocky bare forearms were tanned.

"Hero was sworn to virginity," said Marten. "But not because the Greeks were prudes. They believed that to lose one's virtue was to give up one's power." He paused. "Hero risked everything to be with Leander because she risked losing her gift of precognition. But Leander also risked everything because to defile a priestess was to lose one's honour. He began to visit secretly, at night. There was a channel he had to swim, the Hellespont, a narrow stretch of water but treacherous because of its tides. On the nights Leander came to her Hero lit a lantern in her window. The lamp was no more than a wick dipped in oil but it shone with preternatural light. As Hero's powers began to fade the candle grew dimmer and one night it went out completely. Leander lost his bearings. He was dragged along by the current and quickly drowned. When they brought his body ashore Hero threw herself into the Hellespont and was drowned also. In Ovid's version of the myth the lovers come back to life again as birds."

Finlay had heard of the Hellespont because he had seen a film at school about Gallipoli. He knew it was the ancient name for the Dardanelles. After watching the film Paul Jester the history teacher had put slides on the overhead projector and shown them a map.

"The Dardanelles Strait," he had said. "Thirty eight miles long and four miles wide. The middle point is narrower – only a quarter mile – but the sea there is three hundred feet deep." He had traced the blue line of water with the tip of a pencil and then shown them other pictures, of castles and fortifications on the shore.

"Do you always name your birds after people that die?"

asked Finlay.

"All people die. It's how they live that counts."

Hero was white all over except for the tips of her wings, which were silver-grey. When Marten took her from the loft she did not struggle or flap as the younger bird had done but nestled quietly between his palms.

"I had to sell her brother Leander," said Marten. "I didn't want to but I was short of funds. I was offered a lot of money for him and I was glad of it. Later on I found out who the money had come from and I wasn't so glad but by then there was nothing I could do. In any case I still needed the money. I couldn't have afforded to pay it back"

"Who had the money come from?"

"Nobody important. Just someone I used to know."

On some nights the house was empty. If his father did an overnight to Glasgow or Plymouth he sometimes didn't get back for several days. As a boy Finlay had looked up his route in the AA Road Atlas; the motorways stood out clearly, blue as veins. When Wal Carter was gone Ro stayed out late sometimes. Sometimes she stayed out all night.

There was a girl in Finlay's class called Graczina Carp. Her parents had come to Threep from Bosnia and her mother was a cleaner at the school. Both her parents spoke with strong Eastern European accents but Graczina had been brought up in the village and spoke with a Sheffield accent as broad as Wal Carter's. She had pale blonde hair and almost no eyebrows. On the night after Marten had told him the story of Hero and Leander Finlay had a dream in which Graczina Carp sat beside him in a lorry on its way to the transit depot in Nottingham. When he woke up it was just getting light. He knew at once that his mother was not in the house. Ro rarely played music or listened to the radio, even when she thought she was alone. But the silence around her was somehow full, replete with tawny colours like the light of an autumn evening. The silence without her was different: unstable and brittle as glass.

There was post on the mat, some of it addressed to him. The envelopes contained prospectuses he hadn't sent for from colleges he had barely heard of. The brochures smelled sharply of new paper and had shiny coloured covers like the brochures for the show homes on the Nannerfield Estate. Inside there were Tables of Contents with chapter headings like Admissions, College Facilities and Entry Requirements. There were photographs of young people in front of computer monitors or being shown how to handle medical equipment. Finlay opened the fridge and poured milk into a glass then closed the brochure and slid it back in its envelope. He drank the milk, letting it coat his tongue and the roof of his mouth. When Ro came in she looked composed and unhurried, as if she had been up and about for several hours. She looked at the half empty glass of milk and the colour brochures.

"I know it's too early," she said. "But I thought if you saw all the options you could make up your mind." She took off her coat and laid it on the back of a chair. "I went for a walk up by the allotments," she said. "I sat and had a chat with your friend."

For a moment Finlay imagined Graczina Carp with her pale, mouse-breath eyebrows and the wooden pencil case she had that was really an old cigar box with a picture of Fidel Castro on it but then he realised she must have meant Marten.

"He's got sunflowers growing up there," she said. "He says he only wants them for the seeds."

When a sunflower went to seed the whole of its face crusted over. If you scraped your fingernails across it the striped seeds fell off in their droves. Marten used a tray to catch them, a battered piece of tin with the Maxwell House coffee logo stencilled across it in gold. He would never have described Marten as being his friend. It was hard to imagine Marten as anything but alone.

"He's an interesting man. He used to be a teacher and he once lived abroad. He taught geography," she said. "In a boys' school. He's collected unusual things from all over the world."

"I've never been into his house," said Finlay. "I met him

on the allotments picking seed."

He drained the glass of milk, tipping back his head to catch the dregs. The milk tasted thick and sweet like the scent of a flower. He put the glass down on the table and then went out into the hall. As he brushed by his mother he caught traces of her scent, the pale light blond aroma of summer grass.

Wal Carter worked most weekends even though he didn't need to. He still drove the overnights and the earlies, putting in as many hours as the rest of his men. If you went into the portacabin he still used as an office you could see his name on the roster with everyone else. On his days off he went to the Bedford Arms and played darts or dominoes or rummy with men he knew from the depot. He was often out until the small hours but Finlay had never known him come home drunk. On Fridays he did the accounts. At one time there had been holidays to Whitby or Windermere or Dumfries. Two years running they had rented a cottage near Quimper on the Brittany coast. In the August of the year after Wal Carter registered his business as a Limited Company he brought home three Virgin airline tickets to Cape Town, South Africa. The last trip they had taken as a family had been to St Lucia. In the three years since then there had been no more holidays. When Wal met Ro on the stairs he would stare down at the carpet until she had passed. Ro cooked meals for herself and Finlay which they ate in the kitchen but Wal Carter ate mostly in transport cafes and restaurants. On the nights when his father was at home his parents always went to bed late. Ro would cover the kitchen table with stacks of photographs and articles cut from newspapers or magazines. She sorted them into piles then trimmed off the excess paper and stuck them into scrapbooks. Wal Carter worked on the computer in the small downstairs cloakroom that had been turned into an office. You could only tell he was in there by the thin line of yellow light that shone under the door. Sometimes, at one o'clock in the morning or later, Finlay would hear them talking through the wall. He was never able to make out what they were saying. Once he heard his mother sigh, a long drawn out sound like the sea running backward over pebbles, but whether in exhaustion or pleasure he could not tell.

There was a book of route maps his father had that detailed all the truck stops and transit depots in Great Britain and Northern Ireland. The newest edition had a supplement that showed the depots of Eire and Northern France. The guide had tables of statistics pointing to the most-visited transport cafes and the sections of road that carried the greatest density of haulage traffic. Cities were marked on the map by large red spots. Various arrows ran out from them. In the most densely populated areas to the North of London the mapping lines tangled together like the coloured flare trails at an aeronautics display. Finlay knew many of the maps almost by heart.

"Do the pigeons follow the roads?" he asked Marten. "Do they have it all stored in their heads or are they guided by landmarks on the ground?"

He had read that pigeons could fly for hundreds of miles. In recent years Wal Carter had driven trucks as far as Bratislava and Krakow. Once, when he got back from Poland, he had slept for the better part of twenty-four hours.

"They retain a lot of visual information," said Marten. "There are studies to prove it. But nobody truly knows how they find their way home."

He had separated Hero from the other birds and had started to feed her a pre-race protein diet.

"She knows when there's a race on," he said. "She finds it exciting. She knows she might see her brother."

Finlay wanted to ask how you could tell that but he held himself back. He had discovered that if you seemed too interested in something Marten would sometimes fall silent or change the subject. When Marten had told him about how he had been forced to sell Leander he had always imagined the pigeon would now be dead. He didn't know why he had thought this; Hero was alive after all. Marten laced his fingers into the wire of the flight pen. He gripped the metal hard. The wire left a twisted imprint in the tips of his thumbs.

"In another life I hated that man," he said. "Because he took away something precious that used to be mine. This racing is just a game between us. It's the only real pleasure we both have left." He turned away from the loft. His high forehead was creased with deep frown lines. He looked older than usual and somehow crumpled, like someone reliving the moments of some personal catastrophe. "Would you like to come up to the house?" he said. "I could make us both a cup of tea."

Raisin Terrace was a cul de sac. It looked out directly onto the ring road but to drive onto it you had to go the long way round back up through the village. From inside the houses the traffic noise wasn't too bad. Finlay supposed the long back gardens and the Bounds Hill allotments acted as a buffer. It was strange, almost impossible, to think of Ro coming to Raisin Terrace to visit Marten. She had called him 'your friend,' as if it had been Finlay's doing, not hers, that had brought her there. He wondered what might happen if he asked Marten what they had talked about. He felt hot inside his clothes, sweaty, as if he had been running. He realised that the idea of asking such a question had made him feel vaguely afraid.

Marten's kitchen was old fashioned but very clean. He made tea in a pot and put it on a tray with saucers and china cups. When Wal Carter made tea for himself he brewed it straight in the mug with a dash of full fat milk and a Tetley's tea bag. Marten spooned loose tealeaves out of a hexagonal tin with Chinese dragons on it. In the small square living room at the front of the house there was a dark blue corduroy suite and an oval gateleg table. In the alcove to the left of the fire stood a large teakwood radiogram but there was no television. In the other alcove there was a glass-fronted bookcase full of books. There were pictures on the walls – two small still lives showing wineglasses on a table with a crystal decanter – but no ornaments or mementos of any kind. Finlay wondered what Ro had been talking about when she said that Marten had collected objects from all over the world. He supposed there were other rooms in the house but the thought that Ro might have seen them unnerved him. He ran his eye over the books in the bookcase and saw titles relating to travel and religion and natural history in no particular order. There were novels too, some of which he had read. Teachers at the school encouraged his reading but Finlay had the feeling he was letting them down somehow, that he was something of a disappointment. He received Bs rather than As and his work was always marked 'good' rather than 'excellent.' He had worked hard on his most recent essay, on Will Travis's *The Last Days of Basra*, but the history teacher Paul Jester had marked him only 60%.

"It's good but it's mostly description, " he had said. "I want to be told what you think."

Finlay had liked *The Last Days of Basra* well enough to want to read it again immediately but he had drawn no firm conclusions about it. Paul Jester seemed to think it necessary not only to take stock of the facts but also to make something of them. Finlay felt wary of doing this. He had a fear that in drawing conclusions he might relax his grip on the facts themselves.

"My mother says you were a teacher," he said suddenly. He expected anger from Marten or even denial but Marten simply shook his head.

"I don't believe in teachers," he said. "Things can be learned but I doubt they can really be taught. The best you can do for people is to show them which books to read."

"She told me you've travelled," said Finlay. "Were you ever in the Middle East?"

"I lived in Baghdad for a while," said Marten. "But a long time ago, before the war."

"What will you do if they knock down Raisin Terrace?"

"They won't knock it down," said Marten. "At least not in my lifetime. Some places have a certain quality about them, don't you find? A feeling they've been put there to last."

It struck Finlay as strange that Marten seemed to be asking his opinion, something he had rarely if ever done. As he was speaking he kept his eyes focussed firmly on Finlay. They had an intensity that seemed to belie their colour, the soft pale bluish-grey of summer rain. Finlay looked quickly away, turning his head to one side and staring out of the window. Raisin Terrace seemed bent back on itself, sticking out into the anomalous landscape of Bounds Hill like a jutting finger. It seemed isolated, disassociated, attached to nothing. Beyond the decaying allotments the ring road roared.

"I'd better go," said Finlay. He finished his tea and went out by the back door. He went a short distance along the houses by way of the communal back passage then slipped through a narrow alleyway between two walls. The front of the terrace faced away from the ring road and back towards the village. There was an orange light along the horizon that Finlay supposed was only the sunset but that he nonetheless found disconcerting. He was almost surprised, relieved, to see that the village was still there.

No Man's Land, by Finlay Carter (Essay submitted for Northern Herald Young Journalist's Award September 15 2006)

The Victorian Terraced Cottage was invented as a kind of social housing, as a way of creating a lot of homes in the cheapest and the quickest possible time. The cottages were built for mill workers and miners, farm labourers and machine operatives, people who had nowhere else to go. The houses were small and very different from the earlier Georgian terraces in the spa towns. Some of them had yards or small gardens but many of them were built back to back. As many as a dozen children might be living in the few small rooms.

The wars came and then the boom time. The shipyards and coalmines went under; the cottages turned into slums. Many of them were cleared to make way for high-rise buildings and new estates. When the estates failed people blew up the tower blocks and began returning to the cottages. Every Englishman's home became his castle. The people who lived in them filled them with computers and Victorian furniture and felt proud to be homeowners.

The village of Threep would be a suburb of Sheffield if not for the A399. The ring road has made it into a place that few people would choose to live in and yet it has helped to keep it as it was. At the centre of Threep there is a pub called the Bedford Arms, a post office and a newsagents and an eight-till-late supermarket. The terraces are of the better kind, with square bay windows and gardens neatly fenced at the back. On the outskirts of Threep there is a small council estate, a cluster of new link houses put up in the mid-1970s, and a gravel track leading to the waste disposal site and the postal depot.

The last road in Threep is called Raisin Terrace. The cottages there are much smaller than those in town. Behind Raisin Terrace are the Bounds Hill allotments and then the ring road. The traffic noise isn't so loud in the houses but from the gardens you can hear it all the time.

"It's like a No-Man's-Land," said one of the residents. "If you close your eyes you can almost hear the guns."

He is a retired teacher and he breeds racing pigeons. His house in Raisin Terrace is neat and clean. He has a high steep forehead and looks a little like a newspaper caricature of a maths professor. He wears clothes that make him look older than he probably is. His neighbours are worried about the council proposals for a new incinerator site at Bounds Hill but the plans don't seem to worry him.

"This house will see me out," he said. "These houses were built to last."

Many of the books in his house are to do with war. He said I could look at them if I wanted. I saw photographs of deserted villages and holiday resorts destroyed by bombs. The book I remember most showed pictures of soldiers queuing for water somewhere in the Iranian desert. One of the men had lost both his hands and so his comrade had to fill and hold his cup.

When I asked the teacher if he had ever been to a war zone he said he had, but not while a war had been going on there. I said that some of the people who lived in Raisin Terrace thought of the dispute with the council as a kind of war, as a battle to try and preserve their way of life. The teacher laughed.

"Most people can live anywhere if they have to," he said. "Once you get used to them places are mostly the same."

He ran into Graczina Carp coming out of the post office on Donald Street.

"Hello," she said. "I've just been to buy some stamps."

He noticed her cropped red t-shirt and the small brown embroidered purse she held in her hand. She was skinny under the t-shirt. The skin at the back of her neck was the same colour as her hair. He wondered what the stamps were for, if she had relatives she wrote to or friends.

"Are you sending a letter abroad?" he asked.

She stared at her feet for a moment and then raised her eyes again to look at him. Her gaze seemed cautious now, the green eyes flickering beneath half-lowered lashes. Her lashes were pale like her eyebrows, soft clumps of almost colourless hair that reminded him of the thistledown that got stuck in the hedges at the back of the allotments. He felt a blankness come upon him that was like a panic. His own skin prickled with heat.

"I don't know anyone abroad," said Graczina. "So I've got no-one to write to, have I?" Whenever she opened her mouth it stopped him dead. The robust vowel sounds, the upwardly-tilted, always faintly interrogative intonation was as familiar to him as his own father and yet coming out of Graczina Carp it sounded unexpected, foreign, almost lyrical. Her body, so wiry-pale, seemed inadequate to support it. He spoke in his mother's southern accent and always had done. Even when he started school this hadn't changed. He wondered if Graczina Carp was aware of her fragility but he doubted it. Her eyes looked baffled, injured, but behind the spider-silk lashes they never stopped watching his.

"I just wondered, you know," he said. "If you ever got the chance to go back home."

"This is my home," she said. "I've never known anywhere else."

"I meant Bosnia."

"I know you did. Tell me something I don't know."

He realised there were tears, not visible yet but starting, somewhere in the passages that ran up behind his nose. He pushed a hand across his face and up over his forehead. He felt sweat at the roots of his hair.

"I didn't mean to," he said.

"It's alright," she said, and sighed. "See you at school."

"I'm not going back," he said. "I've made up my mind."

She opened her eyes wide. They were a bright, dense green, like new spring grass. "What will you do?" she said.

"I don't know. I just know I have to leave here." He

pressed the toe of one trainer against the pavement, scraping his foot in a wide repeated arc. "I haven't told my mother yet," he said. "You're the only person that knows." He thought then of Marten and supposed that he had guessed as much too. But there was something about Marten, his age perhaps, or the fact that he had once been a teacher, that put him beyond the count. Telling Graczina Carp had made things real.

The birds were being taken to France. It was what was called a Grand Prix de Cours and was to start from a suburb of Paris called Cergy. The meeting point, where the birds would be registered, was a field behind the motorway services two miles north along the ring road. It was a little after 5 am. They drove out in Marten's grey Morris Minor. It rattled as it went up the hill.

There were cars everywhere. People stood around in groups and talked. The sky had begun to brighten but the air was still. The stillness reminded Finlay of how early it was. There was much less traffic than usual on the roads.

Marten was going to Paris for the start of the race. He was not the only one that wanted to do this and a coach had been hired for them but they had to travel separately from the birds. Once a bird had been ringmarked it was crated and put on the van. After that the owners couldn't touch them. Finlay was staying behind. He was to go to Raisin Terrace and wait there for Hero's return. Once she entered the loft her chip-ring would trigger a clock that recorded the time. Finlay had agreed to take the timer to the club office on Dean Street in Somerville. It was up to the club secretary to calculate Hero's speed. In the week before the race Finlay had handled Hero regularly. He had been surprised at how quickly the bird had grown used to him, coming to rest on his arm at the sound of his voice.

"She can read you like a book," said Marten. "She knows that you don't mean her harm."

Most of the people at the meeting point seemed to know each other and several of them nodded to Marten. Marten nodded back but did not speak. He seemed preoccupied, almost anxious. He stood and watched the first cars driving away.

"How will you get back to the village?" he said to Finlay. Finlay started to tell him that he would walk down the hard shoulder to the transport depot and hitch a ride on one of his father's vans.

"Some of them will just have come on shift," he said. "They can let me off at the allotments." Marten nodded again as if to signify assent but mostly he seemed not to hear. Once he had given Hero over to the stewards he put his hands in his pockets and began walking slowly from one end of the car park to the other. Finlay followed, wondering what might be wrong. The registration of birds seemed to take a long time and Finlay realised that many of the club members were flying several pigeons rather than just one or two. He had no idea what it was that drove Marten to concentrate his attention on Hero. He didn't suppose it mattered, at least not to him.

Marten stood suddenly still. "There," he said. He spoke quietly as if to himself in a voice that was agitated and almost breathless.

"What," said Finlay. He tried to follow Marten's eye. He saw more people and more cars, a hamburger van set up beside the road.

"That's his car," said Marten. "It's an East German Trabant. He's had it for years." He raised one hand as if to point and then drew it back. The car he seemed to be looking at was up on the verge near the hamburger van, a dusty black saloon with a dented rear bumper and spreading patches of rust on the scratched rear doors. Beside it stood three men. They wee talking together but quietly. Finlay watched their lips moving, unable to make out a word.

"I'm going to get a burger," he said. He moved away from Marten towards the van. As he came closer one of the men took a step back from the others and let out a laugh. His face was rubicund under a checked tweed cap. His laugh was loud, rumbustious, straight from the belly.

"That's not like you, Bismarck," he said. "That's going to set the whole thing on its arse."

"They call him Bismarck because he drives a German car," said Marten.

Finlay started. Marten was right behind him. The man they had called Bismarck turned suddenly as if Marten had called out to him but it was not Marten he looked at but Finlay. He was a tall man with a noticeable stoop. He had thin greying shoulder length hair and deep blue eyes. He looked at Finlay as if he knew him, as if he were about to move towards him and voice a command. Finlay took a step forward then stopped. He was suddenly half convinced he knew him too.

"What is his name then, really?" he said.

"It isn't important. Let's go." Marten moved at last towards the coach. He climbed the steps without looking behind him then sat down in an aisle seat on the right. His gait seemed uncertain and stiff. Finlay gazed up at him but failed to catch his eye. On the opposite side of the car park he saw the tall man get into his car. It came to Finlay, suddenly and with certainty, that the man they had called Bismarck was the man who had bought Hero's brother Leander. He looked up at the coach again and this time Marten was looking straight at him. Finlay raised both eyebrows and made a gesture with his head towards the Trabant. Marten shook his head but whether as a signal of denial or lack of comprehension Finlay was unable to tell. The coach began to move. It grunted and roared and then it was on the road. Finlay looked around for Bismarck but could not find him. The black East German car had already gone.

Finlay went home for breakfast.

"The postman's just been," said Ro. "He delivered a card from your friend,"

The postcard showed a photograph of a city street with plane tress and tall flat-fronted houses. On the corner there was a shop marked Bar-Tabac. The picture looked faded and was bent at one corner. The writing on the back also looked faded, as if the card had been left for a long time in the sun. 'By the time you get this card

I shall be here,' it read. 'Drinking chocolate and drowning brioche chez Madame Michelle.' The handwriting was tall and erect with a backslanting swirling flourish on the 't' and the 'g.' The card was unsigned. Finlay realised he had never seen Marten's handwriting. He wondered how his mother had been able to recognise it. He toyed with the idea that she might have received letters from Marten then dismissed it as ridiculous. He held the card to the light, studying the postmark. The place-name was a smudge of black ink blurred beyond recognition but the date stamp was clearly visible. It showed a date two days ahead.

He felt the heavy thump of his heart. He turned the card quickly back to the reverse and looked again at the photograph.

"That's a street in Montmartre," said Ro. "Near where Picasso used to live when he was young." She didn't mention the date on the postmark. Finlay wondered whether she had noticed the postmark at all.

"Have you ever been there?" said Finlay.

"I went to Paris with the school once. We sat around on some steps close to Picasso's house and made a lot of bad drawings. It was more than twenty years ago. It seems unreal when I think of it now."

"Did you tell him about it?" It seemed to him they both knew he meant Marten and not Wal Carter. Ro laughed with her back to him. She started running water into the sink.

"He used to live in France," she said. "In the sixties."

"It's strange that he should come to live here." He laid the postcard aside. It seemed incongruous to Finlay, a lie almost, that someone could travel the world and end up in a place like Threep. The only thing to explain it would be family connections but there was nothing to suggest Marten was local. For the first time Finlay wondered if Marten made things up to impress people. Or maybe to impress just Ro.

"He likes the quiet," his mother said.

Finlay thought of the unending racket of the cars on the ring road above Raisin Terrace and about what Marten had said about it being like No-Man's Land. "It sounds like he's on the run," he said, and then wondered what from or from whom. His thoughts returned to the tall man in the coach park, the man people called Bismarck because he owned some ancient German car. He knew the name Bismarck from Paul Jester's history classes. He had been a man of violent passions, a general who had evolved into a statesman but had remained a soldier at heart. Marten had said something about Bismarck having stolen something from him, having stolen something precious. He wondered if there were other reasons for the nickname aside from the scarred black Trabant.

When Finlay went to Raisin Terrace it was four o'clock. Hero would not return for as much as a day but he had promised Marten to feed the other birds and let them fly for an hour before it grew dusk. He also had keys to the house. When Marten gave him the keys Finlay had understood at once that Marten meant him to stay in the house overnight. He hadn't questioned this even though he didn't like the idea. Even with Marten's permission it felt like trespassing.

It was the start of the rush hour. The ring road was thick with cars. When Finlay opened the trap the pigeons ascended almost vertically as if they had been longing to escape the noise. Marten had told him to fly the pigeons before feeding them. When the birds were hungry they would always return.

The garden was still sunlit. In the gardens to either side Finlay could see variously shaped flowerbeds planted with pink ladies and snapdragons and other flowers he could not name. In the garden to his right there was a greenhouse. Through the dusty panes of glass Finlay could make out the green and bulbous forms of tropical cacti.

Finlay poured seed into the funnel-shaped feeders. As if at a prearranged signal the pigeons began to descend. Finlay recognised the young bird that had been ringed a few weeks previously, the bird that Marten had said was too young to race. She seemed to have grown since he had last taken note of her. Her body seemed more elongated, the tips of her wings were shiny and sleek as knives. Like many of the birds she was grey, the dense mercurial hue of gunmetal or thunderclouds. Unlike them she had markings on her breast, irregular splotches of a pale cloudy rose that made it appear as if her heartbeat had somehow become visible. Finlay remembered that her name was Ginette Neveu.

"Gina," he called to her softly. "Ginny." He extended a finger towards her through the chicken wire. The bird rotated on her perch then returned her attention to the seed. Finlay wondered what it might be like to see such a bird emerge from an egg and to care for it thereafter. Marten had told him they put on feathers in days. He wondered whether all such fledglings carried the potential to become champions or whether it was only a few. Ginette Neveu looked softer somehow than Hero, the curve of her shoulder fuller, the light in her eye more serene. When Hero moved there was an intensity about her, a preparedness for action that seemed to amount almost to purpose. Finlay supposed it was simply a difference in age.

He thought it likely there would be books in Marten's house that would tell him more about the younger pigeon's namesake, the tragic violinist Ginette Neveu. He touched the keys that were in his pocket; there were two of them looped on a ring. One was for the back door and one the front. He had always known he would go into the house the back way because that was the way he knew best. The front door appeared alien and impersonal, not-Marten. It might almost lead somewhere else. He wondered once again why Marten was living in Threep.

Without Marten inside it the house smelled different. There was a sharp, brackish smell from the drains and the dry background odour of dust. On the draining board was a plate with a knife on it and a scattering of breadcrumbs. The kitchen tap was dripping. Finlay turned it sharply to the left and the dripping stopped. Marten had told him to help himself to food from the fridge but he didn't as yet feel hungry. The door leading from the kitchen to the hallway was closed and for a moment Finlay found himself almost afraid to open it. When he did he found only the blue carpet and the tongue-and-groove panelling that lined the hallway. The sun streamed through the fanlight. It ran like spilled gold paint across the floor.

The front door had the chain on and had been locked from the inside. Finlay's skin prickled with gooseflesh, then he realised that it meant nothing. Just that when Marten had left the house he had gone through the back. He undid the chain and thumbed the latch. There was a second lock also, a chubb with a key in it. He turned the key to the right and opened the door.

The light was beginning to fade. There were cars at the kerbside and in the turning space at the end of the road. Towards the far end of the terrace, where the road ran downhill again towards the village, two teenaged boys were playing football. In place of a goal they were using one of the narrow alleyways that ran between the houses. Each time the ball entered the passage it ricocheted off the walls with a hollow ring. One of the boys was tall and dressed in a Sheffield Wednesday football shirt. The other boy was smaller. He wore a plain grey t-shirt and torn blue jeans. He had a bruise on one cheek and lips that were full and rosy like a girl's. As Finlay watched he caught the ball sideways on his instep and pitched it into the goal.

"You crackhead," yelled the tall boy. He flew down into the alley after the ball. The blond boy, laughing madly, swiftly followed. Finlay waited for them to come out again but even after a minute or so there was no sign of them. He stepped back from the pavement and closed the door.

In Marten's sitting room the glass-fronted bookcase was locked. There were other books on a side-table, books that had not been there before. Finlay recognised a new biography of Saddam Hussein that had recently appeared in the school library as well as Will Travis's book on Basra. He opened the Saddam biography at the colour plates and saw a skinny dark-eyed boy in a neat white school uniform transform himself into a filthy bearded figure being pulled from a hole in the ground. He replaced the book on the table and crossed again to the bookcase. He saw that the books inside had been rearranged. They had been divided into categories, fiction and non-fiction, and put in alphabetical order. On one of the shelves that contained non-fiction Finlay could see a three-volume Encyclopaedia of Music. The spines of the volumes were dark blue with embossed silver violins. He tried once again to open the bookcase but was unsuccessful. He found it strange that Marten had removed the key. He looked around the room, searching for places where it might have been hidden. Feeling foolish he lifted the lid of the polished teak radiogram. There was a record on the turntable, Tchaikovsky's violin concerto played by David Oistrakh, but otherwise the cabinet was empty. He stood still and listened. For a moment he seemed to hear the sound of footsteps or voices but then the noises reassembled themselves into the low unstinting mutter of traffic thrashing by on the ring road. The house itself was silent. He came out of the sitting room and went upstairs.

There was a small square landing leading to two bedrooms and a bathroom. The first of the bedrooms was almost empty; it contained a narrow single bed and a chest of drawers. There was a tartan blanket in place of a bedspread and two pillows in square white pillowcases but Finlay found it hard to imagine that the bed was used much. The idea that Marten might entertain guests seemed somehow unlikely to the point of being preposterous. Underneath the bed were a number of cardboard boxes filled with old letters. Finlay made no move to touch them. For some reason he felt certain that Marten would know if his possessions had been interfered with. He crossed to the window. Below him he could see the garden and the neighbouring gardens and beyond them the allotments and the taut grey curve of the ring road. The sun had gone down; the horizon glowed a luminous pink. From upstairs the sound of the traffic was almost inaudible.

The bathroom was tiny: a toilet, a basin, a bath, an airing cupboard stacked with fresh towels. In Marten's room there was a double bed with a high wooden headboard and a tassel-edged candlewick bedspread in parsley green. Above the bed hung a small square painting of flowers that he guessed might be violets. The bulky-looking wardrobe reminded him of the cumbersome antiques in his grandparents' house in Fulton. There was a cast-iron fireplace and a fire screen embroidered with dragons. On the mantelpiece stood a clock under a glass dome with all its workings showing. To either side of the clock stood two framed photographs. The one on the right was a studio portrait of a man in perhaps his late twenties. His fairish, silky-looking hair had been combed carefully in a side parting and there was a small raised scar on his lower lip. The man was good looking in the way of Second World War aircraft pilots and after a moment or two Finlay realised with a shock that it was Marten. The other photograph was also of Marten. In it he looked older by as much as ten years but was still good looking. He had his hand on the arm of another man and both of them were laughing. The second man was taller and darker. His fingers were long and slender but the knuckles were large and heavy and oddly bunched. He had his head turned slightly to one side but Finlay was still able to identify him as Bismarck, the man who drove the battered black Trabant. He was holding a folded yellow handkerchief with an edging of delicate lace.

Finlay went to the window. It was not yet dark in Raisin Terrace but the streetlamps had come on nonetheless. In the house opposite a young woman was leaning out of an upstairs window. She had thin white-blonde hair held back in a blue rubber band. On her right cheek there was a birthmark, a red welt that looked like a shell.

"Dennis," she called out. "Mack!" her voice was high and bright like a cloud. The wispy tail of hair fell from her shoulder and hung from the window. There was the sound of a bouncing ball and racing feet.

There were clothes in the wardrobe, the threadbare jumpers and fraying shirts that were unmistakably Marten's. On the floor of the wardrobe and on the wide top shelf there were other things: a green snakeskin vanity bag, a glass case containing a bulbous-bodied moth with spotted wings. There was a carved wooden footstool in the shape of an elephant and a supermarket carrier bag full of money cowries. Beside this was a shoebox with its lid missing. Inside the box was something heavy encased in bubble wrap. When Finlay unwound the plastic he found a round black metal dial in a wooden surround. The perimeter of the dial was marked with what at first looked like numbers but when examined more closely turned out to be some sort of hieroglyphs. At the centre of the dial was a pointer on a pivot. Finlay prodded it gently with the tip of one finger but it refused to move. He found the thing beautiful despite or perhaps because of its obscurity. He wondered why Marten didn't have it out on display.

It occurred to him that he could steal the object quite easily. The idea exerted a pull on him that he found impossible to explain. He rewrapped it carefully in the bubble wrap and replaced it in the shoebox. There was a serial number on the side of the box and a diagram showing a ladies size 4 red court shoe with the style name Emma. He put the box back on the shelf.

On Marten's bedside table there was a new paperback edition of The Running Man by Richard Bachmann, a heavy gold Rolex, and a ring with an amber gem in a silver surround. It was Ro's ring, his mother's ring, the ring she used to wear before Wal Carter had given her the opal. Finlay recognised it immediately. He felt he would have known it anywhere.

The street seemed completely quiet. A downstairs light had come on in the house opposite but Marten's sitting room lay in darkness. Finlay switched on the standard lamp next to the radiogram. A wan yellow light fell over everything and Finlay saw at once that the key to the bookcase had been in the lock all along. The key turned easily as if the lock had been recently greased. Ginette Neveu was a small slant-eyed girl with dark hair cut and permed in the fashion of the Forties. The photograph was blurred, so her features could not clearly be seen. There was a short paragraph of writing accompanying the picture in which her playing was described as 'an elemental force of a wholly original caste.' It stated also that she had won the International Wieniawski Competition in 1935, a contest in which David Oistrakh had been placed only second. Finlay looked up the entry on Wieniawski and discovered he was a Polish composer who had also played the violin.

There were no precise details of the plane crash. Finlay put the book back in the bookcase then went through to the kitchen. He heated baked beans in a saucepan and toasted two slices of bread under the grill.

Racing Pigeons: a Brief History by David Marten (Pigeon Post, Journal of the Sheffield and Peak District Pigeon Fanciers Association issue 195 March/April 2006)

The Egyptians were the first to keep pigeons. If you go to the museum of the temple of Isis on the northernmost outskirts of Alexandria you can see a stone hieroglyph of a servant with a bird on his wrist dating from 3000 BC. The bird, for years described in guidebooks as a hawk, displays many of the characteristics of the European rock dove, now accepted by most sources as the common ancestor for the modern homing pigeon.

In 1150 the Sultan of Baghdad established a postal system in which the mail was delivered by pigeons. Genghis Khan made extensive use of pigeon post as his Golden Horde swept westwards and south. During the French Revolution pigeons carried dispatches between Brussels and Berlin when the telegraph went down. In the First World War certain birds were awarded medals for bravery under fire. The breeding programme for carrier pigeons became a matter of national security. Details of bloodlines were kept secret and as a direct result of this were eventually lost.

There are more than two hundred species of pigeon in the world. Some of them are exotic, highly-coloured and gorgeous in appearance. The ancestors of the modern racing pigeon were selected not for their beauty but for their abilities in the air. The northern species had dull plumage but long wings and well-developed flight muscles. Some species were high-flyers; others flew better at night. Some birds were fast and others strong. The best of them combined all these qualities. The feature that set pigeons apart from other birds was their inborn instinct to 'home.'

Pigeons are a mystery, just as there is so often a mystery at the heart of that which is considered commonplace. Pigeons are docile creatures and easily tamed. The ease with which they are domesticated is usually ascribed to their need for food. It is less easy to explain their devotion to a single master or their tendency to mate for life. Pigeons have an internal navigational system that is still a bone of contention for naturalists. Radio signals, telephone masts and microwaves can throw them off course but they can adjust to these distractions given time. A racing pigeon in the peak of condition can attain a speed of over ninety miles per hour. The record flight for a pigeon is 2,300 miles.

When I was a boy there was a storybook I loved called *The Mountains and Lady Magdalene*. The thing that first attracted me to it was the front cover, which showed a long-bodied silver-grey bird above blue hills. The book was by Noel Coin and was about a racing pigeon called Maddie. I read the book many times, fascinated most of all by the author's afterword stating that the events described were based on a true story. It was only when I was older that I discovered Noel Coin had been an official war correspondent for the Manchester Guardian. His life had been saved by a carrier pigeon during the 1965 siege of Algiers.

Noel Coin's book filled me with the desire to raise and train racing pigeons of my own but in fact that did not happen for quite some time. I came to know about Noel Coin through his younger brother Simon who was my contemporary at the university of Glasgow. When I asked him what had made him decide on Glasgow he said it was to get as far away from his family as possible. He dropped out in his third year shortly before Finals. Simon of course became fairly well known in certain circles through his crime novels although he had said nothing to anyone at Glasgow about wanting to become a writer. For years I searched second hand bookshops and the stacks of public libraries for a copy of *The Mountains and Lady Magdalene* but nobody had ever heard of Noel Coin.

I came across his brother again years later when he bought a pigeon from me. I recognised him at once although he just as I had been compromised somewhat by time.

There was no need to ask Simon what had re-ignited his interest in pigeons. Pigeons fascinate us and hold our hearts captive because they go where we cannot go, faster and higher and with a singularity of purpose we can only dream of. And yet still they return to us, innocent, undaunted and true.

Finlay woke up to the phone. He thought at first that the sound was part of a dream he had been having about crossing the Indian Ocean on a steam ferry but after a second or so he knew it was real. He slipped out of bed and went downstairs. The voice on the line was Marten's.

"I wanted to be sure you didn't miss her," he said. "She should be there any time now." The line fizzed with static. Marten's voice came and went, interspersed with a record Finlay recognised from a year or so before, Yellow Bird by Conor Oberst. Finlay looked down at his watch. It was shockproof and waterproof, guaranteed to a depth of 250 metres. It had been a gift from his father and he never took it off. The hands stood at half past eleven; he had slept for almost twelve hours. He noticed then how bright it was in the room. He didn't remember having been that tired.

"I'll go outside," he said. "Do you want me to call you back?" Marten did not reply and Finlay realised he was no longer on the line. The record was still playing though, louder and more clearly as if the telephone were somehow connected to a radio station. Finlay replaced the receiver and went out of the room. There was post on the mat in the hallway, a thick buff envelope stamped with the logo of Amnesty International. Outside it was sunny and the sound of the ring road seemed magnified by the clear weather. Marten had told him to feed the birds again in the morning but not to fly them. Some of the pigeons seemed confused by this and several were ignoring their seed. Ginette Neveu was eating normally. Her pink breast was slightly ruffled, perhaps from sleep. Finlay wondered whether she was aware of Hero's absence or if she sensed her imminent return. The Threep and Somerville Gazette often published stories about animals with extra-sensory perception. Finlay remembered one about a cat that could tell the time, and another about a dachshund that had saved its owner from a fire. He had never read anything about birds with telepathic powers. He recalled what Marten had said about Hero being able to read him like a book and supposed that was telepathy of a kind, a form of low-grade precognition that was the experience of many. He stopped looking at Ginette Neuveu and turned his gaze outwards to where the ring road wound its way downhill towards the village. He wondered if Hero knew enough to use it as a landmark, if this road had some resonance for her that helped to mark it out from all the rest.

At first she looked dark against the sky then suddenly she was white. For a moment the sun caught her and made her invisible. As Finlay watched her Hero began to descend. She fell in a straight line, heavily, as if she were made of stone. At the last moment she spread her wings and steadied herself. Their silver tips flashed quickly like two crossed swords.

She entered the trap. The other pigeons parted to make way for her and then continued to eat or preen. When Finlay called to her Hero sidled towards him along the perch, her yellow toes curling and uncurling themselves like long gnarled fingers. Finlay stretched two of his own fingers through the wire and stroked her breast.

"She should have been exhausted," he said to Graczina. "She'd just flown hundreds of miles."

"Perhaps she found a short cut," said Graczina. "Like the one Rae Silcot used on all those cross country runs." She giggled and put a hand to her mouth. Each time she moved her head Finlay noticed her colourless eyebrows. The fine pale hairs lay flat against the taut bluish skin of her brow bone, shiny and sleek as watered silk. Rae Silcot was a large athletic-looking girl who had only entered the school the year before. Finlay knew her by sight but he couldn't remember ever having spoken to her. He knew nothing of what she had done on the cross country runs.

"It doesn't matter," said Graczina. "It was funny at the time but that's all."

"She was named after some sort of psychic. Hero, I mean. She was Greek."

"Hero and Leander," said Graczina. "I used to love those stories. I read them hundreds of times." She folded her arms across her chest and looked down towards the allotments. The buddleia was past its best. The sky was the deep-throated sapphire blue of kingfishers but it smelt like autumn.

"When she came down she looked like glass," said Finlay. "I thought she had disappeared."

"My father disappeared," said Graczina. "The man we live with adopted me but he's my uncle, not my father. He used up all his savings to get us out." Her arms gripped her sides and Finlay saw again how thin she was under her clothes. He half-closed his eyes against the sunlight. Graczina seemed to shimmer as if made from dust. Traffic went by on the ring road. Three lorries passed in convoy. Finlay saw that the one in the middle was one of his father's.

"My mother's not really a cleaner," said Graczina. "She's a doctor. People should know these things and try to write them down before they're forgotten. It isn't important whose side you're on. The only thing that matters is not to forget."

"We could write each other letters after I leave," said Finlay. "You could tell me about Bosnia."

"I don't know anything about Bosnia. I left there when I was two."

"I could send you foreign stamps if you like," said Finlay. "I think they're interesting."

"I saw a set of stamps once with pigeons on them," said Graczina. "There were six of them and all the pigeons were different." She let her arms swing free by her sides. A strand of her whitish hair touched the edge of her mouth. "I'd like to have some of those but you can't get them now."

simoncoin2010@ventura.co.uk
Subject: A399 15/11/2035

Belinda
        Be at the station as we arranged
but there's no need to get on the train. Wait by the
taxi rank and I'll pick you up. I've had the car fixed.
They say it will run and run.

                                                                Simon

It was raining. The HGV's windscreen wipers passed back and forth across the glass in blurry stripes.

"It's a good job I came by," said the driver. "You wouldn't want to be standing out in this." He had a Liverpool accent and curly blond hair tied back in a black bandana. His hands were enormous, half-covered in long reddish hairs.

He was playing a disc of music by Townes van Zandt. The lorry's wheels sent up a trail of spume as they left the depot behind and came out onto the ring road. When they passed the Bounds Hill allotments they were shrouded in mist.

"Where are you off to?" Ro had said. She was in the kitchen, invisible. He imagined her slow firm walk, her magnificent horse-coloured hair and wondered when he might see her again. He put his hand out and touched the door but he didn't go in.

"Just out," he said. "See you later." On Barraclough Road the air felt chilly and smelled of wet rubber. Finlay supposed the summer was almost gone.

"I'm going as far as Birmingham," said the driver. "Will you be alright from there?"

"That's fine," said Finlay. "There'll be plenty of other rides."

"College is it in London then? Or are you running off after some girl?"

"I want to have a look at the city. And then I have to get on a plane." He felt wary of saying more. It was important to him that some time elapsed before he let people know where he had gone. He looked sideways at the driver trying to gauge his reaction but the man's eyes were impassive, fixed on the road. There was a photograph taped to the dashboard, a picture of a smiling girl with waist-length hair.

"Who's that?" said Finlay. He wanted the driver to talk about something else.

"That's my sister, Linda." He took his eyes off the road for a second and glanced at the photograph. "I like to have her with me when I drive."

"She looks nice. Interesting."

"She was christened Linda but everybody calls her Gipsy. I've always had the wanderlust but that girl is even worse than me. She stowed away in my truck once and I didn't know a thing until we got to Athens. She didn't even have a passport. If they'd found her out at customs I'd have been had."

"Where is she now?"

"I'm not sure." He was silent. "But she'll drop me a postcard soon. She always does."

Finlay bent forward to examine the picture more closely. The girl wore jeans and a grey t-shirt with a picture of a racing car across the front. Her feet were bare. It was difficult to guess her age.

"If I'm honest with you she's my hero," said the driver suddenly. "She never gives up on what she wants, not for nothing and not for no-one. She was always like that, even as a baby. I suppose that's just the way some people are made."

When Marten came back from France he had looked different, younger, more like the man in the photograph.

"I don't want her to worry," said Finlay. "When she comes can you tell her that I'm safe?"

"I want to give you something," said Marten. "To say thank you for your help with the birds." He had gone upstairs then and the sound of his footsteps had also been different. Finlay imagined that he sounded lighter and more agile. He had been away for more a week.

When he came back downstairs he was holding the shoebox that had once contained a pair of size 4 ladies court shoes with the style name Emma. Finlay could see bubble wrap poking out of the top.

"What is it?" he said. "A compass?"

Marten laughed. "I suppose it is, of sorts," he said. "If you keep it with you you'll find out."

Terminus

They went into the underground at Mayakovsky Square. As he passed through the barrier Victor glanced back at the statue of the poet. Its concrete plinth was covered in flowers. It was the month of June but even in January the base of Mayakovsky's statue was always covered in flowers. *It's because he makes the people feel immortal,* Victor thought. *Being a poet must be the next best thing to being God.*

On the platform people stood in ranks and waited. There was never a long wait, not in the centre of town, but there was always long enough for him to notice the smell of the metro, the stench of sweating armpits, of stale and spoiled produce, of confined and overheated, somehow artificial air. It was a smell the tunnels seemed to exhale, like the secret dying breath of a second city. *The tunnels are like drainpipes,* Victor thought. *And the people that swarm along them no better than rats.* Victor imagined that he would know the smell of the Moscow metro anywhere, even on the other side of the world.

In less than a minute a train arrived. By the time they forced their way inside the carriage all the seats had been taken. Marisa had been crying. As Victor reached for the grab-rail above his head she leant heavily against him. He could not tell if she had meant to do this or whether it was just the mass of people pushing her close. He glanced across at her but her face was turned away. "Your attention please, the doors are closing," said the tannoy. "The next station is Pushkin Square." The doors slid shut and he train moved off into the darkness. The lights around them flickered but did not go out.

Being in the carriage made it harder to remember what time of day it was. Victor looked at the bent, silent figure of Marisa and wondered whether it would be right now to reach out and touch her. He thought about how it felt to smooth her hair. Her hair must once have been blonde; it had darkened with age of course but hadn't

157

gone all the way brown. It rested against the pale skin of her cheeks, the same dirty yellow as the froth on cups of coffee, the bitter, grainy coffee from the canteen urn.

"You don't need me, Vitya," she had said when he had told her he was leaving. "I think it's true that you love me, but you don't need me, not really." He did not stroke her hair, but lightly touched her arm. She started backwards as if trying to get away.

"No need to push," said somebody behind her. Marisa stared straight ahead, ignoring the angry voice and looking only at Victor. He had forgotten all the things he had meant to say.

"I'm sorry I shouted," he said instead. "I just wish I could decide what we should do."

"You don't have to come all this way," she said to him. "I can go home on my own. It's pointless, you coming too."

"I want to come," he said, and took her hand. There were still a dozen stations left to go. Before he met Marisa he had hardly ever travelled on this line. There was no-one else he knew at Red Guard Fields. When he lay awake at night in his room near Turgenevskaya it was sometimes hard to believe that such a sad grey place actually existed. And yet on a clear bright day such as this one you had a view of most of the city from Red Guard Fields. He imagined it might feel the same to look back at the earth from the moon.

Victor knew that Konstantin Shcherbakov would be at home because he never left the flat he shared with Marisa. The flat had two rooms and a kitchen, and was on the ninth floor of a tower block. Marisa went out to work each day while her husband stayed indoors. Marisa cleaned offices and banks and schoolrooms while Konstantin Shcherbakov wrote peace pamphlets. He spoke to no-one except Marisa although he claimed to have talked with the devil. As the hours wore on he would look more frequently at the clock, his blue eyes glancing at it surreptitiously as if it were something forbidden. Victor wondered if Shcherbakov was still afraid to go outside or if he had simply stopped wanting to.

"People don't realise how badly hurt he was," Marisa

insisted. "I don't just mean his injuries, I mean inside his head. He hasn't always been this way. You should have known him when I first met him. You would have liked him then."

Victor felt angry with her for saying such things. He told her that he could never admire a man who made her live like that, a man who crippled her life because he was afraid to live his own. "He couldn't do it either, if it weren't for you," he said. "No-one can afford to live on an army pension."

Knowing Konstantin Shcherbakov had made Victor want to change his own life for the better. The drifts of meaningless papers and the silent hopeless rooms of the flat at Red Guard Fields had instilled a fear in him that his parents and his teachers had never been able to. It was due to Shcherbakov that Victor had decided to leave. But it was also because of her husband that Marisa would not come too.

"He would die here without me," she had said, refusing to look at him. "You would be sad for a while but you wouldn't die. Maybe you could write to me sometimes."

The train stopped. Victor was surprised to see that they were already at Carfax, out beyond the ringroad. The doors opened and a lot of people got out. Victor sat down and pulled Marisa into the empty seat beside him. With fewer bodies around them it seemed cold inside the carriage even though the metro was never cold, especially in June. When the train started up again Victor linked his arm with Marisa's as if doing that might help keep them together. Marisa was wearing the blue dress he had bought for her with part of his third month's wages from the paper. Over it and despite the warmth of the day she had put on a yellow cardigan that had been donated by her downstairs neighbour. The yellow wool looked horrible against her sallow skin. Victor had noticed that she felt the cold extremely. He had sometimes daydreamed about taking her to live in the south of France, or at least to the Black Sea coast, where Chekhov had gone to cure his consumption. There didn't seem much point in those dreams now.

"I'll look for something better, like you said," she said.

Her eyes were light brown, hazel-coloured, like the little animals that live in the grass or woods. "There's an evening class I can go to at the college. They can show me how to use those new machines." She looked at Victor hopefully, perhaps seeking his approval. *It's all too late*, he thought. *What will all that matter once I've gone.* He released her arm and twisted himself to face her. He put both hands around her neck, displaying her face between them like a jewel. She seemed more bone than flesh. The extra food he bought her had made no difference.

"Please," he said. "Come with me. I can wait another week if you need more time." He had tried to sound sure of himself, like a man in control, but now he heard his words out loud they sounded as flat and useless as before. Marisa bent her head between his hands, forcing him to let her go. In the carriage the lighting flicked off and the wheels beneath the train let out a screech. The people turned the pages of their papers in the dark. "Approaching Kolomenskaya," the tannoy said.

The lights flashed on again and then the doors opened. There was no-one on the platform outside. Victor had never seen a metro platform empty before, not even late at night. The station was completely white like a doctor's waiting room or a hospital corridor. It looked brighter on the platform than inside the train. Suddenly they pulled away. The scene slid from beneath his eyes like a stage set being dragged out of sight. The name on the sign-board at the head of the station was Kamarinskaya, the same as the wedding-dance. Victor was sure the tannoy had said Kolomenskaya but he realised he must have been mistaken. He had never got out at either station before.

Marisa sat silently beside him. Her hands lay in her lap, the small transparent hands of a girl. Victor looked away from her at his reflection in the carriage window. There was no-one sitting opposite them now and it seemed that half the train was empty. The underground plan on the curved wall of the carriage told him there were five more stations between Kolomenskaya and Red Guard Fields. He couldn't see a station called Kamarinskaya. The reflection in the glass looked puzzled in spite of its grief. Victor's stomach churned slightly, the way it always did when he made a mistake. The next station seemed a long time coming. Its name was Bednaya. He felt sure there wasn't a station called Bednaya. Bednaya meant 'poor girl,' a hopeless peasant woman with nowhere to go. The few that were left in the carriage buried themselves in their newspapers. Nobody got out and there was no-one outside to get in.

At the next stop Victor stood up, tugging at Marisa's arm.

"Come on," he said, pulling her to her feet and towards the doors. He was suddenly afraid the doors might close before they could get to them.

"But we're not there yet," Marisa said. "We can't be."

"I don't know where we are," said Victor. "But we need to get out."

There were people in the shadows on the platform but once the train had gone there was no noise. There was light around them but Victor saw it had a faded yellow quality, as of the light from kerosene or gas. Marisa held fast to his hand like a child in an unfamiliar place.

"What are we doing here?" she said.

"There'll be another train in a moment," he said. "The right train." He spoke to her as if she were younger than he was, though he knew that she was older by some ten years. He squeezed her hand but could think of nothing further to say. In the corner by a small closed door a heavy-set man seemed to be talking to himself. After a few seconds of looking at him Victor realised that he was speaking into a radio. *He's just a guard, after all*, he thought. The man wore a dark blue uniform, but over it he had on a thick coat made of navy corduroy, as if he were expecting winter up above. The station smelt the same as any other, only stronger. Victor wondered how deep underground they were. There was an escalator but it seemed to be broken. He couldn't see a station name at all.

"No, no, I don't know," said the blue-coated man quietly into his radio. "I haven't even been there, not today." The radio emitted a crude crackling sound, as if it were about to break down, or as if it had not been working properly in the first place. The guard stared at it and pressed a button. The white noise stopped and the man put the thing away, slipping it in beneath the navy coat. He seemed dissatisfied but not concerned. He stepped forward away from the door, and began pacing up and down at the end of the platform. The sign on the door read 'No Entry.'

"Kostya will be waiting," said Marisa. "He gets worried. I don't want to be late." She tugged at Victor's hand, looking around her as if wondering which way to go. In the end she spotted some benches and made towards them. Victor let himself be led. The guard's feet thumped. The air against his face seemed to vibrate to the sound of it, a grey noise, like a car door being slammed late at night.

He strained his ears, hoping to hear a train. At first he could hear nothing but the feet of the guard. Then at last there was a long, low rushing and the humming of rails. The din came closer and then fled past him, passing through one of the tunnels behind his back. As it faded it merged with a scream. The sound seemed distant, perhaps further away than the train, but it seemed to go on for longer. On the platform nobody moved. The guard broke off from his pacing and took out the faulty radio.

"I told him not to do it," said the man. Busy static answered. He started to pace again, the small black radio dangling from his enormous hand.

"My God, how could anyone do that?" said Marisa. She was whispering, though nobody was close enough to hear. "It's like something you read in a book."

She rummaged in her handbag. She took out a make-up case, a dented silver compact with flowers engraved on the top. When she opened it Victor could see her face reflected in the tiny mirror. In the cloudy yellow light her skin looked grey. *She's nearly forty*, Victor thought, and put an arm around her shoulders. Marisa dabbed a finger in the compact then smeared a little blusher onto each cheek. When she rubbed it in a red stain leapt and spread.

"I didn't know you used that," Victor said. The finger that had touched the make-up had turned the colour of watermelon or old ripe strawberries. As he watched she took out a handkerchief and wiped the mess away.

"I don't, not usually. It's nothing but a waste of time." She turned towards him and tried to smile. Victor found that he hated the idea of that deep wet redness mixing with the paler colours that made up her face. He longed to find a tap and wash her clean. He leaned towards her, causing her handbag to slide from her lap and down onto the concrete. It landed with a thud and he kicked it away.

"I never wanted things to be like this," he said. He pressed her hands together between his own. "I wish things could be different. If only everything had been different." Victor looked her full in the face. It seemed to shine at him, paler even than usual in the strange yellow light. For some moments he gazed at her without speaking, taking in the faded, almost colourless hair, the gold-flecked hazel eyes, the wide unblemished mouth that made her seem like a child. Then the lights went out completely and he could see nothing at all.

It was so unexpected and so total that it felt like going blind.

"They'll have heads roll for this," he heard the guard say. He sounded angry but not overly concerned.

"Let's just sit still," Marisa whispered. "The lights will come on in a minute."

Her thin arm felt warm next to his but Victor was afraid it must just be the cardigan. He held her hands a moment longer then let them go.

"Wait here," he said. "I'm going to try and see what's going on." If she had told him not to go then he would have stayed with her but she said nothing and he could no longer see her eyes. He stood up and began to walk. He scraped his feet against the concrete as if wading through mud. He heard other people shifting in the blackness but none of them seemed close by. He went a little way and then stopped, afraid he might fall from the platform onto the rails.

If I were on the street at night my eyes would have adjusted to the dark by now, he thought. *But there's no light down here in these tunnels, no light at all.* Somewhere in the deeper darkness another ghost train went by. To the left of him somebody coughed. Victor imagined that would most likely have been the guard.

When the child took his hand he almost fell. Its fingers were sticky and hot, its breathing hoarse and somehow desperate. Victor inhaled too quickly, almost choking on the air he was trying to breathe.

"You're not my Daddy," said the child. It was a boy. "I think my Daddy's gone and run away."

For some unknown reason Victor thought immediately of the screaming they had heard, drifting up towards them out of the tunnel. *But that's ridiculous,* he thought. *If he'd fallen under the train he would have died instantly.* He sensed that the boy was looking up at him, perhaps expectantly, though Victor could see nothing at all. He imagined curly dark brown hair and big blue eyes.

"What happened to your Daddy, mate?" he said. "Can you tell me where your Daddy might have gone?"

"My name is Sasha," said the boy. "I'm afraid of the dark."

The tips of his fingers dug into Victor's hand as if they meant to grow a root there. They seemed to drag at him somehow, trying to force him back to a world he'd thought he'd left. They made him feel less alone, even, than Marisa's fingers, soft between the pressure of his hands. He had never even thought of having children. *That's what they do to you,* he thought. *You have them and then you can never get away.*

"I ran out of the train," said the boy. "My Daddy told me not to. He stayed inside."

There was fear in his voice, but there was pleasure too, the rash excitement that accompanies adventure. Victor supposed that the boy was still too young to know that adventures could sometimes end badly. He crouched down beside him, still holding his hand.

"I'm sure we'll find your Daddy. Just wait until the lights come on."

Somewhere on the platform, somebody laughed.

"I don't know what you're doing," said the guard.

Victor had no sense of Marisa. He had no idea by then of where he was. He asked himself if he could wait forever in the dark like this or what he might have to do if nobody came.

The lights came on soundlessly and without warning, exactly as they had gone out. Victor saw that the boy in front of him was pale and thin and very fair, and that his left arm ended at the elbow. His eyes were of a blue so watery that they were almost the colour of quartz. He was older than Victor had imagined. He could have been as old as twelve.

"Just wait," said Victor, dropping his hand. The boy blinked hard at him. A tear formed at the corner of one eye.

"You're not my Daddy," said the child, and ran away.

Victor turned around and thought: *she's gone*. He did not see Marisa at first, coming towards him across the platform. When he finally caught sight of her he saw that she was not looking at him at all but at something else. When he turned to look he saw there was a train. It had come in soundlessly, just like the light. The metal it was made of was old and dark as the walls of the tunnel. It reflected nothing. The people on the platform swarmed towards it, pushing in through the dull open doors. Victor glanced from side to side but there was no sign of the navy-coated guard.

He caught her arm as she came close to him and then drew level.

"Don't get on the train," he said.

"Let me go now, Vitya. Kostya will be waiting." Her voice was soft and gentle as it always was, but already it seemed far away. She withdrew her arm from his and moved away. He gazed at her yellow cardigan, and then her bag, lying open and discarded on the ground.

Once the train was gone he was alone. From the centre of the platform the motionless escalator gleamed sullenly. Victor stared at it, at first doing nothing at all. After a moment had passed he went towards it. Then, very slowly, he began to climb.

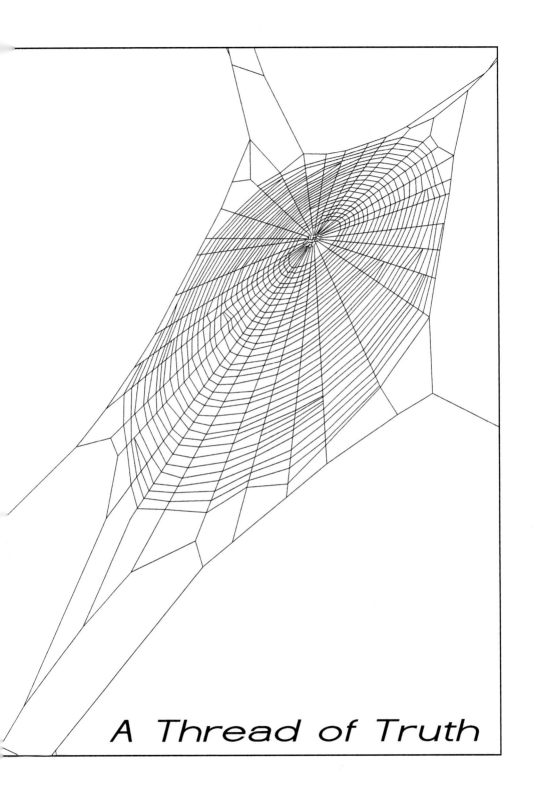

A Thread of Truth

Fear is a subject that obsesses people. There are whole books written on the nature of fear. I have seen them in the bookshops of almost every town I have ever visited, ranged on shelves marked 'Popular Psychology.' Some of these books, hidden for the most part between soft paper covers in inviting pink or invigorating purple, even go so far as to include the word in their title: Fear is a Four Letter Word. Fear Loss, Fear Life. Feel/Energise/Articulate/Regenerate. Others skirt around the subject, pandering to it, as if subscribing to a belief that to deny something is to force it out of existence. Whether the books are prepared to come clean about their content or not is immaterial since inside they are mostly the same. A column of numbered chapter-headings leads you fearlessly forward towards self-discovery, inner conviction, and, finally, success. In the lexicon of the twenty first century fear, more than anything else, is the ultimate synonym for failure.

I first discovered these books at the end of my teens. I had never been a stranger to bookshops, but, like the majority of boys, I had never found myself overly tempted to explore the realms of Popular Psychology or Mind, Body and Spirit. I had seen the pink books on the shiny wooden shelves, pored over mostly by anxious-looking housewives with smudged makeup and chewed fingernails, or other, even more forbidding women with harlequin skirts and masses of cloudy hair. I was more interested in spy stories, exploration, and, later, modern drama. I suppose that my first tentative forays into the inner sanctum of pastel paper and polished veneer were in fact my first attempts at acknowledging to myself that I had a problem.

I would lie in wait, sheltered by the familiar enclave of 'Foreign Travel,' watching until 'Popular Psychology' was entirely empty of browsers. Then I would emerge, head lowered, ready to dart back to safety should anyone suspect what I was doing. I read a little from one book and then another, making dissatisfied noises, pretending that such titles were of no interest to me and no importance; that, indeed, I had taken them down from the shelf by some mistake. I acted, in short, like a schoolboy exploring pornography. And, since I never once encountered anyone in the bookshop that I recognised, I do not even know whom I was trying to fool.

I saw fear analysed by a hundred different methods. I looked at pie charts and pictorial equations and graphs. All the authors seemed to come to the same conclusion: that fear is a disparate illusion created by the unique and particular psychology of the subject in question. I read that the fear of rejection is actually an expression of low self-esteem, that a fear of failure is mostly the misjudged assignment of erroneous goals. I came across the assertion that even the so-called 'logical fears' – the fear of drowning, for instance, or fire, or dangerous animals – arise solely as the result of inadequate preparation for life. You can learn to swim, after all, or fit smoke alarms, or even carry a gun. I came across more than a dozen sets of statistics designed to alleviate the fear of flying. I found a lot of the theories intriguing, and even believed some of them at first, because they did not apply to me. Like most of the people who read such books, I continued turning the pages, hoping to be brought face to face with myself and yet still doubting that I ever would. Anyone who has ever been held in the grip of fear believes himself singularly cursed, an alien, unique. The more I read of popular psychology, the more I came to suspect that many of those who sought to describe fear were actually too unimaginative, or perhaps too stupid, ever to have experienced the real thing.

At first I was almost afraid to turn to the chapters entitled 'Phobias' in case they should describe too accurately, too specifically, the fear that had invaded my life. Instead I found myself discounted as 'someone in possession of an abnormal fear or aversion, an exaggerated loathing, an illogical sensitivity.' The words dissatisfied me, offended me almost, without my being able to understand why. Somewhere in the gulf between logic and illogic the analyst had mislaid the concept of intuition. In the age of the machine, it seems, we humans are duty bound to take on some of the attributes of machines. If there is a problem we analyse it. If something is broken we learn how to fix it. We are expected to surrender that part of ourselves, the beastly core, if you will, that sensed the tiger behind the tree, that smelled out wrongness before it became disastrously visible. The books maintained that all such fears were conquerable given time. They even described instances, case studies, in which phobics came to love the thing they had previously loathed. Ironically that is just what happened to me, but it made no difference. I know now something I did not know then: that the extinguishing of one species of fear may often ignite another. The books seemed not to know this either. They changed nothing. In the end, disappointed, I laid them all aside.

I work as a lecturer in the Department of Zoology, Marchmont College, Petersham. I teach a variety of courses but my field of research is limited to a single sphere: I am an arachnologist. My students call me Spiderman. I have published in excess of forty scientific papers but I am best known – if I am known at all – for my 1995 monograph, 'The Spiders of South West Wales.' I have given lectures all over the world.

It was not a path I set out on, at least not at first. I was possessed of that degree of academic aptitude that made my parents take it for granted that I would attend a university. There was rather less certainty regarding exactly what I might do there. My enthusiasm for Arthur Miller and Ernest Shackleton seemed of little importance in the selection of a future career and I possessed no other particular bent. In the end I decided to enrol on a course in Surveying and Land Management. My father was a quantity surveyor. He did not seek to influence my choice but in the event his apparent contentment with the work made my entry into the profession seem at least possible, even if the *ad hoc* nature of my decision did not leave me entirely satisfied.

If anyone had told me that, less than eighteen months

from graduation, I would be petitioning my tutor for the right to switch to Zoology I would not have believed him. If I had known what would lie at the heart of that desire I would not have believed myself. When I returned to university for the final semester of my second year I knew beyond doubt that what I wanted to do with my life was to find out more about spiders. To read about them, write about them, to come to know their kingdom and their ways. I suppose there are some who would find this vocation perverse. They would perhaps find it even more so were they to know that, a mere three months earlier, I had been terrified of spiders. So terrified that even a picture of one would chill me from the inside out.

It is one of the commoner phobias. In the course of my work I have found that most people share it to a degree, that their distaste can be plotted anywhere on a scale that runs from mild dislike through a sort of self-righteous hatred all the way around to virtual physical paralysis. There are many learned articles on the subject. When I was about seventeen I came across an essay by Primo Levi entitled simply 'The Fear of Spiders.' I had not expected to stumble upon such a thing so unexpectedly and even the look of the word on the page, the spindly black letters seeming somehow to stand in for the dreaded thing itself, caused me to look away. Levi summarised the various theories and expounded upon them, his wryly factual approach doing nothing to alleviate the horror. In the event he described the phenomenon so succinctly and with such a degree of accuracy, so much more terribly than any of the self-help books I had lately been perusing that, admire him as I might, I found myself a little afraid to even have the book in my room. There was one passage in particular that haunted me in which Levi described the metamorphosis of Arachne. I remember that I was initially confused over the identity of Arachne, mistaking her for Ariadne who had, after all, led Theseus from the labyrinth by means of a silken thread. But what I remembered most of all was the image Levi conjured, of a woman's body changed catastrophically, irrevocably, to that of a monstrous spider. It was done as an act of revenge, I remember that too. The thought of it kept me from sleep.

My fear seemed to come out of nowhere. As a youngster I played in overgrown gardens and abandoned woodsheds like anyone else. I must have encountered spiders, motionless at the centre of their webs in the autumn twilight, running from the rays of the sun in the heat of the day. I would have seen them scuttling for cover in the greyed-out depths of the garage, or stranded, a scribble of velvet black ink, in the white enamel belly of the bath. It did not matter. I remained insensible to their presence and ignorant of their world. Perhaps I even kept spiders in jam jars and fed flies to them in the way of other boys; I cannot now remember. Neither can I say for certain exactly when or even why things first began to change. I know only that by the time I was fifteen the sight of a spider made me catch my breath in shock and draw away. By the age of seventeen I was even worse: I could not sleep easily in my bed if I suspected a spider's presence in the room. Instead I would lie rigid on my back, the air moving in shallow gasps from my throat to my lungs, while I imagined what it might be doing, that fat black *Tegenaria*, in the cleft of the rippling curtains or off in the shadowed, marginal netherworld beneath the vulnerable bed.

When I started at university my first worries centred themselves not on the severity of my teachers or the threat of the mid-term exams but on the nature of my lodgings and their susceptibility to invasion by arachnids. I told no-one about my fear. It was a secret thing, something dark, of which I felt somehow ashamed. There were times when I saw others running from spiders, venting their alarm in a volley of cheerful obscenities or a lusty and wholesome shriek. I envied them their openness, their easy camaraderie when under fire, but I felt unable to share it. I guarded my nightmare as if exposing it could only increase its dimensions. So far as I could I pretended indifference, even when I found myself closest to losing control.

The matter came to a head in the spring term of my second year. We were given practical assignments, meaning an extended period of work experience in a professional firm. I was sent as a trainee surveyor to Russell and Bowcock Ltd, a family concern specialising in the appraisal of farmsteads and other rural properties. I was to work closely with Stephen Bowcock, the son of one of the partners. It was my first real taste of employment and I found myself somewhat nervous. To my surprise this feeling soon dissipated; I had done well thus far in my studies and quickly came to understand what was required of me. In the first few weeks of my time there we concentrated on land values and resales. It was not until our journey to Hayman's Cottage at Bidford that I began to realise that my fear of spiders might even stand to jeopardise my future.

It was a probate sale. The cottage had been owned by a Mrs Mead, a widow of more than ninety years of age, and was in a state bordering on dereliction.

"This one'll take us all day," said Stephen Bowcock. "The place is a mess, plus there's several acres of land."

As soon as I saw Hayman's Cottage I felt deeply uneasy. It was built of cob and thatch, the exterior woodwork soft and crumbling through decades of rain and neglect. There were outbuildings, semi-collapsed lean-tos with roofs of corrugated iron. By the back door was a heap of rotting logs. I knew instantly, with a certainty born of intuition rather than reason, that the spiders would have taken the place over.

I followed Stephen Bowcock across the overgrown lawn to the back door. He took a bunch of ancient-looking keys from his jacket pocket, tossed them once from hand to hand and then let us both in. The sour, warm breath of the cottage rushed out to meet us, together with the smell that fills up old houses quickly once they are left alone. It is the smell of damp newspaper and mildew, of the decomposing bodies of moths. I was relieved to see that most of the widow's furniture had already been removed; it left far fewer places for things to hide.

"It'll be right off the scale," said Stephen Bowcock, unpacking his damp-meter. I went with him from room to room, carefully filling in the forms we used to record wet rot and dry rot, subsidence and residual damp. I forced myself to concentrate on small and harmless things: the scratching of pen against paper, the click and flash of the camera, Stephen Bowcock's off-key hummed rendition of Bobby Shaftoe. He sauntered from room to room, running the damp-meter over the walls, shining a pocket torch into the understairs cupboard and the space beneath the sink, pulling back the torn linoleum from its place against the skirting. I listened to what he said but tried insofar as I could not to watch what he did. I was deeply, achingly frightened, but in spite of this things were mostly alright until we came to the second bedroom.

It was the bedroom at the back of the house, and retained the whispery perfume of dying roses. I suspected that it was the room in which the old lady had habitually slept. The far wall was split by a crack. It was a dark, ugly crack, and so wide it had torn the wallpaper. From where we stood, only the top half was visible; the rest had been obscured by a huge mahogany wardrobe.

"I noticed that outside," said Stephen Bowcock. "It's a beast. We're going to have to check it out."

He moved across the room to the wardrobe and I had to do the same. It was a monstrous piece of almost gothic proportions. I supposed it had been left in the room simply because removing it with the rest of the furniture had ultimately seemed too much like hard labour. We grasped it at either end and heaved it aside. We managed to shift it a couple of feet and then Stephen called a halt.

"Stop," he said, puffing. "That's plenty."

Behind the wardrobe the crack ran all the way to the floorboards, widening at its midpoint to a three-inch hole. The edges of the crack were ragged, reddish, like the sides of a wound.

"Thought so," said Bowcock. He pulled his briefcase towards him across the floor, extracting an extending metal probe with a spatulate steel-tipped end. He guided the probe carefully inside the crack. Half of its length disappeared.

"That'll go right the way through to outside," he said. "It's a major structural fault." He rested one hand on the wall beside the crack and made to withdraw the probe. At that moment, a trickle of russet brick-dust cascaded from the wall in a miniature avalanche. I stepped sharply backwards, away from the wall and away from

Stephen. I knew there was only one thing that the dust could mean: that something was coming upwards out of the hole. My mouth was immediately dry, as if I had thirsted for days. I felt great tides of sweat break loose beneath my arms. I saw the forelegs first, tentative, questing, almost tasting the air. In the very next instant the rest of it followed, hauling itself out of the cavern in the wall like a rat exiting a drainpipe. It was huge and ovate, quivering with a life force that seemed almost alien. Its legs could have spanned a man's hand, and in my state of terror its body seemed equal in size to my thumb. I did not know its name, indeed I was unaware that a spider so large could be found in the British Isles. For a single confused moment I wondered if I was in fact seeing it at all, or whether, in my state of heightened anxiety, I had somehow set it loose from one of my nightmares.

In the event the thing we had disturbed was *Tegenaria parietina*, the largest native species, sometimes known as the Cardinal Spider. It is commonplace, indigenous, completely harmless – at least to man. It hesitated for a second on the rim of the crack then rushed over Bowcock's outstretched fingers and up onto the ceiling.

"Holy shit, that was a big one," said Bowcock. "Look at the bastard go!"

He seemed to be speaking from a great distance away. There was a ringing in my ears, a sound that I remembered hearing once before, a long time ago, when I fell off my bike in the road. I had heard that sound, a high, bright whistling like a kettle boiling somewhere in a nearby room. I had tried to stand up and then fainted. I knew that I must not faint now, not because I was afraid of looking foolish in front of Stephen Bowcock but because the monster was still in the room and I was still in the room with the monster. I watched as Bowcock removed the probe from the wall and telescoped it together. He scratched the side of his nose with a pen in a gesture that was common with him and then stepped away from the wall. He looked up then, upwards towards the ceiling. I dared not follow his gaze.

"Let's move it back," he said, and I realised he was talking about the wardrobe. I shuffled and heaved, wondering frantically what the spider might do now that we had shut it out of its hideaway. I felt a tickling and pricking on my scalp, along my arms and in the back of my hair. I reached up, feeling myself begin to suffocate on the ripe, sour stench of my fear. I touched the collar of my shirt, my burning cheek, my clammy nape. There was nothing there.

"We'll write all this up in the pub," said Stephen Bowcock. "We can come back after lunch and finish the rest."

We had our sandwiches and beer and then drove back. It was late March but the clocks had not yet gone forward. Twilight had begun to gather beneath the clouds, making the cottage look unnaturally bulky and dark. All the time we had been in the pub I had dwelt upon the fact that in leaving the spider alone we had lost sight of its position. It could now be anywhere, in any of the rooms. I wondered if the electricity still worked at Hayman's Cottage or whether it had been disconnected when Alicia Mead had died. I fumbled with the car door but it would not seem to open. The palm of my hand felt waxen and beyond my control. I suddenly became aware that Stephen Bowcock was saying something, presumably to me.

"Can you write these up?" he said. "While I finish off inside?"

He was holding out a sheaf of foolscap, the forms I had started on earlier. He was smiling with the sweet, sheepish grin that is used mostly to smother embarrassment. There was an expression on his face that could have almost been taken for pity.

"Have the radio on," he said. "I won't be long."

I took the papers from him, wondering what he knew. The next day we were out in the fields again quantifying another farm. Up until then I had enjoyed my time at Russell and Bowcock but the incident at Hayman's Cottage threw a dark wavering shadow over everything. It was not just the dawning awareness that every working day might present a dozen or more similar obstacles; it was also my sense of fatal inadequacy before Stephen Bowcock. No matter how I tried to tell myself that I had merely imagined his sympathy I remained inwardly convinced that he had spied out the truth. I could hardly bear to look him in the eye.

Luckily for me it was almost the Easter vacation. At the end of two weeks I packed all my things and went home. In previous vacations I had been content to spend my time peacefully: reading and working, seeing the occasional friend. This time was different. I felt uneasy and irritable. I would go to bed early but wake the next morning exhausted, as if I had not slept at all. I felt like walking for miles but instead would shut myself in my room for hours at a time, trying to concentrate on my studies but actually accomplishing nothing. I realised, I suppose, that I had driven myself unwittingly into a cul-de-sac: I had made plans for a future from which I was effectively barred. I could not understand why I had failed to see this before. If I was afraid of spiders then it went without saying that I would be afraid of unknown buildings, and yet I had chosen to study for a profession in which one entered unknown buildings every day. Many of the houses would be old. Some would be old and unlived-in like Hayman's Cottage. In my desperation I began inventing scenarios in which I never went out at all but did all my work from the office. I imagined how liberating it might be if I came to lose the use of my legs.

Perhaps it was, after all, those hours in bookshops that saved me. I had rejected the self-help manuals as childishly inadequate and yet some portion of them must have lodged in my brain. That something would have been reinforced by television, by the increasingly popular reality shows in which people were forced onto aircraft or taken to the tops of high buildings or made to go to parties and enjoy themselves with strangers. I had no real interest in such programmes and yet it seemed almost impossible to avoid seeing them. Maybe it was neither of these things but some half-buried instinct telling me to act, to act quickly before it was too late.

In any case I came to the conclusion that things could not go on the way they were. I decided I had to do something before my fear of spiders became the yardstick by which everything else in my life was measured.

Not unsurprisingly the television documentaries tended to favour the dramatic approach most commonly referred to as aversion therapy. Expert behaviourists would inundate the subject with the object of their fear until the appetite, or in this case the phobia, sickened and eventually died. I understood that there were clinics that specialised in exactly this sort of treatment. I had heard that the treatments worked. Nevertheless I mistrusted them. There was something of the circus about such techniques; I disliked intensely the idea of turning myself into a freak show. The books, on the whole, suggested something different: within the pages of Popular Psychology eminent counsellors maintained that knowledge was power, and that the best way to outwit fear was to drown it in facts. I was already of a studious temperament and the idea had some appeal. Midway through my Easter vacation I put aside my coursebooks and set about learning as much on the subject of spiders as I could.

I started with the Internet. I typed in 'spider,' unsure of what to expect. There were thousands of available sites. I had wondered about instigating a search for 'arachnophobia,' or 'fear of spiders,' but decided fairly quickly against it. I wanted to come to the topic fresh and uninitiated, as if it had never crossed my mind to be afraid.

The first sites I tried hardly moved me at all. They dealt mainly with foreign species: tarantulas, funnelwebs, huntsmen. After the initial shock the graphic photographs of mouse-sized bodies and impossibly enlarged mouthparts, I found myself examining these creatures as if they were stilled out-takes from a science fiction movie or specimens of life on some other planet. I knew that they were no threat to me, that I was separated from them by thousands of miles of land and, better still, ocean. The only chance I had of ever coming across one was penned behind glass in a zoo. Do not think that I was unafraid. There were times when, forcing myself to look at these things, my breathing became harsh and strained, the pads of my fingers sliding, perspiring, from the keypad. And yet the underlying rationality of my mind had already begun to classify all subsequent experience in relation to what I had seen that afternoon in Hayman's Cottage; *that* could happen, and *these* could not. Therefore these were safe.

I cut down my search, confining it to 'British spiders' only. There were many entries. I quickly found out that there were more than five hundred species of spider native to Britain, that they could be found everywhere from cellars to treetops, from heathland to garden ponds. I learned the difference between an orb web and a blanket web. I discovered sites where you could download moving images, film of wolf spiders catching and killing their miniature prey. I did not feel capable of looking at those yet. Instead, I turned my attention to a listing for the British Arachnological Society. There was a lot of data and a lot of words in Latin. There was also a signpost to something they called a Spider Identification Weekend. I clicked on it, and found a photograph. It showed a whitewashed stone house, and, behind it, the greenish-black shadow of trees.

'Fenland, windmills, clifftops – and spiders!' read the caption. 'The British Arachnological Society invites you to take part in a weekend of spider-watching, based at Jessop Lodge, Langwold, in the heart of the Suffolk countryside. No previous experience required.' There was a contact name, Sally Beamish, and a telephone number with an Ipswich code. The dates involved were for the weekend after Easter. It started in three days' time.

I dialled the number with nothing more in mind than to see if I could do it. The idea that there might still be a place available at Jessop Lodge had, I think, not even entered my head. The telephone rang for an age. Just as I was about to put down the receiver I heard the breathless voice of a woman apologising for having been outside in the garden. When I said I was calling about the Spider Identification Weekend she said yes, there was still one place available.

"That's a shame," I said, determined to have misheard her.

"No, I said there's one place left," she repeated. "Someone had to pull out, you see. There was a funeral." Her voice was soft and musical with just a hint of an accent I supposed had to be Suffolk. It gave no hint as to her age.

"I know next to nothing about them," I said. My heart had started to pound in a way I found ridiculous, even for me. Once again my armpits and shirt were damp with sweat.

"We'll soon change that," she said, laughing just a little. "What time do you think you'll be here?"

I found myself giving out my name and telephone number and telling the woman I'd ring back when I had the train times. It would have been impossible for me to do otherwise. My parents had always set great store by manners and as a youth I was often polite to the point of servitude. I couldn't bring myself to say I had changed my mind.

The journey was long and complicated. I had to change trains at Liverpool Street and then take the branch line from Ipswich. Sally Beamish had told me I could get a bus from Newnham to Langwold but if there was a problem I should ring and somebody would come with a car. I had bought a spider book for the train, 'Common British Spiders,' by Kenneth Nugent. It had an *Araneus diadematus* on the front cover, head down at the centre of her web. I know that there are some arachnophobics who cannot even look at the image of a spider without sensing the approach of panic but I was not really one of them. As long as I knew in advance what I was about to see I experienced little more than a marginally increased heart rate and slight dryness of the mouth. Furthermore I had already increased my tolerance of such things through my use of the Internet. The book was beautifully made: pocket-sized, with a red embossed binding beneath the shiny new jacket. I read the text, glancing briefly now and then at the pictures. Perhaps the psychologists were correct in their theories of factual bombardment, perhaps it was just that I had always found pleasure in reading. By the time we reached Chelmsford I was already beginning to come to terms with the various and yet curiously singular conformation of two body parts to eight legs, and as the smaller, branch line train pulled out of Ipswich and began making its way into the sparsely populated countryside of East Suffolk I found I could even look at some of the photographs without flinching.

Jessop Lodge was a surprise to me. I had expected it to be smaller. When I asked Sally Beamish what the house had been originally she told me it had been built by the squire of Langwold Manor as a residence for his son.

"You'll see his monogram over the door," she said. "The manor's gone now, of course. It was destroyed in a fire."

Seeing Sally Beamish in the flesh made it no easier to determine her age. She wore her hair long, in a single grey plait down her back. Her limber-fingered, ringless hands were immaculately white and smooth. She could have been anywhere between forty and sixty. She took me back outside onto the porch, where the massive granite lintel had been carved with the initials C.V.R, and a date, 1792.

"That stands for Charles Vernon Rowland," she said. "There's a portrait of him in the library." She paused, tucking both perfect white hands into the square back pockets of her jeans. "I'm so glad your journey wasn't too difficult. You're almost the last to arrive."

The house had six bedrooms upstairs as well as an adjoining stable block converted to provide additional sleeping accommodation. A printed leaflet on the dressing table of my own room informed me that Jessop Lodge was now the property of the National Trust. There was a list of the organisations that had access to it including the Fenlands Conservation Society and the RSPB. The room I had been given was on the third floor directly under the eaves. One approached it via a narrow twisting staircase that led off the second floor landing. The room had exposed black beams and polished uncarpeted floorboards. It made me feel rather nervous. I left my suitcase at the foot of the bed without unpacking it, washed my hands and face and went quickly back downstairs into the hall. Once again the prospect of meeting strangers seemed far less intimidating than the thought of being alone in an unknown room. When I got to the bottom of the stairs it was to find Sally Beamish opening the front door to an extremely tall young man in a belted green trenchcoat. He had ash blond hair tied in a ponytail and startling eyes the colour of lobelia flowers.

"This is Hilary Arden," she said. "His car broke down in Swaffham. Come through. We're about to have tea."

Hilary Arden nodded to me, raised his eyebrows slightly and then compressed his lips in a smile. He slid out of his trench coat and began to mount the stairs. "Hilary studies in Cambridge," said Sally Beamish. "He's reading for his PhD."

There were nine of us all told: two group leaders and seven participants. Tea had been laid out on a low rectangular table in the downstairs sitting room, a large room but overfull of chairs. There were people in the armchairs closest to the table, some of them already talking amongst themselves. When I entered the room with Sally Beamish the conversation stopped almost at once.

"Hilary's just arrived," said Sally Beamish. She spoke in the direction of a middle-aged balding man in well-worn tweeds. He was sitting by himself on a leather chaise longue sorting a stack of papers into separate piles. When he looked up I saw at once that one of his eyes was green and the other brown.

"This is Simon Barclay," Sally said, turning to me. She spoke with a special emphasis as if she thought I would know who he was. It wasn't until about a year later, when I discovered that his name carried more than fifty page references in the bibliography for the British Quarterly Journal of Invertebrate Science, that I realised Simon Barclay was a world expert on the *Lycosidae*.

"Is he coming down to tea?" said Barclay. He glanced at me briefly and then looked down again at his papers. He was so softly-spoken it was almost a strain to listen. At that moment the door to the room opened again and Hilary Arden came in. He was minus the green trench coat and wore pale patched jeans and a bright blue turtleneck. He stooped low over the table, filling one of the small white plates with tuna sandwiches and miniature sausage rolls. I stepped away from Simon Barclay and sat down in one of the armchairs. It was shaped like a box, with a chintzy rose-patterned cover. Sally Beamish passed me a mug, a white porcelain cylinder with a narrow golden band around the rim. The mug was warm to the touch, and brimming with milky tea. The others in the room gradually began helping themselves from the table, exchanging as they did so the occasional polite remark. In the corner with the chaise longue Hilary Arden started to talk in a low, level undertone to Simon Barclay. I sipped at my tea. A gust of wind rattled the windows. I asked myself exactly what it was that I had hoped for.

"Perhaps we'd all better introduce ourselves," said Sally Beamish. All heads turned immediately in her direction and the atmosphere at once felt perceptibly lighter. There was a sense within the room that the thing we had come for had finally begun. Sally Beamish glanced just once in the direction of Simon Barclay and then told us she had been helping to run courses at Jessop Lodge for the better part of a decade. As she spoke she reached behind her head, pulling the heavy grey plait forward over one shoulder. She wound the braid tightly around her hands like a length of rope.

"Some of my friends think I'm mad," she said, smiling. "No doubt some of yours feel the same."

There was a married couple, Elisabeth and Jarvis Newcombe, who had driven up to Langwold from Worcester. They both taught sixth form English.

"We've always been terribly interested in natural history," said Elisabeth. She too wore jeans, and a multicoloured patchwork top. Gold hoops dangled heavily from her ears.

"We started with butterflies but we thought that was rather a cliché," added her husband. Everyone laughed.

Hilary Arden stretched out his legs, thereby bridging most

of the gap between the chaise longue and the tea table, and stated he was hoping to substantiate a particularly stubborn chapter of his thesis. "Don't let that worry you though," he said. "Mostly I'm here for the wine." He raised one of his refined, almost invisible eyebrows. The blue of his irises flashed like expensive stained glass. Opposite the Newcombes and adjacent to myself an elderly gentleman with heavy dark bags under his eyes made it known that his name was Andrew Lill. The hands holding his cup seemed paper-thin and yellow in colour and trembled very slightly as he spoke.

"Andrew comes here twice a year," said Sally Beamish quickly, speaking for him. "We know him very well. We know you, too, don't we, Gustav?" She turned to the man in the seat next to her. He was slim and pale, with hair cropped so close it was difficult to determine its colour.

"I'm really just a friend of Hilary's," he said. "I can't stand the sight of spiders!"

He spoke perfectly crafted, carefully enunciated English with the merest race of a German accent. His name was Gustav Preisner and he was writing a thesis on Paganism in Europe. Whenever he looked at Hilary Arden his face seemed to soften, like that of an indulgent mother beholding her intransigent child. He had a feathery hairline moustache. All of his movements were tinged with a casual, liquid grace that was almost sinister. I found it hard to believe that he held no affection for arachnids.

"I'm Adam Wetherall," I said, when it was my turn to speak. "Spiders are just my hobby."

Heat rushed into my face. I don't think I have ever felt more unutterably stupid than I did at that precise moment. I fancied that all of them were staring at me, that everyone knew I was lying. I tried desperately to think of something else to say that might obscure the original foolishness but I could not. My mind seemed paralysed. Only gradually did I become aware that somebody else was speaking.

"Jennifer Bristowe," she said. "Spiders are my hobby, too." Her voice drifted softly down to me, weightless, peerless and somehow golden. She leaned forward in her chair, both hands wrapped serenely around the pale blue body of her mug, and I realised that I had previously failed to notice her at all. She was a small girl, almost tiny, with long, skinny arms that left her sleeves behind at the elbow. A fall of mouse-coloured hair concealed her shoulders. The eyes behind her spectacles were hazel, shading to gold. She was flat-chested and colourless, almost like a child. As she spoke she smiled at me. I imagined I saw in her smile not just the fellowship of youth, but also some deeper understanding, a camaraderie born out of like-minded forebodings and mutual trepidation. Looking at her I felt more anchored, more possible, more real. I felt that I had chanced upon a friend.

As we finished our tea Simon Barclay finally broke his silence. Once one became accustomed to the whispery tone of his voice it became apparent that he was a speaker of considerable fluency and power. He recapitulated that which Sally Beamish had earlier told me about the history of Jessop Lodge, adding that virtually the entire Rowland clan had perished in the Langwold Manor fire.

"Jessop Lodge was bequeathed to the nation," he said. "And therefore bequeathed to us."

He turned next to its location, demonstrating an enthusiasm for the place that seemed occasionally to border on the fanatical. Simon Barclay stated that East Anglia, with its undeveloped countryside and paucity of industry, had fulfilled in important role in the preservation of native flora and fauna.

"The very featurelessness of the landscape makes it somehow impregnable," he said. "The Broads and the fenlands, the mudflats, the eroded headlands – one might almost come to believe in an ancient Albion, an indestructible heartland, a kingdom set apart."

I remembered how slowly the trains had seemed to travel once they left Ipswich, and the map I had bought, showing a loose network of minor roads that appeared to lead to nowhere in particular. I thought I could see something in what Barclay was saying but I was not altogether certain that I liked it. When, quite suddenly, he broke off his educational diatribe and suggested that we might begin our journey into the world of spiders right here and right now I liked it even less.

We followed him through the enormous flagstoned kitchen to a long narrow chamber that might once have been described as the scullery. There was an industrial-sized washing machine and drier on one wall, a ceiling-height fridge-freezer on the other. The walls themselves had all been painted white and were hung with an assortment of cast iron cooking utensils that looked as if nobody had used them for centuries. Probably no-one had.

"There she is," said Barclay. "Sally here calls this one Frieda."

He pointed. All eyes followed his finger. In one corner of the ceiling there crouched a spider.

"*Pholcus phalangioides*," said Sally Beamish, brightly. "She's been with us for more than two years."

Andrew Lill shuffled forward, sliding across the flagstones without lifting his feet. "They're dependent on us, you know," he said. "The *Pholcidae* can't survive outside. At least, they can't in England." His voice seemed as fragile as his hands and sounded rusty, perhaps from lack of regular use. To my horrified eye the thing on the wall looked enormous. It was not as loathsomely robust as the monster I had seen behind the wardrobe at Hayman's Cottage but its legs were so very much longer. They were spread in great arcs, casting a complex of invidiously intricate shadows against the pockmarked whitewashed background of the wall. At their centre hung an elongated body, bulbous and pustular, the sickly corpseflesh grey of a toadstool. As we watched the creature trembled and raised one of its legs, slowly, cautiously, as if it sensed our presence, before sidling further back against the wall.

I stood on the threshold of the room, irrationally convinced that if I tried to retreat the spider would come racing after me. I felt rather than saw the Newcombes crowd their way past me, seemingly eager to get a closer look.

"She's beautiful," said Elisabeth Newcombe. "We had one just like it in our wine cellar."

Her words seemed robbed of all meaning as if she had suddenly started to speak in a foreign language. My ears filled up with the high-pitched whine of tinnitus. Once more I felt ready to faint. I put out a hand, meaning to support myself somehow against the doorframe. Instead of the cold painted wood I felt the touch of warm, live skin on mine. I tried to shrink back, terrified by the unexpected contact. Seconds later I realised it was only a hand that I held, a five-fingered human hand just like my own.

"It's alright," whispered the girl, softly, gently, directly into my ear. I turned to my right and saw that it was Jennifer Bristowe. The harsh white light from the overhead fluorescent reflected off her glasses, robbing her eyes of colour. "Just hold on to me," she said, a fraction louder. "You'll be fine."

She moved forward slowly, still holding my hand. I found that I was moving with her even though the concrete floor seemed to shudder beneath my feet, as organic and as mutable as grass. We gathered in a knot beneath the spider, craning our necks upward like sightseers in a cathedral. The *Pholcus* sat motionless in a tangle of gossamer and the play of its own faint shadow.

"People call them Daddy Longlegs Spiders," said Gustav Preisner. "But the cranefly is a bumbling imbecile in comparison."

"I thought you said you couldn't stand the sight of spiders," said Elisabeth Newcombe.

"I can't," said Preisner. "But that doesn't stop me knowing things about them." He took a long, slim, black and gold pencil from his pocket. He reached above his head, using the pencil to gently touch the spider's right hand rearmost leg. In a second the *Pholcus* had tucked all its limbs tight and fast to its sides. A moment later the legs were spread again and the spider itself seemed to oscillate, vibrating rapidly from side to side. The movement was utterly unexpected and deeply uncanny. I clung to the girl's fine-boned hand, feeling sweat breaking out on my palm.

"It's to confuse the enemy," rasped Andrew Lill. "She

thinks she's invisible, shaking herself like that."

"It's a female," whispered Jennifer Bristowe. "The males of most species are a great deal smaller. I wish they hadn't disturbed her." She was standing very close to me again, speaking so that only I could hear. After a minute or so the *Pholcus* became still. She stepped down from the web and rearranged her legs, settling herself head down in the right angle between the ceiling and the wall. I noticed again how long the spider's legs were: tapering silver-grey rods like needles of glass. I found, quite suddenly, that I was breathing more easily. I turned to Jennifer Bristowe and saw that she was smiling.

"How did you know?" I said. I let go of her hand. Her fingers slipped slowly from mine, making my newly exposed palm feel empty and somehow bare.

"I could smell it." She was still smiling, her round, heavy spectacles snatching at the light. "But you can see she's beautiful now, though, can't you." It was a statement rather than a question, and I said nothing. Some of the others had already started to file past us and back into the kitchen. Sally Beamish switched out the light. We turned and followed her out of the room.

The rest of that first evening was spent in the first floor lounge. There was a semicircle of bucket chairs, and, on one wall, a pull-down canvas projector screen. We watched an hour-long film entitled 'The Spiders of the Sceptred Isle – Journeys in an Unseen World.' The voice of the narrator seemed somehow familiar and after twenty minutes or so I realised it was that of Simon Barclay. I sat next to Jennifer Bristowe, watching as the massively enlarged bodies of *Pardosa agricola* and *Thomisus onustus* surged in darting broken arcs across the wall. There were spiders that lived in air-filled bivouacs beneath the water, others that rode the summer thermals on parachutes woven from silk. I had never before in my life imagined such a variety of colours. There were even spiders that, chameleonlike, could match their hue to that of the flower on which they sat. I was enthralled. I have often wondered since that night whether there are people who, after being terrified their whole lives by the very thought of flying, fall instantly and completely in love with it when they finally get off the ground. It was like that for me. From time to time I glanced at Jennifer Bristowe. She did not look at me, but sat motionless, seemingly lost in the film. She had her head propped sideways on one hand, the flickering light from the screen curving itself gently around the softly blurred line of her cheek. In one of the chairs behind us Gustav Preisner slid his black and gold pencil back and forth, making notes in a yellow ring-bound notepad. I heard Elisabeth Newcombe cough, and then whisper something quietly to her husband. It suddenly occurred to me that Jennifer Bristowe was the first person to whom I had openly admitted my fears. Later, in bed, I found myself thinking of her again. I had not yet seen inside her room. I wondered what it was like, and what she might be doing there. My own room felt different from how it had seemed before. In my place beneath the eaves I felt close to the elements, to the threadbare row of beeches behind the house, to the murky-toned expanse of the curiously boundless Suffolk night. It struck me that, for all my boyhood enjoyment of adventure stories, I had largely confined my own explorations to the interior realm of the mind. All at once I felt something shift within me, a crucial movement, as when a boulder overreaches its centre of gravity and begins to roll downhill. I lay on my back under the lightly starched linen, eagerly perusing Nugent's 'Common British Spiders.' I read until almost midnight. From time to time I laid the book face down on my chest and looked about me at the exposed beams, the polished floorboards, and the dark, shadowy space between the dressing table and the wardrobe, half hoping that a spider would appear.

I had never had much to do with women. As a child, the few friends I made had all been other boys. I was not frightened of girls so much as ignorant of their ways. I had little idea of how one might approach them and as I entered puberty my lack of knowledge had eventually hardened into a shyness that I found it difficult to transcend. I observed girls from a distance, unable to shake off the conviction that they were laughing at me in secret. When I was in the sixth form I developed an intense and painful infatuation for a girl named Madeleine Evers. She was studying for the Oxbridge entrance exam, and her hair was long and red like the plumage of some rare bird. Over the course of eighteen months I watched her become friendly with and then engaged to one of my classmates, William Napier. I myself barely spoke to her. I told no-one of my feelings for Madeleine, just as I told no-one about my fear of spiders. I technically lost my virginity during my first term at university but the experience – a clumsy encounter at a party with a second-year student of Economics who disappeared at the end of the night and whom I never saw again – left me miserable and unsatisfied. I felt some relief in the fact that, physically at least, I had been properly able to function. What disturbed me was that nothing had really changed.

I could never imagine what I might say to a woman. The openness with which others of my age expressed themselves appealed to me, and yet I could find nothing in what they did – the light-hearted, flirtatious banter, the exuberant roughhousing that seemed to have taken the place of any more formal courtship – with which I could identify. Once, when I was half-drunk on cheap white wine at a chess club reunion, I tried to explain what I felt to a schoolfriend, Damien Fellows.

"Just be yourself," he urged me. I replied that I was not altogether sure of who that was, but even as I said it I was aware that I was not telling the exact truth. I knew how to be myself; I feared, however, that people would find me dull.

I do not know which was the more important determinant in what happened so quickly between myself and Jennie Bristowe: the fact that she seemed as little versed in artifice as I was myself, or the fact that I had unwittingly revealed to her my most intimate secret and therefore felt bound to her in a manner that could not easily be undone. It could even be that the one had somehow precipitated the other. When I came down to breakfast on the first morning of my weekend at Jessop Lodge I found that I was already tense with the expectation of seeing her. I wondered if she would treat me as a stranger, or, worse still, ignore me completely. I had read of such things, even if my experience in them was negligible to say the least. As I descended the flight of stairs leading from the first floor into the wide parqueted hallway I saw her there, leaning against the newel post and looking upwards into my face as if it were her habit to do so, as if she had done so before on countless similar mornings. She was dressed in jeans and a brown-checked brushed cotton shirt. Her dun-coloured hair was pulled back from her face.

"Everyone's started," she said. "But I thought I'd wait for you."

I was six inches taller than she. In her monochrome wispiness she ought to have appeared frail and lacking in substance beside me but all the same she did not. There was something about her, a self-containment and tenaciousness that prevented this, making her hardy like those garden weeds that conspire to flourish anywhere even in winter. For one bottomless second I found myself tongue-tied. Then, from behind the closed door that led to the dining room, came a flurry of voices followed by the sound of Jarvis Newcombe's robust Home Counties guffaw. I raised my eyebrows slightly; at the same moment Jennie smiled. A small noise escaped her, threatening to become laughter.

"Come on," she said. "We'd better go in."

As she turned away from me towards the door her fingers brushed briefly against mine. I found myself wondering what might happen if I were to take hold of her hand as she had taken mine the day before. I eyed the delicate filigree of bones that made up each wrist and once again I was struck by the length and slenderness of her arms.

Everyone was eating. Gustav Preisner was spreading butter thickly onto a slice of wholemeal toast and holding forth on the medicinal properties of *Tegenaria domestica*.

"These house spiders were used as a cure for influenza," he said. "From Roman times at least. In Shakespeare's day, patients were told to swallow them alive. Sometimes they put them in breadcrumbs to cover the taste. I've never yet tried it myself but then again I'm not often ill." He finished buttering his toast and took a large bite of it, showing his teeth in a grin. Cold, early morning sunshine came through the window, making the cropped bristles of his hair shine a metallic coppery red.

"You're revolting, Gustav," said Hilary Arden. He rocked backwards in his chair, scraping the parquet. He wore a dusty-looking green velvet blazer. His hair hung loose to his shoulders, giving him the exotic look of some minor European prince.

"But he's right, of course," said Andrew Lill. "Although the flavour is very bitter." The old man swallowed a mouthful of tea, as if to replenish his voice. His hands shook slightly as he spoke. "It's all been written down."

"I've heard of a Dr Muffet who used to prescribe spiders for almost everything," said Elisabeth Newcombe. The plate in front of her contained a heap of scrambled egg and two well-grilled rashers of bacon. "Is he anything to do with the rhyme?"

I listened to them, filling my own plate with fried mushrooms, dry toast and tomatoes. I wanted to get outside.

"Did you sleep well?" said Jennie to me, suddenly. She was eating triangles of untoasted, thinly buttered bread, and drank her tea black, with two heaped spoonfuls of sugar.

"Yes, I did," I said. "It feels as if I've been here for ages."

Jessop Lodge was situated at the very edge of the village with no houses beyond it save a modern barn conversion with a 'For Sale' sign on the unmown verge outside. The biggest building in Langwold was the church, whose square flint-block tower dominated the skyline. Aside from the copse of beeches behind the house there were few large trees to be seen. The spring's first growth of cow parsley and stinging nettles clung determinedly to the boundaries of lanes. A cold easterly breeze picked at our clothes, coming at us straight from the horizon. I had heard the countryside of East Anglia variously described as tedious, colourless, and bleak. I found it startlingly new. There was a stark austerity in its simplified planes, an unadorned beauty that was almost grandiose. The landscape seemed virgin, untouched, the chill air invigoratingly clean. I felt that anything might be discovered. Anything at all.

We congregated at the far end of the garden. Out of sight of the house the grounds of Jessop Lodge had been allowed to go wild. Roses and herbaceous shrubs grew side by side with hogweed and cow parsley. In summer the hollyhocks and marsh marigolds would be swamped in foxglove and convolvulus and festoons of red campion. Simon Barclay talked to us for about ten minutes, telling us that on one occasion in late summer he had identified as many as twenty-five different species without having to move more than a hundred yards from the house. Many of his whispered words got lost in the wind. In the end, Sally Beamish produced a large cardboard carton full of small round boxes with transparent plastic lids. I recognised them as collecting boxes, though I had not seen one before outside of the schoolroom.

"It seems that none of you are complete beginners," said Simon Barclay. "Perhaps you can come up with something that I missed."

We had maps of the village and instructions to re-congregate at one. The way things had turned out it was natural for us to pair off into couples. The Newcombes stayed together, as did Hilary Arden and Gustav Preisner. Andrew Lill made his way unsteadily across the grass in the direction of a seething mass of bramble and nettles. After a moment's consultation with Simon Barclay Sally Beamish ran after him. A second later, I saw her shepherd him away towards the conservatory. Jennie and I stood side by side on the path, our shoulders slightly hunched against the cold.

"I'm a complete beginner," I said. "I'm here under false pretences."

"It doesn't matter," she said. "We can look for them together if you like."

I realised then that I wanted to touch her, that if she had gone off with one of the others instead of staying with me I would have felt disappointed and personally diminished in a way that seemed quite out of keeping with the short time I had known her. We went back around to the front of the house, out through the gateway and down into the narrow lane beyond. The lane led us straight into the village. Jennie seemed familiar with the route already and I asked her if she had been to Jessop Lodge before.

"I was born close to here," she said. "In a village called Madeley. That's how I know my way around."

She spoke in a clear, high treble without a trace of the local accent. I wondered if she had been sent away to school. I tried to imagine her as one of a group, contributing to the bustle and clamour of a dormitory of adolescent females. I found it difficult to do. She seemed unique to me, a solitary being. It was hard to conceive of her fitting in well with others.

Langwold was tiny and well-groomed, one of those villages that had become largely given over to commuters. It had a newsagents and a baker's, as well as a convenience store that sold a limited selection of overpriced groceries. There were people on the High Street but they ignored us. I wondered if anyone might know Jennie but none of them said hello. The Church of St Stephens stood on a large plot at the furthest end of Aubury Lane, slightly adrift from the conglomeration of low flint cottages that made up the bulk of the village, and the scatter of newer whitewashed bungalows at its outer edge. The church towered over everything. I shaded my eyes with one hand and stared up at it, wondering why it had been deemed necessary to erect such a colossus on the outskirts of a settlement that was really little more than a hamlet.

"There are churches like this all over East Anglia," said Jennie. "They gave them tall towers so they would be visible against the flatness of the land. The climate here made life hard. People saw the church as a sanctuary, particularly during the Plague."

She pushed open the lych-gate and we went into the cemetery. I have never harboured any fear of graveyards as some do but as a young man I had a tendency to feel somewhat uncomfortable in the vicinity of the dead. It felt like trespassing. In front of the church the plot was well-husbanded and green. There were rows of granite headstones, both plain and adorned, as well as several larger memorials. I noticed almost immediately that one of these, a rectangular marble plinth with attendant guardian angel, bore the name of Rowland.

Of course I had no means of knowing whether the occupant of the tomb bore any relation to the one-time inhabitants of Jessop Lodge but it seemed highly probable, if only because the village was so small. For some reason, the thought made me distinctly uneasy. The gravestones rose out of neatly mown grass and were surrounded by a hedge of tailored yew. The whole was sterile and sedate like some sort of uncanny garden. Even to my untrained eye it seemed inhospitable to wildlife. I wondered why we were there.

Jennie touched my hand. "Come on," she said. I followed. She moved deftly and quickly, in the manner of a fieldmouse. Her long, thin arms moved back and forth in time with her stride. I sensed once again a power in her, a fortitude that belied her stature. Something occurred to me that I had read the night before in the Nugent, about how spider silk has more strength in it than a tension steel wire of a similar thickness and length. I walked faster, wanting to catch her up, to be close enough to her to feel the warmth of her body through the coarse navy wool of her coat. I knew enough about women to realise that to most eyes Jennie Bristowe's nondescript colouring and lack of obvious physical assets would render her ordinary, if not plain. She did not seem so to me.

The rear of the churchyard was a shambles. It was as if the manicured propriety that could be seen from the lane was nothing but a carefully contrived façade. Behind the church, a rusted iron gate let onto a wilderness of weeds that in places was shoulder height. The dry stone wall that formed the boundary of the cemetery had been breached in several places, the green tide behind it overflowing into the red ploughed fields beyond. There was something pagan and almost shocking about such neglect and yet it excited me too because it was so unexpected. The weeds were all new growth, and yet they did more even than the great tower of the church to underline the age of the place. Jennie looked at me with an expression that was almost triumphant.

"Not everyone knows this is here," she said. "Isn't it fantastic?"

"Yes," I said. I looked about me, fascinated, at the monster nettles and Giant Hogweed and the two-dozen other outcrops that I could not put a name to. It was like being in another country. A pungent aroma drifted up to me from the crushed foliage at my feet and I recognised the scent of mint. I reached out, rubbing one of the serrated, elliptical leaves between finger and thumb. For a moment, my skin took on the spicy, bittersweet smell of the plant itself. The place was strangely silent. As I stood and listened I heard a lone car sweep invisibly by on Aubury Lane, while from the tangle of ivy curtaining the back wall of the church there came the muffled scampering of some hidden rodent or bird.

"Shall we make a start?" said Jennie. She stood up to her knees in a thicket of riotous greenery. There were nettles touching her palms but she seemed not to know.

"Where do we look?" I said. I had no idea how I felt. I had the faint sense of fear at the root of my spine but I recognised it for what it was: an echo of a past that even now seemed far more distant than it ought to have done.

"Let's find a web," she said. "Just to begin with."

It did not take her long. At that time I had no idea that to enter the kingdom of spiders you must first become small. I cast my eyes about me in all directions and none, standing fully erect, gazing bemusedly at the entire vista as if in the expectation of coming upon silken ropes as thick as grass stems, their weavers immense, like so many denizens of nightmare. Dark birds flew high above the church, not making a sound. A single raindrop extinguished itself on my cheek. I looked across at Jennie. She had sunk to her haunches, and was running her eyes over a low-lying clump of shrubby weed no taller than my knee. As I watched, she called me to her. Her soft-timbred, flute-like voice was little more than a purr.

"Don't get too close," she said. "Or else she'll know you're there."

At first, I saw nothing. I tilted my head a little, wondering what I was meant to be looking at, and the web flickered into view, hovering on the air like the after-effects of a well-aimed punch to the head. It was stretched vertically between one row of leaves and another, one of those many-sided, cartwheel orb webs that possess such a degree of symmetry that you find yourself perennially surprised to see one outside of a book of children's fairytales. I moved my head one way and then another, adjusting the flow of light onto the skeins. In the end, I managed to count over two dozen unbroken radials, but could fix no final number on the spirals. In a strange moment of epiphany I recognised in the spider's web a construction of such aesthetic perfection, such intrinsic rightness, that it was almost impossible not to take it for some part of a higher, perhaps universal, design.

"Imagine yourself this small," said Jennie suddenly. She held her thumb and forefinger a quarter inch apart, suggesting a creature of negligible size. I found it hard to see what she meant at first, or perhaps I did not want to see, to imagine myself surprised, pursued, ensnared. I have given lectures to my students in which I invite them, in imagination at least, to enter the great backyard jungle, a primitive, uncivilized land in which eight-legged beasts of prey vie for territory with the arrogant centipedes, and where the common alleycat, a monster of gargantuan proportions, is a creature of unspeakable legend. A number of years ago I was lucky enough to collaborate in the making of a short educational film with exactly that agenda. The promotional material called it the Jurassic Park of the suburbs. I enjoyed the work immensely, and the results were a revelation. But it was Jennie who first taught me to see it for real.

The trap was unbroken and empty. I had no idea why a spider might spin such a web and then abandon it, but it seemed like a terrible waste.

"Is it hiding?" I asked. I could not, yet, form the word 'spider.' Jennie smiled at me, sideways.

"You're learning already," she said. She plucked a blade of grass from between her feet, and used it to beat a light tattoo on one of the silken threads, a line that I had hitherto taken no note of, but which I now saw led outwards from the web's very centre, disappearing in a nearby clump of leaves. Almost at once the leaves began to stir, as if a soft wind were moving gently through them. And yet there was no wind, not at that moment. I took half a step backwards out of habit. My breath came shallow and fast as it had always done at such moments. But it was excitement that I felt now, not fear.

The spider scuttled free of its light green canopy, using the stoutly woven signal thread as a lifeline. She was large, more than half an inch in length, and possessed what I later came to recognise as exceptionally well defined markings. Her legs were striped in horizontal bands of light and dark brown, as is usual with *Araneus diadematus*, and her plump brown abdomen bore the characteristic broken white cross. She ran to the centre of her web, where she became suddenly, instantly still, as if aware she had been tricked. After perhaps thirty seconds she turned herself in a circle, like a dog settling itself on a blanket, and hung head downwards, the web shaking minutely in response to her weight. She was beautiful. I leaned forward to gaze at her, hardly daring to draw breath in case the movement of air were to send her once more into hiding. To my surprise and delight, I had recognised her at once from the illustration in the book by Kenneth Nugent. The text had identified her as the Garden Spider, claiming her as one of the most common and widespread of native British species. I found it difficult to believe that such a miraculous creature could be described as commonplace. I stared and stared at her, lost, like a man in love.

"In the Middle Ages, they were said to be holy," said Jennie quietly. "Because of the sign of Christ." She was kneeling close to me, her breath warm and faintly moist against my cheek.

"Are we going to catch her?" I said. As I spoke, I realised that I hated the idea. To trap the creature, to destroy the web – it would seem like an act of betrayal.

"I don't like putting them in boxes," Jennie said. "Let's leave her and look for some more."

We spent more than two hours in the cemetery. Jennie rehearsed me in the art of seeing, of looking into places that a week before I would scarcely have noticed. The leaf litter hosted the Wolf Spiders, *Pardosa amentata* and *Pardosa pullata.* They were lithe grey beasts that hunted their prey on foot, speeding along so quickly that few ground-dwelling insects could outrun them. Under a pile of stones we came upon a gnarled black *Zelotes latreillei.* On being exposed to the light he dashed forward in a series of irregular jerks, waving his forelegs at us as if indignant at being disturbed. In a fissure of the grey church wall we found the tiny pink *Oonops pulcher.*

"They have six eyes, instead of eight," said Jennie. "They only come out at night."

The spider ran over her finger in a flurry of flesh-coloured legs and then disappeared once more into its crack. In the long grass by the dry stone wall we discovered another orb web builder, a graceful *Tetragnatha extensa* with legs so long that I could not resist tickling her belly with a grass-blade just so I could see her in action. She moved a little way up the stem, standing on tiptoe like a ballerina, and then came to a standstill, folding her incredible legs vertically and sideways, making of herself one long knife-shaped whole, all but invisible against her blade of grass.

Each of our finds was enchantingly, stomach-tinglingly new to me. But Jennie knew all of them by name. At one point, I asked her how she had come by such knowledge.

"Did you find all this out on your own?" I asked. "Or is it something that you're studying at college?" She glanced sideways at me, brushed a stray strand of hair off her face and then looked down at the ground. For the first time she seemed almost shy.

"It's just something that interests me," she said. "There are plenty of books." She hesitated slightly and then continued. "I haven't been to college. I've been ill." She looked away from me, as if she did not want to be pressed. Beneath the coarse blue coat the curve of her spine looked fragile and vulnerable to damage. Once more I wanted to touch her but did not dare.

"Let's cut back through the field," she said at last. "There's a place where we can get through the wall."

The land dipped ever so slightly as we pushed our way through the undergrowth, moving away from the church and down towards the broad swathe of farmland beyond. As we came near to the breach in the wall, I tripped against something and almost fell. I put out a hand to steady myself and then parted the grasses, wondering what was there. At my feet was a large, rectangular slab of granite. I bent down to examine it more closely, and was almost shocked to discover that it was in fact a grave marker, similar to many of those we had already seen in the churchyard. I stepped sideways, wanting to let in the light, only to have myself collide with another identical tombstone. I called out to Jennie, who had all but reached the wall. She started retracing her steps and by the time she got back to where I was I had uncovered two further stones, to the right and the left of the others.

"I don't understand," I said. "Did you know that these were here?" The graves in the churchyard had been without exception carefully tended, the stones scrubbed and clean, the monuments set about with flowers. These stones, all but buried in the grass, were covered in mosses and lichen. I knelt beside the stone that had almost felled me, and used a sharp, flat stone to scrape the middle portion free of detritus. There was a name, 'Alison Jane Tranter,' but nothing else, not even the customary pairing of dates. The tombstone bore no decoration. I put down my scraper. Looking at the name, so naked and stark now that the dirt had been cleared away, made me feel guilty of some unconscious act of sacrilege. I had no wish to perform such an operation on any of the others.

"Old families sometimes die out," said Jennie. "Then there's no-one to look after the graves."

"But in a small village like this," I persisted. "It seems strange that she had no friends."

Jennie shrugged and I fell silent. I felt foolish with the

kind of red-cheeked, bumbling foolishness of someone who finds that he has unintentionally stumbled into an affair that does not concern him. As I mentioned before, cemeteries had always made me vaguely uncomfortable and, with all my grandparents having been cremated, I had never had to visit one myself. I could not understand my sudden sense of outrage over the neglect of the Tranter woman. I stood there, gazing down at the stone in an effort to hide my inner confusion. I wondered how old she had been.

"At any rate," I said. "It's odd that these graves are so far away from the others." I had no desire to continue with the subject, and yet I was continuing with it, nonetheless. I did not know why.

"Suicides were often set apart," said Jennie. "Or murderers." She bent towards the grave, wiping the flat of her hand across the carved stone letters, smearing her palm with green. Seeing her that way – her bowed head, her filthy hand – raised a cold, dark feeling in me that trespassed on the boundary between discomfiture and horror. I wanted to seize her, to snatch her to safety, as one might drag a child from the reach of a fire. I will not say that I sensed some secret affinity or relationship between Jennifer Bristowe and Alison Jane Tranter; even though I now knew that Jennie had been born near Langwold, I was not and never had been a man of heightened imaginative susceptibility, the kind of person that looks for hidden meaning and mysterious depths in everyday occurrences. I suspect rather that it was an intimation of mortality, the sudden and crude juxtaposition of a young and sensitive creature – the girl I had already begun to love – with somebody old and forgotten and dead. Perhaps her earlier mention of illness had made me feel afraid. In either case, the smell of the place, with its moist dirt and lichen and crushed rotting leaves, made me rather anxious to be gone.

"Come on," I said. "We'll be late for lunch."

I took her hand, and together we passed out of the churchyard and onto the smooth grassy border of the neighbouring field. Her hand was cold at first from its contact with the stone, but as we walked it took on the heat of my own hand, becoming warm and responsive, a set of shadow-fingers that seemed almost indivisible from mine. I could still feel dirt on her skin. I scraped at it a little with my fingernails, and then imagined taking Jennie upstairs to my room, running a basin of warm water and immersing her hand in it, rubbing at it gently until it was clean.

On the way back to the house we talked mostly about spiders. We had made no use of our collecting boxes and had only our notebooks as proof of our finds. I had begun by writing just the name but Jennie had quickly corrected me, showing me how to properly enter a sighting, noting place and time and weather conditions as well as species and date. Jennie ran her eyes down the list, murmuring one or two of the Latin epithets aloud.

"Some of these are quite rare," she said. "Nobody will believe that we've seen them."

For some reason this struck us as funny. At exactly the same moment both of us started to laugh.

There was lunch and then there was a lot of fuss made over Hilary Arden, who had managed to capture a magnificent *Dolomedes plantarius*. It was a huge beast, with a chocolate brown body the size of a woman's thumb. A week earlier I would have not have been able to look at it without severe disturbance to my heart-rate and breathing. Now I had read enough to know that the Raft Spider was protected by law in Britain and that Hilary would have to return it to its original habitat.

"The name is inaccurate, since they do not build rafts," said Gustav Preisner. "It's a typically English fallacy."

"But of course it's the spider itself that is the raft. The spider can walk on water," said Andrew Lill. He spoke almost into his hands, mumbling away as if in private. I was certain that Preisner did not hear him. The Newcombes seemed to have concentrated their attention on orb weavers, of which they had tracked down half a dozen species. I glanced at them briefly, hunched and motionless in the bottom of the glass-topped containers. I was relieved when they let them all go.

For the remainder of the afternoon we retired once more to the first floor lounge, where Simon Barclay gave an informal seminar on the history of the British Arachnological Society. I listened intently, and made notes. I was filled with a quiet excitement, the excitement of a man who knows he has found his vocation. I spent little time dwelling on what had happened to me or considering the forces that might have wrought such a change. I knew only that the change had happened, that the thing I had hated and feared had become a source of fascination and satisfaction, even joy. If I was concerned about anything it was the future, and how I might best alter my life to accommodate my destiny. From time to time I glanced up at Jennie. She sat in the chair beside me, so close that I could hear her breathing. She had made notes also but the margins of her paper were covered with doodles of spiders. The pencilled creatures gathered and swarmed, detailed and lifelike as photographs. She seemed sunk within herself, inhabiting some intense and febrile world of her own. And yet I felt linked to her, irrevocably, as if by a silken thread. It was difficult for me, and almost frightening to realise, that I had known her for less than a day.

The idea had been that we were to prepare the evening meal as a team. What actually happened was that Elisabeth Newcombe cleared the kitchen of everyone but herself, her husband, and, for some reason, Hilary Arden, and proceeded to mastermind the production of an excellent three-course dinner. By this second evening the dynamics of the group had altered. There was enough familiarity to provide a fair measure of relaxed enjoyment yet not enough to engender open competition. The conversation was led by Elisabeth Newcombe herself, ably supported by Gustav Preisner and Sally Beamish. The rest of us contented ourselves with cameo roles and were glad to be entertained. There was a lot of laughter. Once the meal had been cleared away it was decided to retire to the ground floor sitting room for coffee and armagnac. Simon Barclay made up the fire. It was Elisabeth Newcombe who gave us the idea for the ghost stories.

"Of course you realise we're right in the middle of M.R James country," she said. She swept a gaze around the room, addressing all of us in general and none of us in particular. I suppose it had become difficult for her to stop behaving like a teacher.

"Not only that," said Sally Beamish. "There's a rumour that he visited this house."

I had heard of M. R James but never read him. My enthusiasm for Victorian literature had encompassed the great explorers and men of science but never the masters of Gothic. When I looked at Jennie I saw that she was smiling. She had not spoken much over dinner but she had kept herself close to me, from time to time leaning in so that our legs touched under the table. Now, in the mutable light from the fire, her hair and eyes glowed a phosphorescent tawny-orange. To me, loving her, she seemed almost more spirit than substance.

"Do you know him?" I whispered.

"Yes, I do," she replied. "You can't live in Suffolk and not have read James."

"A master of atmosphere, certainly," said Gustav Preisner. "But for terror with conviction one must turn to Grimm."

"Go on then, Gustav," said Hilary Arden. "Tell us a ghost story. You know you want to." He slumped back in his seat, extending his legs expectantly towards the fire, his large-knuckled hands crossed loosely behind his head. In the shadows his hair glowed almost white.

"What a marvellous idea," said Jarvis Newcombe. "We could all tell one."

His suggestion was met with universal and enthusiastic approval, but in the event only two tales were told. The second, Jennie's story, took us late into the night. When it was finished everyone repaired very quickly to bed. There was a half-spoken consensus that the weird tales would be continued on the following evening but for some reason that never occurred.

Preisner's story was that kind of German Gothic that sets especial store by unequal love between conniving intelligent dwarves and empty-headed but beautiful humans. The hero, if there was one, turned out to be the long-suffering ghost of the girl's dead father. Told in the half-dark, in Preisner's obsessively correct, somehow ascetic English, it proved extremely effective. It was a chilling story, full of cruelty, but it managed to evoke in me also an echo of childhood, of Hallowe'en lanterns and contraband torchlit reading beneath the bedclothes. I felt obscurely comforted. I think we all felt hungry for more.

"Who's next?" said Jarvis Newcombe. His voice was less reticent, more animated than usual, and a clump of his thinning, greying hair had fallen forward onto his forehead, making him look, for a moment at least, like the schoolboy he had presumably been some thirty years before.

"I'll go next," said Jennie. I turned to her, startled. She held my eyes for a second and then looked away into the fire. She folded her arms in front of her, brushing my knee with her fingers as she did so. I could not read her expression but her movements spoke of rigidity, of tension. I wondered if she were frightened. The others, I believe, were as surprised by her offer as I.

"Can such young people know such old stories?" wheezed Andrew Lill.

"Of course, there's a long tradition in England of ghost stories written by young women," said Simon Barclay quickly. "Just think of 'Wuthering Heights.'"

"We'd love to hear you, Jennie," said Sally Beamish. "Does anybody want another drink?"

Glasses were swiftly refilled. Jennie herself declined the brandy but leaned forward, hands empty, long pale fingers locked about her knees. Then she began to speak. Her voice had a high, bright clarity that made it sound almost like song. The others sat immobile, as if spellbound. Nobody said a word.

"There was a young man, Jonathan Merrick," she began. "His father was the manager of a large pig farm on the borders of Essex and Suffolk. He had not done badly for himself, but nonetheless he was determined that his own son should escape the rigours and uncertainties of a life on the land, and instead make a career in the Professions. He saved hard, so that Jon could attend the grammar school in Colchester rather than the free school in the village. He wanted Jon to study for the Law.

"Jon won a scholarship, and a place at a college in London. When he turned eighteen, his mother packed a battered leather trunk with clean linen and a brand new travelling cloak she had ordered especially from Watt's Bespoke Tailors of Chelmsford. His father booked him a seat on the overnight coach. On the day before he left the village Jonathan Merrick paid a final visit to the girl he looked on as his intended, one Alice Teresa Chilcot. He fastened a golden locket around her neck, and promised to write to her as often as his studies allowed. Alice cried. She gave Jon six silk handkerchiefs, each one embroidered by hand. The handkerchiefs were wrapped in pale green tissue. The tissue exuded the soft yellow scent of Chinatown roses. It was a scent he had sometimes noticed on Alice's skin.

"He was fourteen years old when he first met her. He was a quiet boy by nature. This, and the fact that he had been sent away to school, had earned him few friends in the village. At weekends and during the holidays he kept mainly to himself, reading quietly in his room, or, sometimes, taking long circuitous walks across the fields. Had it not been for the Christmas party at the Lambcocks he might never have met Alice at all.

"The Lambcocks owned most of the village. Stuart Rowland Lambcock was a gentleman farmer with an extensive store of wealth. Every year, on the last Saturday before Christmas, he threw a party for all of his tenants. There was a fiddle band, and dancing, and a wealth of exotic food. There were gifts wrapped in silver paper for every child. Jon's parents looked forward to the party; for Jon it was an ordeal. He found it hard to talk to strangers, and nobody talked to him. The village children ignored him, and the five dark-headed young Lambcocks spoke only amongst themselves. Jon moved slowly between the revellers, looking only for somewhere to hide. In the end he slid behind the curtains. There was a narrow space there, between the long red velvet and the glass. The alcove was cold and cramped. He found the place was occupied by Alice.

"She was a thin child, with ungainly, gangling limbs. Her complexion was pasty, her hair a shade of undistinguished brown. The dress she wore was plain, not a party dress at all. Jon could not remember ever having been alone with a girl before. He stood there in front of her, holding back the curtain. The noise behind him in the room grew dim. She stared at him without smiling and then turned away again towards the window. 'Look at the grass,' she said. 'It's like diamonds.' He stepped forward, pressing his face close against the glass. On the lawn outside a hard frost had turned all the stalks into needles. 'It'll cover the windows later,' said the girl. 'In the morning there'll be patterns, like paintings made out of snow.'

"He knew that it was true, because he had seen it before. For some reason it amazed him that the girl had noticed it too. He sat down beside her, their backs against the velvet. Jon felt at ease, as if he had known her for years. 'At my school, all the windows ice shut when it's cold,' he said. 'Except for the headmaster's. He always has a fire.' He pictured the icicles that hung from the taps in the first floor washroom, water turned to glass in the midst of its fall. Quite suddenly he felt like running and dancing. He wanted to go outside, to see the crystallized lawn laid out like silver netting beneath the moon.

"They met on the following day and again on the day after that. On New Year's Eve he kissed her on the lips. He told her which books he liked best, and the nicknames of the teachers at his school. She taught him the names of the stars in the belt of Orion. Jon, who had never before exchanged a confidence with anybody, grew used in time to telling her everything. On some nights he dreamed of her, her slight, pale, overlong limbs, her round hazel eyes, the fringe of fine fair hair that hung about her face. When he went back to school she gave him a bookmark, a strip of cream silk that had been stitched to resemble the pale, peppered wings of a moth. He kept the bookmark beneath his pillow and came to think of returning home as returning to Alice. At sixteen he supposed that he must be in love with her, although the bond they shared seemed somehow much deeper than that.

"Alice Chilcot lived with her aunt at Adsetts, a low, red, rather ugly house that overlooked the church. Some people said that her parents were dead. Others maintained that Melanie Chilcot was not the girl's aunt at all, that she had taken the child in out of pity. 'The girl's not even a real Chilcot,' said the egg woman, Eleanor Brady. 'Nobody knows what she's called.' The villagers seemed to agree that Alice Chilcot would one day be rich, that her father had made a fortune importing silk and porcelain from China.

"Jon listened to the stories, because he enjoyed hearing her name in the mouths of others. He placed little value on what was actually said. 'My parents live abroad,' said Alice, when Jonathan asked her. 'My mother got very ill, so my father took her away. It's not safe for her in this country because it's too cold.' In the schoolroom Alice was shunned. Jon put this down to her shyness, although he had heard it said more than once that Alice Chilcot had once been prone to rages, that she had assaulted Wilbur Collett, the boy from the smithy, by throwing the lad to the ground and snapping his wrist. 'I pushed him and knocked him down,' said Alice. 'Because I saw him kill a spider in the yard. It's bad luck to kill spiders, and cruel. But I didn't really mean to break his arm.'

"She never seemed to mind his questions. The life he had had before knowing her appeared, in retrospect, empty and somehow frightening, and it seemed to him sometimes that he had always, in some way, had a secret, innate knowledge of her existence. When the weather allowed, they walked, often for miles. Alice liked to collect things – pine cones and beech nuts and empty snail shells – and to quote the names of flowers, insects and birds. If it was too wet or cold they secreted themselves for hours in Alice's room on the upper floor of Adsetts. It was a large room, approached by a private staircase, with a separate curtained alcove for her bed. The furniture was old, and stained with a thick, dark, heavy varnish. There were shelves stacked with books, and closets full of teasel-heads and sheep's skulls and pressed, dried flowers. When Jon took down one of the books, he found it illegible. The words looked familiar but different, as if they were an anagram, or puzzle. 'That's Middle English,' said Alice. 'My mother taught it to me when I was small.' The book was bound in stiff red leather, and was full of engravings that reminded him of the pictures in fairy tales. He laid it aside, without looking at any of the others. He found it hard to believe that Alice was able to read them, and supposed she held on to the books because they had once belonged to her mother.

"As well as the books and collections, there was Alice's workbox. It stood on carved wooden legs, like stilts, and had a plush pink velvet lining. There were three shallow drawers stacked one inside the other. In the top drawer there were a number of small round wooden boxes containing needles and buttons and pins. Beneath this lay the silks. There were many different colours, all in rows. Whenever he looked at the hanks of neatly twisted yarn Jon found himself thinking of the soft shiny hair of girls standing in line for church on the eve of some great festival. Alice sewed large tapestries, wide vistas of interlocking colour to which she gave titles like 'Crystals,' or 'Plantain,' or 'Beehive.' They had no obvious design, like the samplers that his mother sewed, or the embroidered antimacassars in his old headmaster's study. Alice said she saw them inside her head. She quite often talked while she worked, not even looking down at her fingers. Jon occasionally wondered if the silks Alice used had any connection with the silk imported to England by her father but it was a question that he never liked to ask.

"Sometimes, when the time came for him to leave her, she cried. Rather than swelling her eyes and reddening her features, the tears drained her face of all colour, turning her skin the uneven, porous white of blotting paper. Whenever this happened, Jon found himself helplessly caught between anguish at parting and the desire to be gone as quickly as possible. Her tears frightened him, although once he was away from her he often felt like weeping himself. In all the time before Jon went to London he never once saw Alice naked. Through the brown wool of her dresses he had felt the soft, slight weight of her breasts, the masked, damp heat in the cleft of her narrow thighs. In his dreams, when he possessed her, her skin was gossamer-fine, like that of some other, less human creature. It bruised easily beneath his hands like the pollen-dusted wing-skin of a moth.

"Almost from the first Jon felt at home in London. It was not the great city itself that captivated his heart so much as the fact that, for the first time in his life, he found himself in the company of many like-minded men. To his surprise he made friends easily, and soon moved from the spartan Halls of the University into more comfortable lodgings at the home of a fellow student, Edwin Ryder. Ryder knew a lot of people, and found much enjoyment in bringing them together. There were card parties and dinners, with eating and talking and drinking until the small hours. Ryder's parents were often present, and also his sister, Helen. Helen Ryder was twenty years old, and already engaged to be married. She played the piano, and was said to be serious about it. She wore her hair long, gathered in at the nape with a band of blue silk ribbon. She beat everyone at cards. When she laughed, she threw back her head like a man, spinning the stem of her wineglass between her fingers. She was somehow so different from Alice. He sometimes found himself remembering how Alice had injured the smith's boy, Wilbur Collett. He wondered how Alice might react to Helen.

"He returned to the village for Christmas. By the time the coach drew in it was long since dark. The houses on the Green seemed smaller, cramped narrowly together on the bald black frost-bitten ground. Jon stared up at the sky. He had forgotten, in London, how crushing a night could be. All at once he felt heavy with gloom and a longing to return to the city. The village seemed irrelevant, part of his past. He walked home over the meadows, not wishing to meet with anyone. After supper he went back across the frozen fields to Adsetts. Alice seemed paler even than before, her thin hair colourless and limp. Upstairs in her room, she laid both arms tightly about Jon's neck and clung to him, making a low, soft moaning sound from somewhere deep inside her. When she finally drew away, her eyes were dim with tears. Jon held her without looking at her, gazing instead on the room itself, on the birds' eggs and the pine cones, the frames of pressed flowers, the spools of silk in ochre and sienna and cerise. Everything seemed unchanged. If anything, it was a more concentrated version of itself, more intensely full of innumerable nameless objects. There were some things he had not seen there before: a glass-fronted cabinet full of bottles, and a pen and ink line drawing in a frame. The bottles were empty and unstoppered. By the discoloration of their interiors Jon thought Alice had probably dug them out of the ground. The drawing showed a young woman, bent backwards in some sort of agony, clutching at the air with outstretched arms. Her clothes were in tatters, and, from her tensed, hunched shoulders another pair of arms appeared to be growing. 'I copied it,' said Alice. 'It took me forever. It's from an etching by Gilles DeLore.' 'I don't think I know it,' said Jon. 'What's it about?' He found the thing hideous and deeply disturbing. He thought it might keep him from sleep. 'It's the Judgement on Arachne,' said Alice. 'She was a mortal woman, yet she challenged the goddess Minerva to a spinning competition.' She broke away from him, crossed to the picture and lifted it gently down. 'Arachne won the contest, but Minerva had her changed into a spider. The gods don't make good losers, I suppose.' She rested her fingertips briefly on the glass as if she were stroking the image and then hung the frame back on its hook. 'Of course, that myth was probably created to illustrate another,' she said. 'Or maybe even to hide it. Ordinary people have always been terrified of shapeshifters.' For a moment she seemed to become a brown pool of nothingness, merging seamlessly with the peripheral shadows at the margin of the room. Then she was herself again, edging towards him into the light thrown down by the lamp. She had always been full of such stories and he had always listened, fascinated by the esoteric breadth of her knowledge. Yet this tale seemed to him morbid and distasteful, her thoughts burdensome and backward, just like the village itself. Nobody had said such things in London. He could not help remembering that there had been another rumour surrounding Alice's orphaned state: that her mother was not in fact dead, but mad, and confined to some foreign asylum.

"Jon found that he had run out of words. He took the girl in his arms and laid her down upon the bed. When he put his hands beneath her garments, he was almost surprised to find her skin downy and suffused with warmth, pulsing with secret life. She lay beneath him, drawing air through her mouth, noisily, as if finding it hard to breathe. He reached out and touched her breasts, thinking of the blue silk ribbon in Helen Ryder's hair. When he entered her, she cried out, arching her back and baring her teeth, like the damned, mutated woman in the picture. Afterwards, she lay completely quiet. Jon took her head between his hands, stroking her hair with his fingers until she slept. He wondered if the act he had just committed constituted more of a promise to Alice than his earlier gift of the locket, or whether it was the other way around.

"Alice refused to go to the Lambcocks' party. Jon went to please his father, intending to leave before ten. The house was resplendently lit and visible for miles. By the time he arrived the dancing had already begun. Jon took a glass of wine from one of the silver trays and lost himself in the crowd. Here and there were people he recognised. Several of them stopped him as he passed, and asked how things were turning out in Town. Whenever he spoke people listened. Somebody brought him more wine. The fiddle band were playing a country set. Jon sipped his drink and stood watching the dancers. He wondered what it might feel like to spin and twist in the lamplight, holding fast to somebody's silk-gloved, delicate hand. 'You should try it,' said a voice close beside him. 'If you fall over, you can always get up again.' The girl's hair was dark, almost black. She wore a red velvet dress with a white lace collar. Jon thought he recognised her from somewhere but had no idea why. 'We learned to dance at school,' he said. 'But I've never tried it out.' It was a round dance. At first, Jon heeded frantically to the caller's instructions, panicky with the fear of committing some immortal blunder. Only gradually did he become aware of the tune. The room wheeled about him, the eight foot Christmas tree reduced to three dozen points of star-shaped candlelight. For a second he saw his mother, smiling up at a fat man in a pirate's hat and eating a candied apple. The black-haired girl was laughing, creasing the corners of her chestnut-coloured eyes. 'You're Winston Merrick's son,' she said, as the music came to an end. 'You used to be terribly shy.'

"It was only then that Jon knew who she was. He remembered other Christmases, the images resurrecting themselves in his brain like pictures in an album. There had always been the great hall and the throngs of dancers, just as there had always been five beautiful dark-haired children handing out the presents from the tree. With each year that passed the children had grown taller. 'You're Stuart Lambcock's daughter,' he said. 'You have four older brothers.' His cheeks felt hot but he thought it was just the wine. 'Yes,' she replied. 'But I wish you'd call me Anne.'

"To cover his confusion he asked her to dance again. While they were dancing they talked. He found her easy to talk to, unaffected and open to merriment like his new friends in London. 'Living in Town must be heaven,' she said, as they finally approached the refreshment tables. 'There's nothing to do here, and nobody to see. I'd like to leave the lot of it behind.' She was already aware that he was hoping to sit for the Bar. 'The whole village knows that,' she said, smiling a little. 'You're a success story. It's not very often that somebody gets away.' They stood in front of the windows, side by side, their lips moist with the residue of goose liver patties and fruitcake. Beyond the curtains the wide lawns sparkled with frost. Below them in the village dim lanterns cast their aura at the moon. To Jon the lights of the houses seemed pathetic and hopeless, the diminishing embers of a yellowed and dying world.

"When Anne asked him to attend a drinks party later in the week Jon accepted, telling Alice he had been invited to play whist with some long-standing friends of his father. Alice seemed content to wait for his return, using the periods of his absence to add hundreds of minute blue stitches to a huge new tapestry she called 'Libellula.' She said that Libellula was a species of dragonfly, and showed him a picture of it in one of the leather bound books with the illegible foreign script. Its body was bright blue, with venomous dabs of yellow. Jon found the thing ugly and wished he had never seen it. Alice seemed like a child to him, someone whose company he had long since outgrown. He disliked being alone with her in the overflowing room beneath the eaves. He wondered what it was that they had once found to talk about. The desire to touch her had gone.

"He grew accustomed to well lit interiors and congenial voices. In the days between Christmas and the New Year he saw Anne Lambcock often. On New Year's Eve as the clock struck twelve he took her in his arms. When he kissed her, he found himself almost overcome by the soft refinement of her person, by the rich and exotic scent of her perfume. She had silky-fingered, fine-jointed hands that he loved to hold. She laughed often, making deep, chocolate slits of her eyes. She liked to sprawl on sofas or in armchairs, discarding her slippers, as comfortable inside her skin as some young greyhound or foal. The Lambcock boys involved her in their games and banter as if she were a younger, more beautiful brother. They were friendly to Jon, accepting his presence as if he were one of their own. 'They like you,' said Anne. 'You're clever, but you don't make them look stupid. They like that. So does my father.' Jon wondered whether Stuart Lambcock would continue to like him if he asked Anne to marry him. It was something he hardly dared to think about. There was also the question of Alice. He saw her as little as possible, knowing nonetheless that whenever he was away from her she would be waiting for him in her room, sitting beside the window while she worked on one of her incomprehensible tapestries. He remembered the unexpected heat of her body, the febrile, passionate intensity of her embrace. He wondered what would happen if he were to simply return to London and never come back.

"The trouble was, she knew him too well. 'There's

something wrong,' she said to him one evening. 'You're different. It's as if there's another person living inside.' She placed both hands on his chest, rested her head between them and began to cry. 'I need to go,' he said. 'I'm going to be late for supper.' As he walked away from Adsetts, he was aware of Alice watching him from the window. He went onwards without turning round. The next morning he went to meet Anne. He cut through the churchyard, not wanting to be seen from the road. As Anne came towards him he was struck once more not just by her beauty but by the force of young life that was in her. She seemed to exude light, just as Alice seemed to somehow suck it in. 'You looked miles away,' she said, taking his hand. 'I wonder where you were.' She was wearing a red woollen bonnet trimmed with ermine. Her flared grey coat came almost to the ground. Even encased in its black leather glove, her hand felt polished and perfect like that of a doll. 'These young philosophers,' she said to him, smiling. 'They're awfully attractive.' Behind him in Adsetts Lane something stirred in the bracken. Jon started and turned his head. He realised then that he was almost afraid, that he expected to see something, without daring to wonder what that thing might be. The lane stood empty. In one of the adjoining fields he caught a brief sight of a rabbit scampering for cover under a hedge. In the evening when he called on Alice her aunt told him she had gone out. Such a thing had never happened before. Jon hid himself in the porchway of the church and waited there for almost an hour. Alice did not appear. He ran home across the fields, his emotions caught in a no-man's-land somewhere between foreboding and relief.

"He slept badly; the little rest he had was plagued by uneasy dreams. He rose early and went straight to Adsetts. 'She didn't come back last night,' said Melanie Chilcot. 'Her bed's not been slept in. I don't know what to do.' The woman seemed dazed, or only half awake. She looked up at Jon with deep-set hazel eyes that were almost identical with Alice's own. He had never paid much attention to Melanie Chilcot, perhaps because he had never truly believed in her relationship to Alice. There was no way to doubt it now. He took her into the parlour and made her sit down. 'She can't be far,' he said. 'There's nowhere for her to go.'

"It was the fifth day of the new year. There was a hush on the village and a depth of cold that seemed somehow to seal it in time. Jon walked without really knowing where he was going. Icicles hung from the trees like crystal daggers. He could not imagine anyone choosing to remain outside for long. He made for the hay barns and the grain store. The grain store was padlocked but he knew where his father kept the key. He undid the padlock and swung the door wide on its stiff rusty hinges. A diagonal shaft of white winter light stabbed into the darkness. There was a hasty, muffled scrabbling that he knew was probably rats. He smelled the familiar, sweetish odour of winter corn. Apart from the wheat bins the grain store was empty. He followed the line of the hedgerows until he came once more to the churchyard and the narrow muddy runnel of Adsetts Lane. On the pavements the overnight snow had melted to a thick brown slush. The silence oppressed him. He had the enervating sense that he was watched. He opened the lych gate and searched among the tombs. Here and there he found flowers, their frozen heads silvered with ice. There were names on the graves he recognised but no sign anywhere of anything living. The church towered above him, levelling a black accusing finger at the sky. A single breath of wind parted the slime-dark foliage of the yews. Once again Jon felt afraid. He left the churchyard, increasing his speed until he was almost running. The cold air burned inside his lungs, and his mind, made numb by fear, was filled with a sea of thoughts that he dared not examine.

"He headed out of the village, climbing the shallow incline towards the wavering line of poplars that marked the boundary of the Lambcock estate. Between the bottom fields and the gamekeepers' cottages he could see the grey stone walls of the Lower Byres, a series of dilapidated outbuildings that had once been used to shelter the Lambcock cows. The buildings were ancient; in places, the roofs were gone. In summers that seemed long past he had spent hours up at the Byres, mostly with Alice. They had sometimes stayed until the sun set, and the dusk turned all the grass from green to blue.

The heat of the soil had fled skywards, seeming to seep away to nothing beneath his hands. He had rubbed her fingers between his own to warm them. Around them in the darkness, the crickets had hummed and chirred. They had never been to the Byres in winter because of the cold.

"Jon crossed the field, the frozen grass shattering like glass beneath his feet. In the Great Byre there was nothing. Dead leaves mouldered in the corners, mildew coated the walls. He stood in the doorway, watching as a great black spider emerged from a crack above the lintel and began lowering itself slowly downward towards the ground. It went cautiously, hand over hand, its hind legs paying out the silk. Jon fought the urge to knock the thing to the ground and crush it beneath his heel. He had never cared much for spiders, and the sight of such a one, such a huge, dark beast and so monstrously secretive, made his heart contract within his breast. He turned away quickly, making his way along the narrow cobbled path that led from one ruined barn to another. The second byre was smaller, with no sign of life in it at all. The last building was little more than a hut. It had once been a wood store, a low construction, with angular, stoneblock sides. There was a single narrow window high up under the eaves. Rotting logs were piled haphazardly against one outside wall, an invitation to vermin. Jon moved slowly towards the entrance, not knowing whether he could bring himself to go inside. The place was so desolate it seemed almost evil. It was inconceivable to him that anyone could remain here, even for a single hour. As he made to leave, a movement caught his eye. He started and looked upward. In the bare black socket of the window something fluttered gently in the breeze. He went closer, craning his neck. Issuing from the gap in the wall was a mass of greyish filaments or fibres. It looked like the Old Man's Beard that grew amongst the hedgerows every autumn, or the swatches of cotton muslin on jars of jam. The stuff seemed somehow dirty. It trailed down over the ivy towards the ground.

"Acting without thinking, Jon stepped over the threshold of the hut and stared upwards into the shadows. The partially obstructed window afforded little natural light, but Jon's eyes were young and very soon adjusted to the dark. A tangled, fibrous mass of the ambiguous greyness clung like wadding to the uneven flintblock stones of the inner wall. At its edges, the mass was gossamer-fine, a network of silvery wires. Towards the centre, it seemed almost solid. Jon ventured closer, wanting in spite of himself to reach out and touch it. The stuff looked soft and tactile, almost like velvet. He put out his hand, brushing lightly at the surface of the great, spun bulk of grey. The threads clung in droves to his outstretched palm. Jon recoiled at once, wiping his sticky fingers against his side. For one split second he imagined he saw a movement, the minutest of tremblings at the heart of the tangle of grey. Then everything was still. Jon stood motionless in the gloom as if held captive. He continued to stare, and as he stared he perceived a deeper, darker greyness within the cloud of monochrome nothing, a greyness that seemed to have weight, and bulk, and maybe even form. In the end, he found he could quite easily make out the blurred and hazy outline of a flared grey floor-length coat. Somewhere above the coat was a flash of red. The colour was covered by grey. It shimmered through the haze like a sunset through clouds. As Jon watched it, it seemed to glow brighter, a crimson woollen hat with ermine trim.

"There was a rustling somewhere behind him. His blood-heat seemed to vanish, as if all the clothes had been suddenly stripped from his body. He dared not turn; when he finally did, he saw Alice. She was wearing an over-large, mud-coloured greatcoat. There was part of a dried-up oak leaf clinging to the back of her hair. 'Spider silk is stronger than steel,' she said. 'People don't believe that, but it's true.' Her gloveless hands looked cold. There were strands of silver thread stuck to her palms and something a little darker beneath the nails. She stumbled on the stones then came towards him. She felt frail in his arms as though her substance had somehow diminished. 'You know me best,' she said. 'No-one else knows me at all.' Her body trembled as if from the cold, and he realised she was crying. She said something else, but he did not hear what it was. Her thin hair chafed his fingers. He sensed that if he looked at it properly it would be grey like the stuff on her hands. He felt a vague disgust as if he had discovered a stain in his clothing. 'Let's get you home,' he said. 'You must be very cold.'

"He went back to London the following day. It was more than a decade before he returned to the village. From his mother's letters, he learned that Alice Chilcot had died in childbirth although nobody had known that she was pregnant. The baby was named Teresa, and cared for by Alice's aunt. He learned also of the fire that destroyed the Lambcock house, and that killed Stuart Lambcock and three if his sons. It was thought that the fire had begun in the attics, although no specific cause was ever found. About Anne Lambcock he heard nothing. He felt that it was safer not to ask."

There was a silence. The fire in the grate had burned down so low that it was really nothing but embers. Hilary Arden was the first to move. He sat forward in his seat, the refined contours of his face catching the sluggish red light from the expiring coals. His hair had come loose from its binding, lending him the delicate androgynous beauty of a young messiah.

"What happened to the little girl?" said Elisabeth Newcombe suddenly. "Teresa."

"She wouldn't know that," said her husband. "It's just a story." There was a sharp undertone to his voice that quite surprised me. I had not thought him capable of speaking that way to his wife. Perhaps the others felt the same. There was a tension among us that was entirely new.

"Teresa grew up in the village," said Jennie. "She was fifteen when her grandfather came to collect her. His name was Persimon Tranter. He owned a *castello*, in the south of Italy."

Jennie was curled in the armchair, her feet tucked neatly beneath her. When I looked I saw her black lace-up boots placed side by side on the hearth. I had not seen her remove them. For a full minute nobody spoke. Then Sally Beamish clambered noisily to her feet, almost overturning a tray of drinks. "I'm going to bed," she said

"I can't keep my eyes open." She yawned, tipping her head back so that her long grey plait dipped below her waist. Everyone started to move.

"Come up to my room," Jennie said to me quietly. "I'll make us a cup of tea." She turned round in the armchair, looking me full in the face. Someone had put on a lamp. In the artificial light she appeared somehow less than three dimensional, a figure in a sepia-tinted print. The hallway was already empty. I followed her, climbing the stairs. There were lights on the second floor landing, tiny wall-lamps with four-sided, needlepoint shades. They made the patterns in the carpet shift and dance like the pieces of coloured glass inside a kaleidoscope.

Jennie's room was larger than my own, It overlooked the garden. There was a huge pedestal washstand in one corner, a massive French armoire in another. The rest of the room was dominated by the bed. It was higher than usual, with wrought iron legs in the shape of eagles' talons. I found it vaguely unnerving. It looked as if it belonged in a museum. Jennie walked to the bed and lay down. I noticed a coin-sized hole in the foot of her sock, and a pale patch of flesh showing through. I realised she had left her shoes behind in the lounge. I sat next to her feet, then took off my own shoes and lay down beside her. The huge bed creaked and groaned. Jennie's eyes were closed. Her eyelids were pale to the point of being colourless, with a network of fine blue veins. I put my hand on her hair. The heat of her head came through it, as if she were bald. I thought of the cold, low-lying wind that had come at us all morning through the churchyard and wondered vaguely if Jennie were sickening for something.

"Are you alright?" I said. I realised as I said it that this was almost the first personal question I had asked her. We had spoken of many things but as yet we had exchanged no confidences. The immediacy and depth of the empathy between us had made it seem unnecessary and yet asking such a question now made me feel inwardly naked. Unstable, as if I had removed some final barrier to complete intimacy.

"What did you think of the story?" she said, and opened her eyes. Her pupils had expanded against the semi-darkness. The hazel bands around them glimmered an opaque gold.

"It was strange," I said. "It felt like it really happened." I had found the story sinister and claustrophobic. It left a bad taste in the mouth, acrid and sour like bad black olives. I felt tight across the chest, taut with anger against whoever it had been of the company that had persuaded Jennie to tell it. Then I remembered that no-one had tried to persuade her of anything, that Jennie herself had offered. She had not so much told her tale as unburdened herself of it, in the way that a survivor of some fatal accident or catastrophe might relate what had happened to them. Gustav Preisner's delivery had been the tightly-controlled craftsmanship of the practised raconteur; listening to Jennie had been like eavesdropping outside a confessional. I did not like the idea of her being so badly upset. She had made mention of an illness. I had already begun to think of her as delicate, like some non-native organism that could only survive within the specially heated atmosphere of a vivarium. I suppose I thought that any excess of negative emotion could well do her some harm.

"Were you frightened?" she said. I wanted to reply that there had only ever been one major source of fear in my life, and that had now been banished, seemingly by her. I could have added that I had never been the kind of person to be troubled by ghost stories or horror films, that my imaginative powers had always been more prosaic than fantastical. And yet I hesitated to say any of that because part of me had been frightened. Not by the story, but by its effect on Jennie. She had turned on her back. I watched her chest rise and fall with the rhythm of her breathing. I wanted to put my hand on one of her breasts, to feel the warm, pulsing life of her, to prove to myself that she was still alright.

"It was a good story," I said at last. "It could be made into a film."

For a moment she said nothing. Then she sat up, moving with a suddenness, almost a violence, that nearly made me recoil. She faced me on the bed. Her lips were tight, stretched to transparency.

"What would you say if I said it was true?" she said. "That there was a thread of truth running through all of it?"

I thought she meant that she had been hurt that way, that she had trusted someone and that they had betrayed her, let her down. Her hair clung to her shoulders in a criss-cross of shimmering fibres. Her long, freckled arms were bent at the elbows, one hand on either knee. There was an intensity about her, a concentrated energy that seemed disastrously out of place upon the surface of this world. It occurred to me how tragic it was that for the majority of people strangeness was a source of fear rather than inspiration. I supposed it would be fairly commonplace for individuals to experiment with strangeness and then find it not to their taste. I wondered if she was testing me in some way. I could not believe that she had damaged anyone but maybe she had wanted to. She would have felt bad about that; bad enough, perhaps, to make her ill.

"I would say that people do bad things all the time," I said. "Terrible things, sometimes. That doesn't always mean it's their fault."

I put both arms around her shoulders and leaned forward, so that our foreheads were touching. She stayed still while I held her, but cast her eyes downwards as if she found me difficult to look at. After a little while she lay back down. I lay beside her, listening to the over-rapid beating of her heart. Gradually it slowed, in the end matching my own. Some hours later I woke with a start. The lamp was still on, shedding an anaemic yellow light around the room. The house was deathly quiet. The clock next to the bed read half past three. I looked at Jennie. She lay facing the wall, her long limbs bundled together like so much dry kindling. She was so still that her body seemed uninhabited and husk-like, as if her spirit might somehow have left it behind. I was tempted to shake her, simply to prove myself wrong. I laid the palm of my hand on her back, to the right of her spine. She felt warm through her clothes, and she was breathing. It was a strange hour of the night. Time itself seemed motionless, poised on the brink between yesterday and the day after.

I rose from the bed and switched out the light. The room was plunged into a complete blackness that only slowly became grey shadow. I reached for the folded coverlet at the end of the bed and pulled it up over our bodies. I lay on my back, eyes wide open on the dark, thinking about Jennie and the story she had told. I think I already knew, absolutely and without any doubt, that there was something wrong with her. I think I knew also that were I to ask her outright she would undoubtedly have told me what it was. I did not want to ask in case I was unable to cope with what she said. I had known her for no time at all and yet I, who had never been much of a one for certainties, was certain that were I to give her up the rest of any time owing to me would pass away uselessly and almost unnoticed. I turned on my side and slept. I dreamed of a house on a clifftop, with long red velvet curtains and without any stairs.

On the next day the drizzle abated. During the night westerly winds had blown the cloud cover out to sea, leaving the sky a clear, soft, chalky shade of blue. We crammed ourselves into the large four-wheel drive belonging to Sally Beamish and drove it to the coast not far from Dunwich. There were a series of cliff paths and lanes. Simon Barclay showed us where we could find the orb web builders *Larinioides cornatus* and *Mangora acalypha,* and took us to see a derelict granite barn where a multitude of *Amaurobis similis* lived in silk-lined tunnels between the stones. We had lunch in a roadside pub, the Ostler, an ancient building with tiny windows, its walls covered with mementos of its coaching past. After lunch we went into Dunwich itself. Elisabeth Newcombe had expressed a wish to look at the church whose bells had supposedly foretold the death of the town by drowning. It was a small building, smothered in ivy. To the rear of the church was a square walled cemetery with a sign informing visitors that the graveyard had once been the preserve of St Ninian's Charitable Refuge.

"That was a leper colony," said Simon Barclay. "I've found more species of wolf spider here than anywhere else in the county."

The cemetery was impenetrable, protected by high iron gates. I wondered how Simon Barclay had managed to get inside. The idea of the lepers was slightly unnerving. I had always connected leprosy with faraway places, with an unhealthy amount of sunlight and inadequate sanitation. The others drifted away from the graveyard and began poking about in the dense shrubbery at the side of the road. Jennie and I stood side by side with our faces between the bars.

"It's a dark place," Jennie said. "The sort of place you never really want to come back to, even if it's beautiful." She was holding onto the railings with both hands, as if she were inside a cage. I prised her fingers free and turned her around to face me. The skin of her palms was covered in coppery rust.

"You mustn't be frightened," I said. "The dead can never do you any harm." She looked at me, and her hazel eyes seemed to tremble slightly, as if perhaps they doubted what I said. A week before it would never have occurred to me that the dead could be capable of anything, let alone injuring the living. I put my arms around Jennie and supposed that my beliefs, on that score at least, remained largely unchanged.

What little heat there had been seeped out of the day. By the time we returned to Jessop Lodge the sinking sun had set fires all along the western horizon. Directly above us clouds had gathered, their underbellies the varicose, blunted blue of stainless steel. They swept rapidly across the sky, banishing the sunset's orange luminescence, bringing down the night like a curtain. The hedgerows smelled of rain, and the tarmac glistened with moisture. The house was completely dark. I wanted to get inside and light the lamps. I wanted to go upstairs and be with Jennie.

Her pubic hair was silky and fine, like the hair on her head. I stroked her down there, feeling the strands part beneath my fingers, a criss-cross of pinkness and crinkled golden fur. She had her fingers twisted in the hair at the nape of my neck. Each time she moved her arms I could smell her, a greenish odour, like lawn clippings or muddied leaves. I parted her legs and she gasped, as if I had caused her pain. The skin of her thighs felt warm and slightly moist, like fallen petals. When I penetrated her she locked her ankles together behind my back and pulled herself hard up against me. She came almost at once, as if she had been tormenting herself with the thought of the act and needed only the briefest moments of physical sensation to bring it to fruition. She let her breath out slowly, through her teeth. I closed my eyes, dissolving in liquid crystal.

"I forgot who I was," she said, once I was still. "I thought that I might have been you."

Some time later I went to the bathroom. The second floor landing was dark except for a thin line of light trickling from beneath an invisible door. A floorboard creaked beneath my feet. There was a subdued murmuring of voices. I thought that one of the voices belonged to Sally Beamish.

"There's more to these things than meets the eye," said the other voice, quite distinctly. I recognised Andrew Lill. I paused for a second, and then moved on along the corridor. I wondered if Sally Beamish had let down her hair. I imagined it quite clearly: a fall of raw grey silk against the mottled but still firm flesh of her back.

Sally drove me back to the station. We left the house later than had been planned, due to some matter of a misplaced book, and so I nearly didn't make the train at all. I was glad of this because it gave the journey an urgency and focus that would otherwise have been lacking. As we pulled out of the driveway I glanced into the front right hand wing mirror and saw Jennie. She was wearing her navy coat and had her back to the car. Hilary Arden had offered to take her home.

"It's just down the road," he had said. "It'll only take fifteen minutes." She had thanked him, and then waited while he fitted her small green canvas holdall into the boot. I found that I could already imagine her getting out of the car in front of a foursquare ugly house made of coarse red brick and standing still at the side of the road while Hilary Arden's dented Volvo shot off once more towards Cambridge. When everything had gone quiet she would turn around and go indoors. She loved the smell in the lane, the scent of spring earth and wet cow parsley.

Half an hour earlier she had given me a folded slip of paper on which I supposed she had written her address and telephone number, together with a postcard picturing a large female Diadem Spider, head down at the centre of her web. I put both things into my wallet and did up my coat. Jennie's eyes followed the movement of my fingers on the buttons. The irises were cloudy, the colour of weak milky tea. I kissed her eyelids with their pellucid, nacreous skin and their spiderweb of threadlike blue veins. I did not tell her I loved her. It would have sounded like saying goodbye.

I signed off the surveying course and began to study zoology. My tutors made something of a fuss at first but in the end they gave in. There was no real precedent for my request and so, I imagine, no reason to turn it down. I already had an 'A' level in mathematics. They told me I had until the end of the year to prove I could catch up. By the time I came back to start my third year in the autumn I think they had stopped making distinctions.

There are couples who survive long absences intact, hopscotching their way from one weekend to another. There is no question that Jennie and I could have survived this way also but it seemed somehow imperative not to waste any time. Two weeks into term I moved out of halls into a studio flat on the third floor of a building that also housed a fish and chip shop and a theatrical hairdresser's. I paid the rent by coaching recalcitrant schoolboys on an 'O' level mathematics crammer. A month later Jennie joined me, and things became easier. She took a job waitressing in a Cypriot lunch bar, and then, later, at the mock-Victorian tearooms that adjoined the Viceroy Hotel. I wanted her to try for something better but she refused.

"I like it," she said. "You see new things every day." When she returned to the flat in the evenings she would take off her coat and shoes and lie down on the bed, watching me through half-closed eyes as I sat at the table, marking quadratic equations or correcting an essay. If I sat down on the bed next to her I would sometimes feel her long, pale limbs trembling with tiredness. Occasionally she would fall asleep, her nebulous, mist-coloured hair coating the pillow like strands of solidified cloud.

She read as much as I did, maybe more. I presumed that she would eventually express the desire to embark on some course of study, but when I asked her about it she said that she didn't see any point in going to college. In the time that was left over from working in the restaurants she circled the town on foot, hunting for spiders. Mostly there were common species, found in the network of dustbin alleys that ran behind the houses, or on the patches of wasteland that formed a boundary between the small industrial estate and the sterile, iron-grey river. Sometimes she collected things – dock leaves and broken bracelets, the shiny toothed caps of old beer bottles – and made drawings of what she saw. The drawings were intricate and intensely detailed. There were paintings, too: intense still lives in concentrated, jewel-like colours, immaculately rendered on six-inch squares of cotton duck, or silk. One day shortly before I graduated she came home and told me that some of her paintings were to go on display at the municipal library. The pictures were of single diamante earrings and yellow matchboxes, all except one, which was of a *Marpissa muscosa*, a squat, heavy hunting spider with powerful, hairy legs. I myself had never encountered one outside of a textbook. When I asked her where she had seen it Jennie said she had found her under a brick in the fenced in alleyway between the sports centre and the Weigh'n'Save.

"They like the dark," she said. "They usually hunt at night." A month after the exhibition Jennie received a commission to illustrate a children's book, a simple field guide to garden birds. She had work all the time after that. Sometimes, if she had a deadline, she would sit up half the night under the powerful anglepoise lamp she used, laying down tiny dabs of colour with brushes so fine that the paint seemed to be hovering in mid air. When she finally came to bed her fingertips were stiff and cold, like stone.

She had one close friend, a heavy, slow-moving girl called Laura Piedmont who worked in a bookshop. She had very clear, almost white skin and wore dark voluminous skirts that went all the way down to the ground. Laura occasionally came to the house but more often than not Jennie met up with her somewhere in town. She gave Jennie presents sometimes, boxes of homemade shortbread, velvet gloves. I liked Laura, but I found her difficult to talk to. There was another friend of Jennie's I got on well with, someone she had met while working at the Turkish restaurant. Her name was Clarissa Paules and she ran a haberdashery shop in the precinct. She had curly blonde hair and a riotous, bawdy laugh. She liked to play whist or backgammon and usually won. We saw a lot of her for a while, then suddenly nothing at all. Jennie said she had moved. I went past her shop once or twice after she disappeared. The blinds were down, and it was impossible to see inside. Six months later it reopened as a delicatessen.

Almost every culture in the world sees fit to include shapeshifters somewhere in its mythology. Perhaps people feel a repressed longing to escape the bounds of their human form, to find a new depth of expression in brute strength or weightless flight. Perhaps they seek to explain the sometimes duplicitous nature of strangers or neighbours. The Roman scholar, Juvenal, wrote a treatise on the mysteries of lycanthropy. Bohemian legend tells of a prince who took the form of a bat two hundred years before Bram Stoker invented his Dracula. In South America the Incas worshipped the Sun Dogs, enormous, great-eyed hounds with the souls of men. Stories of the Silkie people, girls and youths who can enter the sea as seals, are common to the folklore of both Iceland and Great Britain. Depictions of such aberrations in art and literature are numerous. I know all this because I have read about it. I read about it still from time to time. I am fascinated by the subject, as some others are fascinated by racehorses or steam trains. I had studied Kafka's

Metamorphosis at school. At the time it meant little to me and yet when I re-read it a few years ago it disturbed me profoundly. I found myself unable to shift certain of its images from my mind, and for a while it gave me nightmares of an intensity and persuasiveness that I had never imagined existed. Eventually, however, the dreams went away. The tale of Gregor Samsa and his transformation into a giant beetle slipped from my daily consciousness. The book that contained it sat largely unregarded on the shelf.

There was something else I read that, although it horrified me less, stayed with me longer. It was an article in one of the Sunday supplements, a report of a young man in America who was convinced that he was descended from an alien bloodline. There was a photograph showing a lean, rather bloodless youth with a prematurely receding hairline and a curiously distorted right eyebrow.

"I know there must be others like me," ran the quotation. "They need to wake up to who they really are." I remember staring at the photograph for a long time, trying to work out whether there could possibly be any truth in what the boy had to say or whether it was all simply an excess of emotion, another of the delusional states that often seem to come with adolescence. I wondered whether such a madness, if indeed it were madness, might be somehow contagious, or transferable by reason of genetics. That led me to meditate on the nature of genetic mutations, the kind of biological accidents that can produce a sheep with two heads or a baby with twelve fingers. I wondered what else they could produce, whether all such mutations were so immediately visible.

Jennie first became pregnant in the summer following our second wedding anniversary. She lost a lot of weight. The skin of her face took on a papery texture and seemed to separate itself from the flesh, so that it hung on her, slackly, like some sort of mask. Her arms, because of their thinness, seemed longer, their rash of summer freckles standing out starkly like the blotchy discolouration of disease. By the sixth month, and in contrast to the rest of her, her belly was hugely distended. The taut, stretched skin of it had the same delicate translucency as the skin of her eyelids, and the same prominent tracery of bright blue veins. I noticed a fine line of transparent hairs, running from her crotch to her navel. The whole looked painful to the touch, as if it might fracture or burst. She seemed not so much distracted as directed entirely inwards. She would sleep for hours, her arms and legs drawn up around the colossal bulk of her stomach, on some days rising only to paint for an hour or two in the early afternoon. Occasionally on waking she appeared momentarily unsure of who or where she was. I was terrified for her safety. It was not so much the fear that she might die – although that too was present – as the idea that the trauma of the pregnancy would change her in some way, that even after the birth I would not get her back. I was reminded of the illness she had had before she met me. I wondered what, exactly, that had been.

In the event, she went into labour at ten o'clock on the morning of her due date and gave birth less than three hours later. There were no complications. The baby was a nine-pound girl. We named her Rebecca. Two years later our son Benjamin was born. Jennie's pregnancy seemed somewhat less of an ordeal the second time around although it could simply have been that I knew what to expect. By the time Benny came into the world Beck had grown into a sturdy, talkative toddler with a shock of thick, dark hair that lent her a touch of the exotic. For some reason people seemed to think she looked like me. Benny had fine pale hair like Jennie's, and eyes the liquid, willow-leaf green of peridots. He hardly ever cried. Beck, by contrast, made enough noise for the two of them put together.

In an autobiographical essay entitled 'Rumpelstiltskin,' the great American arachnologist Cedric Hathaway stated that he had never entirely conquered his childhood fear of house spiders. "There is something stealthy in their movement, in their invisibility-made-suddenly-visible," he wrote. "Something that is inescapably, almost mythologically horrific." I was somewhat surprised when I read that, but could not help but admit to more than just a trace of fellow feeling. I have studied spiders all over the world; it goes without saying that the *Tegenaria* that inhabit the attics and understairs cupboards of Northern Europe are mere pygmies when compared with the Huntsman Spider of Australia or the Bird-Eating Spider of Brazil, either of which could cover a grown man's hand. Nonetheless there is something endearingly benign about these larger species, a plush and characterful, almost hamsterlike quality that is entirely lacking in the hunched, skittish, soft-bodied arthropods so graphically described by Hathaway. I am not afraid of house spiders yet something within me grows cold at the sight of them. It is as if they were not made to be looked upon and therefore resent our scrutiny. One might almost imagine, in the manner of the alien boy in America, that they serve some god quite other than our own. Perhaps I am prey to a shadow, a trace-memory of the creature behind the wardrobe in Hayman's Cottage. Perhaps it is nothing more than the baseless, residual loathing observed by Levi. It is something I am slightly ashamed of. Perhaps it will fade with time.

There is one evening I particularly remember. It was at the end of September, at that exact day in the year when the summer finally gives in to autumn. I remember that Jennie was upstairs with Beck, making plasticene animals with her, or reading 'Sad Sarah,' or going over her collection of shells. I was downstairs in the room that had been turned into my study, marking a pile of first year essays on the prehistoric origins of the common housefly. I had lit the gas fire for the first time since early April. Benny was sprawled on the carpet, dressed in a blue-grey romper suit with twin white rabbits appliquéd onto the knees. He was playing with a collection of coloured plastic cubes called Sticklebricks, a species of modified building blocks that could be locked together by means of soft, rounded spikes that reminded me of the upstanding quills of a porcupine. Even as a baby he liked to build things, and showed an aptitude for the practical that, I suspect, had been entirely lacking in me. He mumbled to himself as he worked, carrying on a one-sided conversation in his own private Benny-language that occasionally bordered on English. It was a restful sound, quite different from the excited, gossipy tirades that had once poured forth from Beck. As I have said, he hardly ever cried. From time to time I spoke back to him. When I did this, he would look up for a second, staring at me out of his liquid crystal eyes with an expression that looked like concern.

"Da," he would say, or something that sounded like da. Afterwards he would return to his work. I would do the same. We worked side by side for the better part of an hour, until, quite suddenly, I became aware that his chattering had stopped. I started in my seat then, as if a loud noise had disturbed me. I got up, hurriedly, all but knocking the chair to the ground. He was sitting with his back to me, cross-legged. The fine fringe of his hair had fallen forward, hiding his eyes, and his cheeks looked ruddy in the dull orange glow from the fire. He had his hands held out in front of him, moving them slowly one over the other as if he were turning a wheel. At first I thought he was playing with something he had made. Then, as I crept quietly closer, I saw that he was handling a house spider, an enormous *Tegenaria duellica* with a coal-coloured, hairy body that had to have been almost two centimetres in length. It was the kind of creature that might be glimpsed crouching amongst a stack of half-empty paint pots in a garden shed or garage, that might emerge from behind a wardrobe in some ancient, abandoned house. I froze, watching as it ran over the back of his hand and then dropped swiftly down to the waiting palm below. Its legs rose and fell in a characteristic, jerky rhythm that made the creature appear almost mechanical. Benny stared down, seemingly entranced, managing the thing's movements in the manner of a much older child. It was obvious to me he felt no fear.

For a moment I was almost afraid to touch him. Then, as if released from some spell, I swooped down and snatched him up into my arms. The spider passed over his kneecap then dropped to the carpet and scuttled away. Benny gazed up at me, his green glass eyes full of wonder.

"Mouse," he said, or something that sounded like mouse.

"Not mouse," I said. "Spider." I enunciated the word slowly and carefully, separating its twin syllables one from the other.

For the briefest instant I almost regretted letting him have it. I knew that Benny would retain the word, as he seemed to retain everything. There was silk on his palms. I brushed the threads quickly away. There seemed to be a lot more of it than there should have been. It clung briefly to my own fingers, viscous and slightly sticky, like grey spun sugar. I clasped Benny to me against my chest. He nestled into me, gripping my shirt tightly with his ten long, mobile fingers. But I caught him glancing downwards, just once, searching the carpet, the skirting board, the dark, trapezoidal kingdom beneath the chair. His green eyes shone as if harbouring a secret.

The door opened and Jennie came in. Her long, speckled arms were encased in the blue knitted sleeves of a hooded pullover. Her dust-pale hair fell forward, half-covering her face. She looked so much like Benny. More like his sister than his mother.

"What have you boys been up to," she said. She reached up a hand, tucking the straying hair behind one ear. In the hissing red light from the fire her hazel eyes glowed gold.

"We're discovering strange new worlds," I said, looking down at Benny's agglomeration of sticklebricks. A complex construction in blue and red and green, it could have been a castle or a ranch-house or some extraordinary breed of spaceship. "We've also been learning new words."

"Spi-der," said Benny, reaching out his arms towards his mother. He spoke the word quite clearly, almost as if he had known it all along.

Fragile things can sometimes be dangerous. A bumblebee can sting. If a crystal goblet is shattered the shards of glass produced could kill a man, or render him dumb and blind. It is difficult to say, sometimes, in harbouring such things, whether one protects them from the world or protects the world from them. Perhaps the only important thing is the safeguarding of something unique and irreplaceable, something that one loves. Maybe, in most cases, there is no danger at all.

A few years ago I returned to Langwold. The British Arachnological Society had enlarged its programme of Spider Identification Weekends, and now ran six yearly programmes instead of the former two. They asked me to direct one of them, a three-day course taking place at the end of June. I found Jessop Lodge unchanged, even down to the magnificent *Pholcus phalangioides* on the ceiling of the utility room. Sally Beamish did her best to convince me that it was the same spider, the one she had once christened Frieda.

"They live a long time, you know," she said. "Sometimes for many years." What she said was true, and I was happy to go along with the joke, to amuse myself as well as the others. There was a retired banker from Leicestershire, a Canadian postgraduate lawyer, and two couples from somewhere in the Home Counties who already knew each other. The daughter of one of them, Amelie Richards, spent the whole weekend trying to engage the attentions of Matthew Ravenscourt, a university student from Durham, by pretending to be terrified of anything larger than a money spider. This might have been annoying had it not been for the fact that Amelie Richards was actually one of the most adept spider hunters I had ever encountered. Sally herself appeared hardly to have aged at all.

"I moved down to Langwold, when Andrew died," she told me. "He comes to the house most days." I examined her face for signs of madness or grief but could find neither. Her long braided hair, once grey, had turned completely white.

On the second morning, while the Ashtons and the Richardses were compiling a photographic record of habitats, and Amelie Richards had gone off with Matthew Ravenscourt in his dilapidated Morris Minor, ostensibly on the hunt for Raft Spiders, I made my way into the village and thence into Aubury Lane. It was a hot day and there were people everywhere, even in the churchyard. I had no wish to talk to anyone so I continued along the lane and into the fields. I approached the church from behind. The gap in the wall was still there, as was the unhemmed carpet of weeds, the rampant outcrops of bramble and dock, the stands of giant hogweed. There was a greater profusion of all than there had been in spring. I had to hunt awhile to find the graves.

I did not look at what was carved on the others; I am sure they would have meant nothing to me. At the grave of Alison Jane Tranter, or Alice, as Jennie had called her, I knelt down in the leaf litter and unwound the spools of green that covered her name. At the head of the stone there were nettles growing, their leaves heavy and dark with the fully-grown caterpillars of the Peacock butterfly. The lack of any date made it impossible to determine whether Miss Tranter had been Jennie's grandmother, or great grandmother, or a person even greater than that. It could be she had been some other, more distant relation – a great-great aunt, perhaps, or a cousin four times removed. Perhaps she had just been somebody Jennie had read about once, and remembered. There are people, like the parents of the American boy who claimed to be an alien, who insist that too much reading acts as a dangerous stimulant to the imagination.

I had thought to leave flowers on Alice's grave, but in the end I did not. I replaced the leaves, obscuring her name, and left the place the way I had come. I thought that, like Jennie, Alice might not like cut flowers, that she would prefer me to leave them growing in the ground.

AFTERWORD

A lot of writers groan at the mere thought of being asked where they get their ideas from, some because they've heard the question so many times, others because of a natural unwillingness to disrupt the creative process by talking about it. I think the issue is confused further by the widespread misconception that ideas arrive out of nowhere, fully-formed and packaged ready for use. I myself have always found ideas in the same way I might find whelks along the strand line: by being attentive to my surroundings and adopting the habit – perhaps I was born with it – of being attuned to the particular rather than the general. Ideas, in other words, are little more than beach combings – more commonplace than you might think and free for the taking in greater quantities than you could ever hope to make use of. If there is a story behind the story at all it is usually to be found in a chance alignment of oddments or circumstances rather than a lightning bolt from the blue – although there are of course exceptions to the rule.

Amethyst is a story about coming home. A year ago I spent a weekend in Porlock, Somerset, and was struck by the contrast between the hustle and clamour in the cramped interior of the village and the still timelessness of the lanes leading out of it, upwards and away into the hills. I was in the process of buying my flat in London and my thoughts idled towards what it might be like to return to a smaller place after a long time spent in a larger one. Once I began writing, Porlock transformed itself with a steady inevitability from the quaint Exmoor village it is to the somewhat baleful Victorian spa town that seems to be a recurrent setting in my fiction, but the story's central themes remained the same.

Ryman's Suitcase was a story of two halves. The title, as far as I can remember, really did come out of nowhere, but I liked it so much I kept it hanging around on a scrap of paper in the hope and trust that a story would eventually turn up to accompany it. A year or two later I came across a competition flyer tucked inside a magazine, an invitation from the Friends of Arthur Machen to compose a modern fable inspired by the work of the Master. I knew at once that the time had come for me to tell the tale of Derek Ryman and his itinerant luggage. The story didn't win the competition – the Society's panel of judges must have found the traces of their hero present in it to be distressingly meagre – but fans of Machen will recognise a few place-names and I like to think my narrator bears some distant kinship to Machen's earnest and well-meaning men of science.

Bird Songs at Eventide is the title of a song by Eric Coates with words by Royden Barrie, the father of the English composer Richard Rodney Bennett. It has the same elegiac tone as a Victorian parlour song, and although I first heard it on CD I found myself imagining a crackling 78 recording sung by John McCormack, perhaps because the words themselves are almost unbearably nostalgic. In view of this I wrote a story about the far future set on an alien planet.

Queen South was another story directly inspired by music. I first came across Aaron Schmidt's band The Ashtray Hearts about three years ago and immediately fell in love with the imaginative beauty of their lyrics and the wide open spaces of their music. Aaron Schmidt is a poet, pure and simple, and his song Queen South, with its perfect seven-line lyric followed by an extended tone-poem for accordion, guitars and drums, seemed to me at once so enigmatic and so whole that I couldn't stop playing it. Middlehampton might as well be a million miles from the American West – and as that's a part of the world I've not yet had the fortune to visit it would perhaps be strange if it were otherwise – but nonetheless I can never think about this story without hearing alt-country music in my head. It was written in the dog days between Christmas and New Year and did everything to ease my state of mind.

I dreamed about **The Vicar with Seven Rigs** – the title anyway. I forced myself awake to write it down and then fell asleep again. By the morning the dream itself – so vivid while I was experiencing it – was reduced to a vague shimmer of uncomfortable sensations and dissolving images but at least I still had the title. As with Ryman's Suitcase it seemed incumbent on me to find the story that went with it. The narrow thoroughfare behind Nonie's house is an extension of the 'two fences,' a green lane between two strips of barbed wire that ran the length of the canal close to my sometime childhood home in Whittington, Staffordshire. For the children of the village it was an endlessly fascinating place, one we would play in for hours. You could find anything you wanted there: giant toads, discarded tractor tyres, even old jam jars.

When I was about five years old one of my favourite storybooks had to do with a racing pigeon that was struck by lightning. I became fascinated by the idea of a bird that could find its way home across hundreds of miles and a few months later a man from down the street gave me a pigeon of my own, a tiny naked squab that had fallen from its nest. My mother managed to rear it on bread and milk and as an adult the bird was as intelligent and loyal as I had presumed he would be. He couldn't race, of course – he was an ordinary fat park pigeon – but he used to follow me to school along the pavement and he always flew home at dusk. A month after completing **Heroes** I made a trip to Buxton and was delighted to see that the special lorries used for transporting racing pigeons are still a common sight on the highways of the north of England. A recent re-

reading of H. G. Wells's The Time Machine – another childhood obsession and still my favourite among his novels – may also have had some impact on this tale.

Terminus is a story about the Moscow underground, one of the deepest metro systems in the world and the one that dealt permanently with my fear of escalators. In fact I am rarely more at ease than when travelling on the Tube – it's just that the stories it brings out of me somehow never seem to reflect this. I was in Russia for the entire summer of 1987 although I only got to spend two days in Moscow itself. It was blisteringly hot. The city seemed agitated, nervous, poised for political change. The weekend was too much of a rush. I stood and listened to a student singing guitar-ballads at the foot of Mayakovsky's statue, wishing I could stay longer and wanting to get out of the heat.

A Thread of Truth was written for my friend Linzi Hathaway, who is an arachnophobe. We've discussed the subject of spiders several times and on one such occasion were joined by another friend who went online to show us images of some of the more spectacular species she had encountered on a recent trip to Australia. Whilst browsing the various sites I came across a posting by the British Arachnological Society advertising 'Spiderwatch Weekends' somewhere in East Anglia. A lot of the business of writing is so concentrated, so *technical*, that you only realise you've been enjoying yourself once a piece of work is actually complete, but in the case of A Thread of Truth I can honestly say it was a pleasure. I think a lot of that had to do with the fact that Linzi knew what I was working on and was impatient to see the result. I felt honoured by her faith in what I could do.

In the event she seemed to enjoy the story, although I don't think it did much for her arachnophobia.

Printed in the United Kingdom
by Lightning Source UK Ltd.
118557UK00002BA/1